THE

GENTLEMAN'S
CONFESSION

THE
GENTLEMAN'S
CONFESSION

A
MATCHMAKING
MAMAS ROMANCE

ANNEKA R. WALKER

PROPER ROMANCE

SHADOW
MOUNTAIN
PUBLISHING

Visit us at shadowmountain.com

Proper Romance is a registered trademark.

Library of Congress Cataloging-in-Publication Data

Names: Walker, Anneka R., author. | Walker, Anneka R. Matchmaking mamas series ; bk. 3.

Title: The gentleman's confession / Anneka R. Walker.

Other titles: Proper romance.

Description: [Salt Lake City, Utah] : Shadow Mountain Publishing, [2024] | Series: Proper romance | Summary: "Inexperienced Jemma seeks advice from her friend Miles, unaware of his love for her. To fulfill a promise, she courts Mr. Bentley with Miles's help. However, Miles struggles with his feelings, torn between friendship and revealing his love before it's too late. Will their bond survive Jemma's pursuit of another, or will it lead to a revelation of their true feelings?"—Provided by publisher.

Identifiers: LCCN 2024012996 (print) | LCCN 2024012997 (ebook) | ISBN 9781639933020 (trade paperback) | ISBN 9781649333018 (ebook)

Subjects: LCSH: Dating services—England—Fiction. | Man-woman relationships—Fiction. | Triangles (Interpersonal relations)—Fiction. | Unrequited love—Fiction. | BISAC: FICTION / Romance / Historical / Regency | FICTION / Romance / Clean & Wholesome | LCGFT: Novels. | Romance fiction. | Historical fiction.

Classification: LCC PS3623.A4343 G46 2024 (print) | LCC PS3623.A4343 (ebook) | DDC 813/.6—dc23/eng/20240326

LC record available at https://lccn.loc.gov/2024012996

LC ebook record available at https://lccn.loc.gov/2024012997

Printed in the United States of America

Publishers Printing

10 9 8 7 6 5 4 3 2 1

To all the hopeless romantics
May this book give you all the happy sighs.

CHAPTER 1

London, England—December 1821

WITH A SIZABLE INHERITANCE TO her name, Jemma Fielding had intended to be a fine spinster, advocate to the poor, and lady champion of justice. However, such dreams rang vastly unimportant to her now, deteriorating at the same rapid pace as the health of her grandmother. The pale, slender person tucked under a lavender quilt hardly resembled the strong, vibrant woman who had raised Jemma from the tender age of three. Jemma's sole dream now was for Grandmother to be well again. Nothing else mattered.

Softly stroking Grandmother's age-worn hand, bent knuckles and corded veins from a lifetime of living and loving, Jemma whispered yet another prayer, then said, "Please, don't abandon me." She was the only mother Jemma had ever known.

Grandmother stirred, and Jemma lifted her bowed head. She hastily pushed aside her rumpled brown hair falling from its chignon in long, straight strands, then leaned forward in anticipation of meeting any need that might arise.

Grandmother's heavy lids blinked slowly open, connecting with Jemma's. "You're still here."

"Of course I am." Jemma had spent seven weary days as a permanent fixture at Grandmother's bedside and would commit to many, many more without a second thought.

The drapes were parted a few inches, and the early rays of sunshine poked through, alerting them both to the news that another day had passed without improvement.

"I told you to rest," Grandmother whispered.

"And I didn't listen."

Grandmother's laugh came out in a weak huff of air. "You always were a headstrong little thing."

"I intend to apply the same will to seeing you better." She smoothed Grandmother's white, matted hair.

Grandmother's head gently swayed from one side to the other. "No, dearest. Not this time."

"You mustn't speak so. I will do whatever I need to help you. Don't you dare give up." Jemma captured Grandmother's hand again.

Grandmother closed her eyes, breathing so softly that Jemma thought she'd drifted off to sleep again. "Jemma . . ."

"Yes?" Jemma slid off her chair and perched on the edge of the bed so Grandmother would not have to speak louder than necessary.

The translucent blue of Grandmother's eyes peeked through again, half-lidded, as if the subtle movement exhausted her. "I'm worried."

"About what?"

"About leaving you. I know it's my time, and I cannot keep holding on. You have to let me go."

Guilt snaked around Jemma's aching heart. Unwittingly, she had kept Grandmother suffering to satisfy her own needs. If God willed Grandmother to return home like He had Jemma's parents, nothing could stop Him. The least Jemma could do was offer Grandmother peace in her passing. She wiped at the sudden moisture dripping down her cheeks. "I don't want you to suffer."

"The greatest pain is not in my body but in my mind." She paused to catch her breath. "The townhome in London is unentailed, and it shall be yours, but leaving you behind, unmarried and alone, torments me."

"My aunt and uncle will take me in. You know how good they are to me. If leaving me must be done, you can be assured, I will be well taken care of."

"But you will not be happy there for long. I know you, Jemma. You must have a place to call your own, as independent as you are, and a husband to walk through the ups and downs of this life by your side. I so dearly wanted to see this union and future with my own eyes. I'm afraid my worries about your happiness will follow me to the grave." Grandmother's chin quivered, breaking a piece of Jemma's heart.

How meaningless Jemma's goals seemed now. She had never intended to marry because she hadn't the same upbringing as those with two living parents in high Society. Grandmother had given her autonomy, leading her to become a rather well-read bluestocking. The freedom had emboldened her to dedicate her free time to Rebel charity causes—causes her group of friends, known as the Rebels, had embraced. Ideas spiraled from there, and now she was attempting to sell her fashion sketches to magazines under a fictitious name so she might increase her donations. She enjoyed focusing on others' needs and her own ambitions instead of pining for suitors. Grandmother had often encouraged her to accept a courtship, but Jemma wasn't interested. Not when it had meant exchanging independence for the role of a submissive wife.

Perhaps being alone was worse than the alternative. Jemma no longer wanted independence. She wanted what Grandmother had given her—a family.

It wasn't Grandmother's way to nag or coerce Jemma, which made this last wish all the more impactful. Jemma reached down and kissed Grandmother's forehead. It was cold, as if her life were fading before Jemma's very eyes. There was no time to consider it. "Would it ease your heart if . . . if I agreed to marry?"

Grandmother's hand came up and rested on Jemma's cheek, the effort no doubt exhausting her. "I don't want you to simply marry, Jemma. I want you to find *love*. I know you believe otherwise, but if you can open your heart, it is a relationship unlike any other." She coughed, and her voice turned shaky. "It's been twenty-five years since my husband died. It would bring me the greatest happiness and reassurance to see your heart carried up with a good man by your side."

Jemma could somehow find the strength to marry. But find love? Her? She swallowed. "I don't even know where to start."

"He must be someone good and kind. Someone devoted to you and your happiness."

A basic recipe for love but hardly easy to agree to. With her grandmother's heart as her focus and the rest of the matter in her own purview, disagreeing seemed impossible. She forced a consoling gaze through blurry tears. "Very well, dearest, *scheming* Grandmother," Jemma teased, hoping to see one last smile. "I will marry for love if you promise you'll watch from heaven."

Grandmother squeezed her hand with what seemed to be the last of her strength. "I wouldn't miss it." A soft, peaceful smile touched Grandmother's lips, and sleep washed over her once more.

Not two hours later, Grandmother's spirit slipped away from her frail body at Fielding Manor and was reunited with her dearest love and Jemma's angel parents.

Through heavy tears of grief, Jemma cried away the remaining hours of the day. When the sun began to set, dragging with it all the light and color of the world, Jemma resolidified the promise she made to Grandmother. Witnessing the fragile moment between life and death had changed her. Loneliness had always been a stranger to her, but now it clung, its soulless fingers wrapping her with darkness. But when she remembered the peace that accompanied Grandmother from this world, it renewed her hope. Humanity, while not always kind, offered a companionship that made the heartaches worth enduring. She would mourn first, as was proper, and then she would seek out the Matchmaking Mamas of Brookeside to request that they find her a husband. The local, not-so-secretive society had proven to be extremely meddlesome in the past, but they had also produced ideal matches for several of her friends.

Whomever they chose, she would make herself love.

CHAPTER 2

Six Months Later
Brookeside, England—May 1822

WHAT DID IT MEAN THAT Vicar Miles Jackson received more romantic confessions than he did confessions of a sinful nature? The women of Brookeside were desperately lonely. He'd received three declarations of affection just this week. Two had been made by young ladies he had already politely rejected in the near past. The third was delivered by Mrs. Fortescue, a seventy-five-year-old woman—fifty years his senior. All three had hinted heavily for a proposal of marriage.

However, Jemma Fielding's entering the chapel just now was *not*, he was absolutely certain, a quest to confess her love.

A shame, that.

Her intelligent eyes gleamed when they met his, and her brunette locks bounced with her purposeful steps. She was easily the prettiest woman of his acquaintance as well as the boldest.

"Miss Fielding." Miles tipped his head, his black curls falling into his eyes for the briefest of moments. "What can I do for you?" The formal address was necessary since the elderly Mrs. Fortescue was still within listening distance, though he was beginning to think the older woman hard of hearing. He had rejected her confession in a firm but kind voice four times in the last quarter hour, and even now, she lingered.

"Mr. Jackson," Jemma greeted with equal formality, a business-like posture in place. When she reached him, she whispered through a smile. "I have come to make a confession."

Amusement teased his mouth. One did not smile in preparation for the humbling practice of admitting one's trespasses. Miles lowered his voice and leaned toward her. "I doubt you have done anything serious enough to warrant speaking to me." He knew Jemma better than just about anyone in the world. They had spent nearly every summer together. She was fiery on occasion but harmless. "Besides, you don't even attend church. There's no sacramental rite I can offer anyway."

"I attend occasionally, and I never miss Christmas and Easter." She pinched her delightfully shaped lips together. "And I *have* done something serious—dreadfully serious. I insist on speaking to you in private and clearing my conscience."

He chuckled under his breath. There was no putting Jemma off. She generally persisted until she got her way. Whatever it was she had to say, it would be far better than waiting for Mrs. Fortescue to vacate the chapel. "Forgive me, Mrs. Fortescue, my attention is needed elsewhere. I hope you do not mind seeing yourself out?"

"What?" Mrs. Fortescue leaned sideways and cupped her ear.

He repeated the words carefully, with practiced patience. Even so, Mrs. Fortescue's pout went so deep it was nearly lost in her wrinkles.

"Good day, Mrs. Fortescue." He dipped his head and turned back to Jemma. "Just this way, Miss Fielding." He waved her into his small office, with enough room for a small oak desk, two sturdy, plain chairs, and a very narrow bookshelf below an oblong window. It was cramped, but Jemma had seen it before and wouldn't mind. He noticed at the last moment the freshly printed book on the shelf and quickly snatched it up and shoved it into his desk drawer.

"What was that?" Jemma frowned, her eyes darting from the shelf to the desk to him.

"Just tidying up," he answered, hoping she would leave the matter be. "Please, sit."

Once they were settled in their respective chairs across his desk from each other, Jemma's smile returned. Whatever she had done, she held no remorse. "Go ahead. Tell me what you did that was so dreadful."

"Well, it isn't a sin exactly."

Miles folded his arms across his chest, feigning impatience. "I gathered as much. Then, if not a sin, tell me what is so important you had to corner me here?" During her summers in Brookeside, she always came running to him whenever something bothered her, and while he did his best not to encourage it, he wouldn't want it any other way.

"I'm not cornering you." Jemma crossed her legs while her mouth formed a straight, stubborn line of pink—a look that often both exasperated and enthralled him. "This was the only way I could speak with you alone without your lady entourage jumping to conclusions about us."

He smirked. "Mrs. Fortescue is hardly part of any lady entourage. Her husband died this time last year, and she misses him. And I happen to remind her of him."

"You remind her of an eighty-year-old man?"

It was a bit of a stretch but far easier than explaining how Mrs. Fortescue found him attractive. He cleared his throat. "At any rate, Jemma, we could have met at the Dome." They had not had reason to gather together at their mutual friend Ian's Grecian temple for a secret meeting in some time; it was usually the place their friends discussed anything urgent or serious, and with the way Jemma was acting, Miles guessed this was just such a matter. It would have been more appropriate to speak there about whatever Jemma had on her mind than in his clerical office.

"Heavens, no. I am not ready to tell the other Rebels about what I have done."

"The Rebels are your closest friends." His too. They made it their job to right Societal wrongs. It could not be good if she would not confide in the group at large. His amusement slipped. "You did do something, didn't you? Well, so long as you did not kill someone, it cannot be too dire."

"It's worse."

Miles coughed. "Worse?"

Jemma nodded emphatically, then followed it with a grimace. "I'm getting married."

His next breath did not come. Or the next. When he finally inhaled, his head swayed from dizziness. "You are . . ." He cleared his throat. "You're getting married?"

She propped her elbow on the desk and rested her hand upon it, releasing a deep sigh. "I told you it was dreadful."

A weight settled in his stomach. This meant one thing. "Have the Matchmaking Mamas found you a husband?" He did not care for their unusual methods, even if they were upstanding members of their community.

"Not yet, but I do hope they hurry. It's been three months since I requested they find someone for me. I know it was in the middle of the Season, and they are down to only five members with Grandmother gone, but they are not being at all helpful by drawing this out."

Miles pinched his nose and shook his head. "Wait. You're telling me you solicited their help . . . of your own free will?" This was not the Jemma he knew. Was this the result of her mourning for her grandmother? Mrs. Fielding's death six months ago had upended the entire community but especially Jemma and their dear friend Lisette—Jemma's closest cousin. Miles had also felt the loss acutely. It had resurrected old feelings of loss from when his father had died. Miles had been but a boy then, yet it had forever changed his life.

No, Jemma couldn't have wanted this for herself. It contradicted her long-standing hopes for her future. Her life's dream was to be a rich spinster who spent her days changing the world for the better.

"If you don't believe me, the others never will." Jemma stood and started pacing, which was quite difficult, considering the small perimeters. "It's not like I want to be married. It's more, I *have* to get married. I promised Grandmother over her deathbed that I would put aside my recalcitrant ways and settle down."

Miles shook his head, his normal, calm presence fading under his mounting shock. "You would never promise something so absurd." Mrs. Fielding was not the type to blackmail her own granddaughter, but nothing would have made Jemma change her mind so easily.

"She was in so much pain, Miles. She would not give up the ghost until I agreed. What was I supposed to do?"

"Lie," he blurted.

Jemma glared at him. "This is not the time to be sarcastic. Honestly, a vicar telling me to lie. I hope no one overhears you."

He had forgotten his position for a moment and where he was sitting. "Forgive me. It was a very poor joke." He loved Mrs. Fielding. He missed her. Of course he didn't mean what he'd said. But Jemma couldn't marry. It would ruin everything.

"There's more. I promised to . . ." Her mezzo voice, like music to his ears, dropped into a contralto tone before fading completely.

Miles leaned forward in his seat. "You promised to what?" What could be worse than Jemma's requesting the matrons of the town to handpick her spouse?

"I promised to fall in love with him."

Those slowly spoken words made his jaw slacken. She might as well have announced she had a fatal disease, for this revelation gutted him all the same. *Say something, man. Anything.* "Oh."

It was the best he could do. Just the thought of Jemma loving someone else made his blood run cold. He supported marriage— even performed marriages—but with Jemma, it was different. She had been untouchable before, safely secured from any persistent suitors or vile men wanting her dowry and beauty for selfish reasons, and mostly thanks to her own unflappable determination. There had been no reason to worry overmuch about his own position being so far beneath hers. A lowly vicar for a friend suited well enough, but not for a husband, not when she could have a titled man, if she desired. She could never have been his, but at least she would never have been anyone else's either.

When he caught her eye, she stared right back. "You have to help me."

Relief surged through him. She regretted her choice. Good, at least she saw the error of her plans. He blew out his breath. "It won't be easy. The Matchmaking Mamas are relentless. But I shall do my best to convince them of your mistake. The other Rebels will help too. You can depend on us."

Jemma frowned. "You haven't been listening."

How he wished it were so. He never missed anything Jemma said. Unlike other debutantes, she never pretended to be anything other than exactly who she was. She was both intelligent and innocent, brave and kind, fierce and gentle. What she said always carried value. Yes, he always listened.

"I don't need you to save the day, Miles, or step in as my clergyman. I am quite determined to marry whomever the Matchmaking Mamas choose. I could never trust myself with such an overwhelming decision. No, I am here to request a favor. I am in need of *Mr. Romantic's* assistance."

His friends still bandied about his adolescent nickname, but he did not like the way she employed it now. Without any effort of his own, women seemed to think him some Adonis. Whatever charm he possessed, it worked on everyone but the lady in front of him—the only one who truly mattered. "You've made up your mind? There is no convincing you otherwise?"

She shook her pretty head, the tenacious, unyielding pink line of her mouth haunting him.

He relented and collapsed back in his seat, still reeling from shock. "What . . . what is it you expect of me?"

She came to his side and tapped his chest right over his heart. He winced, though her touch had been light. When she pulled away, he quickly covered the aching spot with his hand.

"No one is as in tune with people and their feelings as you are. I want you to teach me what you know. I want you to teach me to love my betrothed."

His eyes bulged. Teach her to love a stranger? The devil, he wouldn't! His obligation as her good friend did not include such utter nonsense. He stood and straightened his jacket, his tone controlled and professional. "I sincerely regret, I won't be able to help you." He reached out and took her arm. "I'm a busy, busy man." He propelled her toward the door. "However, if you change your mind about this ridiculous deal you have made, I will do all I can to remedy it." He opened the door and practically pushed her out.

Or he would have had she not gripped his arm. "Miles! You cannot abandon me in my time of need!"

He glanced around to make certain no one had witnessed their familiarity. The church was blessedly empty. Thank goodness Mrs. Fortescue was no longer in the vicinity. He was not acting very priestly. Taking a moment to collect himself, he answered calmly. "It is not abandonment; it's deflection." He tried to pry her fingers off his arm, but she clung all the tighter.

She straightened, and the hardened look in her eyes commanded his attention. "If you don't help me, I will tell the Matchmaking Mamas you are ready to plan your wedding to Lisette!"

Miles froze.

If watching Jemma marry someone else would torture him, marrying Lisette would possibly be worse. Beautiful, kind, sweet Lisette. She deserved the very best in a husband, and somehow, the town had conjectured him to be her equal. If saving her life as a child and being her friend meant this, then he was guilty. But despite being honor bound by Society's expectation to marry her, Miles could never love her.

Not while his heart beat for only one woman.

Not when he'd secretly loved Jemma his entire life.

He relaxed his arm in defeat. "What do you want me to do?"

Jemma squealed and jumped up and down. "I knew you would help me!" Her enthusiasm waned for a moment, and her glare was back. "But it does not mean I do not think it horrid how you keep Lisette waiting and pining for you. It is quite wrong of you to let all these other women trail around you while she suffers at home. Oh, I know, I know. You are a young vicar, and the women are merely bored and lonely. I have heard all your excuses. I do believe you have been dutifully focused on getting your career in order, but it is high time you swept my cousin off her feet and posted the banns."

This was not a discussion he had ever wanted to have with Jemma, of all people. "Don't get distracted. Explain to me the expectations of your request."

Jemma's lips broke into a grin, her dazzling smile threatening to undo him as never before. "Lessons."

"Lessons?" Her smile forgotten, he studied her, searching for signs of madness.

"I haven't any specifics in mind because I wouldn't know the first place to start. I will depend on you completely to teach me everything I need to know."

A small groan slipped, and he leaned against the doorframe. "I've never been married. Isn't there someone better suited?" Their Rebel friends would gladly offer assistance, and without an inner battle tormenting them in the process.

"When the Matchmaking Mamas Society originated and shortly after ensnared Paul in their grasp, you were the most vocal in support of marriage, remember?"

He never thought he'd regret stating his beliefs. "I have nothing against marriage. It's a Godly institution, and those who treat each other with respect find it quite fulfilling. If you recall, I also endorse people selecting their spouse *for themselves.*"

"I'm letting them select a spouse for me. Isn't that close enough?"

His head swung like a pendulum from side to side. "Not for me."

She frowned again. "You're acting needlessly protective of me."

"I'm acting sensibly."

She squinted at him. "It is not like you to put off helping someone. Are you feeling well?"

He rubbed his temples. "I might be taking ill, yes. I'm afraid that leaves Tom and Paul, then, since they are the sole married Rebels."

She wrinkled her nose. "Nonsense, I could never ask a *married* man to teach me. What would their wives think?"

"Then, ask their wives." He could barely stomach this conversation, let alone what it would entail should he agree.

"But I do not know them like I know you. I'd be so embarrassed. Besides, it has hardly been more than a day since they returned from London, and we need time to become reacquainted. And I cannot ask Lisette." She tossed him an angry glare. "It would serve to remind her of her own loneliness."

Miles's jaw flinched. "You cannot mean to come to confessional every day. Someone will catch on."

Jemma's brow danced up and down. "Ah, this part I did plan. Go about your business, and I shall find you when you're needed."

He straightened. "I cannot give myself to all your whims."

"Of course not. I will coordinate my daily walk with your schedule. I have already been insisting on taking long walks alone for the last month in preparation. No one will be the wiser."

Miles ran his hand through his hair but snagged a finger on an obnoxious black coil of hair. "Very well. One lesson, but that is it."

"It will take at least ten."

"Five and no more."

"Done!" Jemma released him and skirted out the door. "Get some rest. We have a great deal of work to do!" She knew she had trapped him, the little vixen, and wasn't going to stay long enough for him to change his mind.

He shook his head after her. This was all Mrs. Fielding's fault, God rest her soul. Her death now seemed suspiciously convenient. She exacted a promise from Jemma and then hid in heaven, where she could safely watch without taking responsibility. He sighed. He did not really think such terrible things about Mrs. Fielding. But would that he could change places with her now. He had a feeling teaching Jemma how to love another man would kill him anyway.

CHAPTER 3

JEMMA PACED THE STRETCH OF the Manning House drawing room, hoping to stir up a breeze. Normally, the cozy space dressed up in crémes and soft pinks was a favorite of hers. Not today, however. There could be no comfort found on the day she was to meet her future husband. Lifting her hand, she fanned air into her face. "I fear the room is overheated," she said sheepishly to Lady Kellen.

"Oh? I am perfectly comfortable." The countess sat regally in her chair, not a blonde hair out of place and likely not a gland in her body even capable of sweating. She was the head of the Matchmaking Mamas in Brookeside, and Jemma had long been in awe of her. Unfortunately, while Lady Kellen was a paragon of women for all to emulate, Jemma was a walking anomaly—a bluestocking who had cried off marriage and the confines of Society only to come crawling back to its comforts and the sudden appeal of a lifelong companion.

Jemma batted her hand all the harder, producing very little reprieve. The contrast between Lady Kellen, the matchmaking goddess, and Jemma, the lonely orphan with ideas far bigger than herself, felt especially acute today.

Jemma ceased her pacing. "Should I request chilled lemonade be brought up for you instead of tea?"

"Truly, I am at ease, Miss Fielding. I have always found the late spring weather in Brookeside suits me." Lady Kellen motioned to the large bay window behind them.

Was the weather one of the reasons Lady Kellen spent such little time in London with her husband during the parliamentary Season? Would Jemma soon avoid her husband for the weather too? She followed Lady Kellen's gaze to the window, half dreading to see a carriage pull up. It *was* a fine spring day. A soft breeze lifted the newly grown leaves on the trees, which meant the infernal heat was coming from inside her.

She went back to pacing and hoping for improved air circulation. After another few moments, she asked Lady Kellen, "When did you say Mr. Bentley was arriving?"

"I expect him at any moment." Lady Kellen smoothed her perfectly pressed dress, a classic white muslin that appeared far more expensive and beautiful because of the wearer.

Jemma adored the minor distinctions of fashion, but her mind couldn't focus on what made the dress so perfect. Not when at *any moment*, her life would change dramatically.

The door opened, and her heart jumped into her throat.

Miles walked in, his black locks atop his head better suited for a palace painting than a man so soon off a horse. And not another sight could be more pleasant to ease her anxious self. Simply knowing he was near allowed her to breathe again. His kind, brown eyes found hers, and his lips moved up on one side, revealing a hint of a dimple. More relief soared through her, fueling her legs toward him and the comfort his presence brought. She wasn't going to face this alone after all.

"Miles," she whispered when she reached him. "I wasn't certain if you would arrive in time."

He frowned as he observed her, keeping his own voice low. "Are you well?" He lifted one hand to cup her elbow, but she grabbed it, squeezing it with all her might.

"In body but not of mind." She was doing her utter best to keep the dramatics to a minimum, but she could not recall being more nervous in her entire life. "*He* is supposed to be here soon, and I cannot seem to collect myself."

Miles glanced around the room, his eyes settling on Lady Kellen. "Where are Lisette and Mrs. Manning?"

Jemma hesitated. Of course he would want to see Lisette while he was here, but Jemma had regretfully sent her away. "I asked my aunt to take Lisette to town this morning." While her aunt had known about the arrangement, Jemma had begged her not to tell Lisette just yet. She would probably turn into a watering pot and beg Jemma not to shortcut her happiness. Since Jemma would do anything for Lisette, it was better to keep her away as long as possible.

Miles squeezed her hand back, the warmth there not at all intolerable, like the rest of the room. "You need to tell her."

"I couldn't!" she mumbled. "You know how close we are. I hate to disappoint her." It was probably hard for Miles to keep a secret from Lisette when the two were so loyal to each other. She supposed real love did that to a person. She quickly added, "But your presence is all I need, so I am certain I will feel better soon. And I so dearly want to hear your opinion." Miles was more than an older-brother figure in her life; he was a man who held her greatest esteem. He'd been there for her since they were children, even though half the town had come to rely on him for one thing or another.

"Jemma . . ."

Before he could lecture her, she turned to include Lady Kellen in their conversation. She hastily dropped Miles's hand, hoping Lady Kellen hadn't seen. "Lady Kellen, I hope you do not mind, but I invited Mr. Jackson to join us this morning. I thought he could welcome Mr. Bentley to the neighborhood with us."

"Welcome him to the neighborhood? I must have misheard," Miles said, stepping forward. "This Mr. Bentley . . . he is to *reside* here? In Brookeside?"

"Then, you didn't know," Lady Kellen answered. "The Kensington House has been purchased at last. Isn't it delightful?"

"No one seemed to know the name of the new owner," Miles said.

Jemma had been one of the few made aware of Mr. Bentley and his plans. "It was all very hush-hush until everything was in order."

"I have to respect a man who prefers his privacy," Miles said.

Jemma smiled, pleased that Miles thought so. She wanted him to like Mr. Bentley.

Lady Kellen took up the conversation again. "If all continues to fall into place and there is a union between them, Miss Fielding will remain amongst us. It's rather perfect. I dare say, none of us could bear to part with her."

Did it sound too perfect? A compliment from the esteemed Lady Kellen was no small thing. Jemma *should* be thrilled with her situation. After all, she prided herself on being quite brave and forward thinking. So, why had her anxiety given birth to a horde of angry bees storming her insides and humming in her ears? She found she'd rather walk on nails or leap through a ring of fire at the circus than meet Mr. Bentley.

They settled into their seats, she in a chair and Miles on a sofa opposite Lady Kellen.

Miles's calm voice broke through Jemma's troubling, consuming thoughts. "Miss Fielding has not made me fully aware of the situation here. Is Mr. Bentley a full participant of this intended match?" Jemma caught a strain in the fine smile lines by his eyes. He needn't be so worried for her. If she were sick on Mr. Bentley's boots, she'd surely live through the embarrassment. She hoped.

"Mr. Bentley is a full and *eager* participant," Lady Kellen answered. "After three years spent in the West Indies supervising his holdings, he has returned to England for good and is intent on finding someone to share his future with."

Miles leaned forward, propping his forearms on his thighs and clasping his hands together. "Did he make his fortune? Or does he desire Miss Fielding's?"

"Mr. Jackson," Jemma chided.

Lady Kellen held up her hand. "A perfectly respectable question, considering the situation. Mr. Bentley has five thousand pounds per annum. He has no need of Miss Fielding's money."

Five thousand pounds was a staggering amount. Miles did not so much as blink at it, not one to have ever cared much for money. It was clear, he did not want her taken advantage of.

Miles pressed for more. "I assume his character is upstanding?"

Lady Kellen gave a single nod. "I was thorough in my assessment. Besides providing well for Miss Fielding, his family name is well known. He also shares Miss Fielding's desire for serving the less fortunate."

The last part had eased some of Jemma's concerns. She loved the work she and the Rebels did, and she wanted a man who would support her in her efforts. However, being charitable meant different things to different people. Some men did not care to have their wives involved in any matter outside their front door. Time would tell if Mr. Bentley measured up to her own expectations.

"Excellent," Miles added, though there was no enthusiasm in his voice. "And if Miss Fielding has a change of heart and desires to remove herself from this arrangement, what contingencies are in place to allow this?"

Lady Kellen flicked a glance at Jemma, who had not even thought to ask such a thing. She hadn't wanted an out. The sooner they were married, the better. Otherwise, Jemma feared she would change her mind and disappoint herself and Grandmother. This way, her promise would be kept, and she could dive into her new life.

"Mr. Bentley requested a month to acquaint himself with Miss Fielding first. I had hoped the two of them could sort out the particulars together."

"Six weeks, at the very least," Miles said rather decisively. "Don't you agree, Miss Fielding?"

Jemma studied his raised brow as he waited for her response. He did know more about people than she did. And they would need time for their lessons together . . . "Six weeks might be best."

"We will let Mr. Bentley know your preference." Lady Kellen grinned, completely in her element. Matchmaking brought her far too much pleasure. Until her own unique situation, Jemma hadn't been very happy about the Matchmaking Mama Society. Seeing two of her best friends happily married because of their mothers' machinations had softened her a little, but she still thought the Society's arrangements somewhat unusual. Unlike her friends, everything had been perfectly transparent from the moment she had contracted with Lady Kellen. It was a small but needed comfort.

The housekeeper brought in the tea things before removing herself from the room again.

Jemma glanced at the clock on the mantel. Mr. Bentley was a quarter of an hour late. Was it a bad omen or a good one?

Miles caught her eye. "Miss Fielding, are you certain this is what—"

There was a rustle in the corridor. Miles had left the door open. All their gazes swung toward it now, leaving Miles's unfinished sentence hanging in the air.

This was it. Jemma had to pull herself together. She could not make a poor first impression if she hoped to win Mr. Bentley over and fall in love with him in a mere six weeks. Facing the door, she couldn't muster any excitement. Every limb of her body became heavy with dread. Did she really want this? No . . . no, not completely. But Grandmother did. And a promise was a promise.

CHAPTER 4

MILES STARED AT THE DOOR as Mr. Bentley's tall form filled the span of the doorway. There was no doubt Jemma would think the man handsome. His tanned skin contrasted with his lighter hair, and his expensive clothes gave him a sort of foreign-prince aura. Not to mention his expressive eyes and much-too-happy smile. Apparently, with one glance at Jemma in all her loveliness, Mr. Bentley was certain he'd made a conquest.

Miles stood to greet the newcomer, determined to be nice. Jemma deserved to have the best, and if Mr. Bentley was the best . . .

He let his thoughts fade, not ready to address them. He'd pour them out onto paper later, as he always did, and try to make sense of them before he attempted to forget them completely.

The ladies stood a moment after him. Jemma, however, didn't quite make it to her feet. She tripped on either her gown or the leg of her chair—Miles couldn't be sure—and with a high-pitched squeak, she stumbled to the floor.

He stared. Jemma was not clumsy, so he was certain she was hurt.

"I'm all right!" she said quickly, bounding up into a sitting position.

Despite her reassurance, Miles hurried to her and extended his hand. When she reached for him, he couldn't help but whisper, "Could this be a sign? Should I send him away?"

"Don't be ridiculous. I tripped," she hissed. Taking his hand, she climbed to her feet, hesitating before fully straightening. She dropped his hand and reached behind her back. "Good heavens!" she hissed under her breath.

"Are you hurt?"

"Worse!" She waved him closer.

Miles stole a glance at Mr. Bentley over his shoulder, who was waiting to be invited in. At least he was a gentleman—even if he was about to steal the woman of Miles's dreams.

"It's my gown. I ripped it."

He took the measure of her lavender gown with puffed sleeves and waistline that dropped slightly lower than an empire cut. It was likely made from one of Jemma's own designs. He didn't see anything wrong with it beside its being new and in the height of fashion. She had a flair for adding beauty wherever she went, but her passion had always been in clothing. Knowing she would dress up for Mr. Bentley made Miles's stomach turn. "I don't see anything."

Her whisper came out higher and more frantic. "It's in the back! If I ruined this dress for a man . . . Oh, do something!"

"Are you certain you aren't hurt?" Lady Kellen said, taking a step toward them.

"No, not hurt," Jemma clarified loudly, stopping Lady Kellen's progression. "I just need a minute!" She dropped her voice again. "He's going to think I am a clumsy idiot!"

"If this is a bad time," Mr. Bentley called from the door, "I can return on the morrow."

Miles straightened. "I think it would be best, Mr.—oof!" Jemma had kicked him in the shin. "I mean, please, come in." He glared at Jemma. What was wrong with her? She was acting completely mad. Granted, it was not his house, to invite guests in or dismiss them, but clearly, this was not the best time.

"Help me stand!" she whispered, ever the stubborn one.

Was she hoping to entertain with her gown falling off her back? He bent over again and offered her hand once more. She clasped it this time, and he gave a tug, aiding her the rest of the way to her feet.

"Make yourself comfortable, Mr. Bentley." Jemma waved him into the room.

"How bad is it?" she said into his ear as she stepped to Miles's side.

Did she really want him to look? "Shouldn't Lady Kellen—"

"Just look," she muttered under her breath.

Good heavens. He was a vicar, not a lady's maid. He reluctantly leaned over her shoulder, bracing himself for the worst. The stitching on the back of the waistline had come undone a good five inches across, exposing her white . . . er, underthings. His cheeks were shading red, he knew it.

Mr. Bentley crept closer, his smug smile now quite hesitant. "I didn't mean to startle you. You must forgive me."

"It's the gown, not you," Jemma answered as if nothing were amiss in the world. With how readily she masked her situation and adopted her poise, one would think her royalty. "It requires a shorter hem, but I was too impatient to wear it." Her laugh that followed was not at all natural, but only those closest to her would notice the obvious strain.

"It is exquisite, so I do not blame you for wanting to wear it." Mr. Bentley's words, while complimentary, rubbed Miles wrong. Did he have to mention her gown at all? It was crass coming from a man who had not even been properly introduced. But, of course, Miles couldn't fault him for the unusual situation.

"Lady Kellen," Miles said, "will you do the honors of introducing us?"

"Pardon my manners." Lady Kellen stepped forward. "Miss Fielding, this is Mr. Bentley, our new neighbor." She pointed to Miles. "And this is our vicar, Mr. Jackson, who has come to greet you, Mr. Bentley."

Mr. Bentley dipped his head, and Jemma bobbed a curtsy. As she did, Miles reflexively put his hand on her back to hide the gap there. If complimenting a stranger's gown was improper, this had to be much worse.

Mr. Bentley raised his brow, and Miles gave him the best innocent face he could muster. He'd done his fair share of acting as a Rebel, so he wasn't exactly the most pious of laymen, but he wasn't sure what his role was supposed to be here. It certainly wasn't to send Mr. Bentley running for the hills, even if it was what he wanted to do.

"Tea, Mr. Bentley?" Jemma pointed to the tea things.

"Yes, please," he replied.

There was no way she could serve tea without exposing herself.

"Lady Kellen, would you assist?" Miles asked. "I think Miss Fielding ought to *stay seated* after her fall." Clearly, she had not seen the damage of the gown for herself. Was her first impression so important that she must risk her modesty? Or was she so smitten by Mr. Bentley that she was beyond good sense?

Jemma glared at him, and then her eyes widened. "It might be best, Lady Kellen. If you do not mind?"

With no chair by Jemma, Miles took a seat on the end of the same sofa as Mr. Bentley while the tea was served. He collected a cucumber sandwich and shoved it ungratefully into his mouth, repeating a psalm of patience in his mind.

The hour passed uneventfully, with Mr. Bentley's surprisingly entertaining stories. Jemma laughed too loudly, but she had no reason to stand up and reveal anything untoward, which Miles considered a win.

When Mr. Bentley stood to excuse himself, Miles knew it was time for him to go too. He didn't care to hear what Jemma thought of Mr. Bentley, nor to be forced to give his own opinion.

Miles spoke quickly. "I ought to take my leave as well. Why don't I see you out, Mr. Bentley."

Mr. Bentley nodded, but instead of going to the door, he walked straight to Jemma. Miles jumped on his heel, following him toward her.

"It was a pleasure making your acquaintance, Miss Fielding." Mr. Bentley looked sideways at Miles, probably wondering why he was hovering so closely.

Miles's adopted his most contrite look he saved mostly for serious sermons but especially for funerals and dipped his chin.

"As I was saying," Mr. Bentley continued. "I hope you might accept an invitation to dine at Kensington House with me Thursday night next."

Jemma's smile wavered. "I, uh . . ."

"Of course Lady Kellen is invited to come, Miss Fielding, as well as your uncle's family."

Miles cleared his throat.

"And . . . Mr. Jackson"—Mr. Bentley's smile went tight—"I hope you will join us."

Jemma met Miles's gaze, and her smile steadied itself, even grew a little. "I would be happy to come."

Miles smiled, too, but as a natural consequence of seeing Jemma's. "As would I."

"Good." Mr. Bentley stepped back.

"Come, Miss Fielding," Lady Kellen said. "You may see me out as well. I have a meeting with Brookeside's musical club this afternoon, and I must be on my way."

Both Miles's and Jemma's heads came up. The musical club was a guise for when the Matchmaking Mamas met. Nothing good ever came from their meetings. And this time, it was certain Jemma would be the subject of their conversation.

"I . . . will see you all out, then." Jemma gave Miles a meaningful stare.

It was time to play hero. Miles motioned for Mr. Bentley to lead the way. Jemma stepped forward next, and Miles placed himself directly behind her. This near proximity was going to be the death of him.

Mr. Bentley suddenly turned. "What a fine house this is. My compliments to Mrs. Manning." His gaze caught on how close Miles and Jemma were standing, and his eyes widened a fraction.

Miles kept his face passionless, a definite chore. "Yes, but a mite drafty."

Jemma's lips pursed tight in an obvious attempt to not laugh and directed her response to Mr. Bentley. "Thank you. I will certainly pass on your kind praise to my aunt." Jemma shuffled forward, forcing Miles to shuffle at the same pace.

Jemma owed him. Their friendship had boundaries for a reason.

Somehow, they all made it to the door without another mishap, although it had been an awkward dance, because it appeared as though Jemma did not want Lady Kellen seeing her dress either. Miles hardly dared wonder what Jemma would do next. She wasn't one to care deeply for other's opinions of her, but her promise to her grandmother had her on edge and acting out of character. Maybe she did need a lesson or two to help her. For someone naturally confident and beautiful, she was trying much too hard to win the wrong man.

CHAPTER 5

THE BEST AND WORST PART of the town of Brookeside was its small size. The consuming thought bounced in Jemma's head with every step of her horse. She had made it only until dinner yesterday, the very day she had made Mr. Bentley's acquaintance, before she had received a written summons to the Dome for a Rebel meeting today. It was signed by Lord Reynolds. She had not even known Ian had returned from the London Season, but it seemed he'd discovered her news upon his arrival.

She had yet to see Tom and Paul and their wives since their return, which meant the Rebels were to be reunited at last. The thought of being surrounded by all her dearest friends warmed her heart. But who had spilled her secret to Ian? Miles wouldn't have said anything, and not just because of his clerical position, so Ian must have heard it from his mother, Lady Kellen. He had a way of gleaning information when he wanted to.

Despite Jemma's excitement to be with her friends, she wasn't ready to face the onslaught of opinions about her choice to marry . . . or the method to find said husband. Ignoring the tug of wind at her bonnet, she leaned into her mare and urged her faster, even though it meant losing Lisette somewhere behind her. She wanted to gain enough speed for all her problems to blur into oblivion.

The sun warmed her back when she reached the mounting block at the Dome. She slid off her mare to the block, then jumped to the ground. Despite her hasty finish, she'd taken her time in leaving, and her friends were already inside waiting—except for Lisette, who had not kept pace, as Jemma had predicted, and had yet to arrive. Tying her horse up with the others, Jemma leaned against the slender white posts to wait for Lisette. She untied her bonnet and tipped her head back, daring the sun to leave a map of freckles on her face. The dratted things would be easier to face than a discussion about her decisions.

By the time Lisette arrived and dismounted, Jemma had resigned herself to the inevitability of what was coming.

"That was some bruising ride." Lisette came up beside Jemma, removing her own bonnet and taming her fair blonde hair before linking their arms together. "You must be eager to hear what the meeting is about. I know I am curious. Miles did not have the least idea either when I saw him early this morning."

Lisette regularly dropped by her charitable offerings to the church, but everyone knew it was their excuse to see each other.

Jemma touched her own dark hair, realizing it must be a mess too. She forced the brown tresses into submission before giving a guilty nod. "We will know soon enough what Ian has gathered us for." She stole a glance at the Palladian-style Dome. Was it just her, or were the gray-white pillars a little prison-like in appearance today?

Lisette tugged Jemma through the door. Once inside, they both put their hands over their hearts and curtsied, a recommitment to their rebel pledge to help those in need.

"Please, don't stand," Jemma said quickly, grateful the Dome allowed some freedom from the constant social protocols. "You all look terribly comfortable."

Ian, sitting on his lime-green throne of putrid, as they had called the decrepit chair for years, met her gaze. With his tall form stretched out, he rubbed his chin, his whole expression deeply perplexed.

She quickly broke connection with him. He knew. He definitely knew. Miles was seated next to Paul and his wife, Louisa, on one of two sagging sofas. Paul's russet hair was combed neatly, but his usual serious demeanor was more relaxed than past years. Louisa had much to do with it. Her heart-shaped face and warm smile could charm anyone into happiness. Jemma met the couple's smile with one of her own, but Miles's head was bent over his prayer book and did not lift to greet her. Her cheeks warmed suddenly, remembering his heroic efforts to keep her underthings from being seen.

The heat of his nearness behind her had sent her head into a tailspin. How was she ever going to get married when she couldn't even handle her dearest friend so near her? Was he as embarrassed as she? He couldn't even meet her gaze.

She was dying to know his thoughts about Mr. Bentley, too, but it would have to wait a little longer. She tore her eyes away from the top of his curly head and waved at Tom and his wife, Cassandra, who sat together on the sofa opposite the others. Tom appeared merry as ever with his wide grin and mischievous glint in his eyes. Cassandra was much demurer in comparison, with her modestly trimmed dress and elegantly coiffed blonde hair. But underneath her prim appearance was a strong, capable woman who managed better than anyone to keep Tom in line at the same time as their capricious son, Alan, who they'd taken in to raise.

Seeing everyone together was a balm for her soul. For a brief moment, she forgot the reason they were gathered. Until she sat down. She was seated with Lisette on the chairs opposite where Ian sat, completing their makeshift circle. Unfortunately, from this position, it was hard not to meet Ian's studious gaze.

"Well, Mother Hen?" Tom said, employing Ian's nickname. "We're all here now. Did you simply miss us and our meetings, or were you eager to converse about something in particular?"

Ian didn't look away from Jemma for a second. "Why don't we let Jemma tell us?"

"Vixen?" Tom whipped his gaze her way. The sharp way he said her nickname made her squirm. "Have you been keeping a secret from us?"

Cassandra nudged her outspoken husband with her elbow. "If she has a secret, there is probably good reason."

Tom gave an exaggerated wince and rubbed his side. Jemma nearly laughed. Finally, someone had reined in their club's insufferable tease. He might turn out to be a decent baron after all.

Paul cleared his throat, reminding her that the topic was still at her feet. "Well, it's not going to be a secret any longer," Paul said. "The Matchmaking Mamas had a meeting last night, and Ian and I managed to catch the sum of their scheming."

Good heavens, Paul had his official barrister look about him. He definitely knew too.

"Jemma doesn't have any secrets," Lisette said decisively, putting her arm around Jemma's shoulders. She was a little taller and a few months older and had the tendency to mother Jemma. Which was one of the reasons Jemma hadn't told her the truth yet.

Lisette continued, her soft voice sweet and soothing. "If our mothers are mixed up in some grand plan to find her a husband, we will have to put the idea to rest at once. No one is more adamant against marriage than Jemma is. Well, except for maybe Ian. And I insist on her being left alone."

Lisette did not insist on much, so Jemma's guilt multiplied.

Ian shrugged. "I would say the same *if* Jemma were still against the idea of marriage."

"What do you mean *if*?" Lisette shook her head. "Of course she is." She squeezed Jemma's shoulders, giving her a side hug. "We will take care of everything."

Jemma didn't cry much, but she was on the verge. She would never intentionally hurt Lisette. Not for the world. Lisette was her hero. The older sister in her life.

"Why not let Jemma answer for herself?" Ian straightened in his seat, his gaze piercing hers. "Whatever you say, there isn't a wrong answer. I certainly won't understand it, but you won't be the first nor the last to cave to the Matchmaking Mamas."

Jemma swallowed. "I, uh . . ." She looked up at Lisette, who let her arm fall away from Jemma's back. "I am sorry I did not tell you sooner."

Lisette's light-blue eyes blinked several times. "Tell me what?"

"I know I have boldly declared I have no need of a man in my life, but I humbly retract the statement. I am soon to be engaged to Mr. Walter Bentley, the new owner of Kensington House." The words cut when they tore from her mouth. She had betrayed everyone in the room, including herself. There was more than one gasp, but only one mattered: Lisette's.

"Jemma, I don't know what to say," her cousin managed.

"Please, don't be angry with me, Cousin. I promised Grandmother on her deathbed that I would marry and . . ." She hesitated, deciding in the last moment to omit any mention of love. She couldn't bear a discussion on that too. "And I couldn't tell anyone because I was afraid you'd talk me out of it."

Silence followed her announcement, and a heavy air of unease settled around the room. A year ago, she had been one of the ones most against arranged marriages. Her friends knew that. They knew the idea of marriage in general had never suited her. What must they think of her now?

"Did they give you time to become acquainted with Mr. Bentley?" Louisa asked, her ever-constant smile warming the room. Paul set his hand on his wife's back, no doubt his silent support of her participation.

Louisa and Cassandra were as much Rebels now as the rest of them after the last year, so Jemma had no qualms answering. "We have agreed on six weeks. In fact, I met him just yesterday for the first time." She glanced at Miles, but his eyes were still on his prayer book. Was he trying to keep his part a secret? She was grateful to have at least one person on her side.

"What did you think of him?" Cassandra asked.

"He was nice." Jemma shrugged her shoulders. He *had* been nice, but why could she not think of a single other descriptor of him?

"Handsome?" Cassandra prompted.

She thought on how to answer. His features were not so perfectly sculpted like Miles's, but it was not fair to compare anyone to Miles. "I believe many would call Mr. Bentley handsome."

Lisette touched her arm. "Is this really what you want, Jemma? Because if so, you know we will support you."

"It is," Jemma reached over and took Lisette's hand. "I know it's hard to believe, and I know you must be angry, but I've been warming to the idea since Grandmother's death. Now that I have met Mr. Bentley, I can truly invest in my decision. I know it sounds impossible, but in the last six months, I've started to see myself and the world differently." She did not dare admit to any of her reservations. This was the time to convince them of her way of thinking, not to give them reason to sway her otherwise. "I hope you can all understand my decision. Not all my goals have changed, but I want what Grandmother had—a family—a legacy to leave behind. And after watching Tom and Paul, I've learned I can still be me and be married."

"So long as Mr. Bentley is the right man," Miles said, and all their gazes swung to him. His prayer book was closed on his lap, his expression blank.

Jemma frowned. What did Miles mean exactly?

Lisette reached for Jemma's hand. "Listen to Miles. There is not a better judge of character." She smiled at him, her eyes crinkling in adoration before returning to Jemma. "You ought not rush into anything."

"I concur." Ian rubbed his thumb across his prominent, dimpled chin again. "We must all get to know Mr. Bentley to see if he is Rebel material. Jemma deserves to be yoked to an equal partner in marriage, and we all know how rare that is." He was likely speaking of his parents. Despite Ian's grievances against his father and his parents' marriage, Lady Kellen was a strong figure in Brookeside, who seemed content with her situation. If that was all Jemma was allowed to be after her marriage, certainly she could find a way to live with it.

"I am happy to help however I can," Lisette said. Her cousin had earned her nickname of Angel a million times over, but this time might mean the most. Lisette's happiness and friendship were everything to Jemma, and she had spent most of her life fiercely guarding their close relationship. She committed to never hurt her cousin again.

Looking across the Dome, Jemma beamed with relief. All her friends were the best in the world. Why had she doubted telling them?

Jemma met Miles's gaze, and he held it for a moment. How she wished she could read him in moments like this. Was he prompting her to tell them about the second half of her promise? The part about falling in love? No, she wouldn't do it. She couldn't possibly confess such a thing to anyone else. It was silly and . . . personal.

But how she wanted to know what he was thinking. Did he detest Mr. Bentley? Approve of him? Why had he questioned Mr. Bentley's worth? His brown eyes swung away from her, and she was left wondering. Tomorrow's walk would give her the answers she sought. There was no time to waste. She needed Miles's guidance if she were ever to figure out this love business, and dear heavens, he had his work cut out for him.

She believed a woman ought to make a fool of herself at least once in front of a man, if only to assure him she was indeed human and imperfect. She had accomplished that feat her first day in front of Mr. Bentley. But such a task was not usually the *first* impression. Now she must enamor him before her awkwardness seared itself into his mind forever. She was depending on Miles to save her.

CHAPTER 6

MILES GENERALLY DID NOT ENVY those who traveled to London for the Season, but he had missed gathering with all his Rebel friends while they'd been in Town. They hadn't rallied together since Mrs. Fielding's funeral, but now they were together in Brookeside again at last. They spent over two hours swapping stories, groaning, and laughing. Apparently, Tom had made a spectacle in the ballroom, kissing his wife in the middle of a dance set. Miles almost wished he could have been there to see the shocked and disapproving faces of the attendees. To Cassandra's chagrin, the scandal had hit the Society papers, insisting the future baron had been inebriated. Tom thought the whole thing hilarious and showed not an ounce of regret.

Miles's favorite story of the afternoon might have been the one Ian told. During a musicale, Paul, their friend who did not voluntarily touch anyone except his wife, had tapped Ian on the shoulder to tell him something. Ian, so accustomed to giving Paul his personal space, had been confused and tried to move out of the way. In the process, he'd knocked over his chair by the window. The back of it had hit the glass and cracked what had once been a beautiful stain-glass image of a candle.

Paul said the candle now looked like it had been lit and the cracks improved it.

Ian, on the other hand, insisted interrupting a musicale was not worth improving the appeal of a window and requested that Paul continue to keep his hands to himself.

To be with good friends was to be happy.

While the others exited to return to their homes, Miles leaned back in his seat to digest their conversations. With their joyful reunion over, he could better reflect on the initial reason for their gathering.

He had depended on his friends to tell Jemma how foolish she was being. Instead, their support, while well meant, had suffocated him. But since it had been the right thing to do, he had kept his mouth shut. Shutting out his feelings was another matter entirely. It unsettled him worse than a bad meal. He wanted his friends—and their distraction—to return.

Ian was the last in line to reach the door to the Dome, but instead of filing through, he pulled the heavy door shut. He turned on Miles and slung his arms across his chest. "Explain yourself."

That demanding, intimidating expression might work on the rest of England, but not on Miles. "Merely cataloging my day before heading out." Miles stretched his arms for good measure. "The Goodmans delivered a new baby last night. Mr. Reed, a new widower, if you recall, requires a visit. And I am to collect items for charity baskets again." Miles stood and straightened his waistcoat. "Enough resting; I had better get to it."

"Sit."

Miles immediately obeyed, perching on the edge of the sofa. Perhaps he wasn't so immune to Ian's ways as he'd thought.

"You knew, didn't you." It wasn't a question.

Miles kept his face impassive. "Why do you say that?"

"You came in without the curiosity of the others. You buried your nose in your prayer book while the rest of us were engaged. Not to mention, your prayer book was upside down."

Miles drummed his fingers on his leg. "Is it a crime to keep a friend's confidence? If so, I am guilty a thousand times over."

Ian crossed the room and took the nearest seat to the door instead of his usual throne. "It's not a matter of keeping Jemma's trust; it's the tension about you. Why is this match any different from the others?"

"I have no idea what you mean."

"From the beginning, you were the strongest advocate for marriage. I am supposed to be the surly one."

"Are you implying I am surly?"

Ian raised his brow. "You're not championing her cause, are you?"

Miles looked over his knees to the tips of his polished boots. How could he champion the idea of Jemma marrying someone besides himself? He could not.

"Dash it all, Miles, if I have to support her, I want to know I am doing it in good faith. Is there something about this Bentley fellow I should be concerned about?"

Miles shrugged. "I hadn't heard of Mr. Bentley until I met him yesterday. He made a decent impression. Afterward, I asked around a bit, trying to learn all I could about him. You know how it is in Brookeside. We have our trusted circle, but people like to talk. The man's been out of the country for the last several years, and his wealth is significant. And you know your mother. She is nothing but thorough when choosing her matches."

Ian's toe bounced. "So, what is bothering you?" It wasn't said in a compassionate tone but more as an order. Ian's heart was far bigger than he let on, but he wasn't the best at expressing himself. "Do you feel the anxiety to marry yourself? You know Lisette will be ready the moment you are. I daresay, she has been waiting since the day you played hero to her as children."

He had never wanted to marry Lisette—not then or now. He'd vowed not to a thousand times to himself. But somehow, it had become expected of him. He'd been young and had thought the idea of him and Lisette would blow over, but he'd stayed silent too long. Impressions had been set. Plans made. How could he compromise his honor as a gentleman? Or worse, Lisette's reputation should he snub her?

It pained him to think that someday, a proposal would be imminent. He would do *anything* to delay that day forever. "I will leave the anxiety you speak of for my mother. She enjoys worrying about that topic enough for the both of us." The pressure from every corner in his life was maddening. "No, it's Jemma." Saying her name felt akin to a confession. He couldn't meet Ian's eyes. He wasn't ready for his friends to know his greatest secret.

Ian sighed as if those three short words said it all. "I know."

"You do?" Miles quickly looked up.

"I didn't believe it at first." Ian shook his head. "I thought Jemma would be devastated, not determined."

Miles repeated the words in his mind, realizing Ian hadn't picked up on his true feelings at all. He cleared his throat. "Yes, her decision is baffling."

Ian rubbed his chin again, his signature thinking pose. "Can a person so adamant against marriage change their mind so easily?"

"They can when faced with the mortal separation from the one they love most. The death of Mrs. Fielding ripped Jemma's feet out from under her. Overnight, she lost a grandmother, a parent, a friend, and a home."

Ian scoffed. "So, marriage is her way of finding security again? I cannot believe it. Jemma is the most independent woman I know in every sense. She retains her sizable dowry, and through harassing our favorite Rebel barrister, I learned she has an impressive inheritance to her name. She's three and twenty and has access to the funds should she want them."

Miles hadn't heard of any inheritance beyond her known dowry. It merely put him more beneath her than ever. He cleared his throat. "Knowing her, she will give it all away to charity."

"Paul cautioned her against it, advising her to be wise so she might support a variety of causes. She cannot help someone if she, in turn, becomes the one in need."

"I appreciate his guidance."

"Yes, but none of this explains Jemma's motivation. Can this all be in the name of grief?"

Miles had observed many different responses to death, and he felt he understood Jemma, even if he did not agree with her. "You heard what she said. She wants a family. It's more than security." It hurt to finish his thoughts, but it had to be said. "Jemma needs affection—love."

"Love." Ian spat out the word.

Miles gave a slow nod. "She has been displaced. She might be resilient, but she still has emotional needs like the rest of us. She might not even know it herself, but love is what she wants more than anything right now."

No response formed on Ian's lips. He wouldn't like knowing Miles was right. No one was against marriage more than Ian. But even he was softening. First, Paul, Ian's closest friend, and now Tom had married—and both were undeniably happier than they had been before their unions.

Ian's sigh was long and tired before he finally spoke. "Let's say I believe you. It brings me back to my initial question. What is bothering you?"

Miles clasped his hands together, his lips unmoving. Part of him longed to unburden the secret he'd carried for more than a decade. He'd penned his thoughts in journal after journal because talking about it wouldn't change the situation for the better. It would inevitably bring certain pain to their otherwise amicable group. For as much as they loved Jemma, they loved Lisette. No one would see their sweet angel friend hurt. "I am not ready to say goodbye to how things were before, I suppose." It was a partial truth.

Ian sobered. "I understand. We've been lucky so far with Louisa and Cassandra. They have readily melded into our group. But even so, our friendships are not the same. We are not needed like we were now that they have each other. A good problem, even if it's hard to swallow."

Miles rued the day when Jemma wouldn't turn to him first in her hour of need. She had always come running to him—whether to vent about some political wrong or to argue about moral rightness of opinions or to share her fears and dreams. The very thought of her distancing herself stabbed at his chest, sending a resounding ache through the whole of him.

Some change would always be bitter.

CHAPTER 7

THERE WAS NOTHING WORSE THAN being a guest in one's home. Jemma loved her time at the Manning House with her aunt, uncle, and cousin, but after all these months, she still felt like it was another summer visit. No one expected anything of her, but she lacked other freedoms she had grown used to before her grandmother had died.

Mrs. Manning, sweet and well intentioned, coddled her. Lisette followed her lead. Mr. Manning touched on the lightest of subjects, careful not to mention any suffering or loss and quick to overapologize if he did. There was nothing natural about any of it. And so it was because Jemma loved them so much that she wanted to marry and leave them—to give them back their home and their lives without her stuck in the center of them.

Grandmother had known it would be this way, while Jemma had had to learn it for herself. Such knowledge might have solidified her motivation to marry Mr. Bentley, but it did not make the long days pass any faster. And she still had six more weeks to endure. Thankfully, she had an escape every day with her reading and long walks.

Today would be even better, too, because she had a destination for her walk in mind—the next step in her new life plan—her lessons on love. So at the noon hour, Jemma set out walking to the church in search of a certain vicar. Miles had been a constant in her life, much like the Mannings, but because he was not a relation, nor was he driving her half mad from his hovering presence, she needed him more than ever.

And she knew exactly where to find him. Not many were aware, but Miles was a creature of habit. Taking the narrow, winding path behind the church, she weaved through the trees in search of him. He always took his midday meal outside when the weather permitted, having a great love and reverence for nature.

The trail ended at a little stream. Years ago, someone had placed a simple backless wooden bench on the bank that overlooked the blue-green creek and the mossy hill behind it. Most days, a trickle of water chased down the hill in thick, majestic tears streaming into heavy rivulets. But after a good rain, it turned into a small but beautiful waterfall. She spotted Miles on the bench, his legs extended in front of him and a sandwich in his hand.

"*Mr. Jackson.*" She made her voice boom, making Miles jump in his seat and drop his sandwich.

She smothered her giggle with her hand. "Sorry, it's just me."

He gave her a sheepish shake of his head and reached for his sandwich, now covered in dirt. "For what reason do I owe the honor of your presence in this humble corner of nature today, *Miss Fielding*?"

"I had to thank you. You know, for the way you handled the horrific turn of events Monday afternoon at the Manning House. I should never have asked you—or any man—to assess the damage of my dress."

"It was mortifying," Miles said plainly. "I may never sleep again."

She smothered another laugh and approached the far end of the bench. "Good, then it wasn't so very bad after all. I am quite relieved."

Miles smirked. "If it had been anyone else, Jemma . . ."

"I know, I know. My reputation. I feel terrible about it. Honestly, I do. Thank you for coming to my rescue. For . . . everything."

Miles gave a slow nod, breaking a piece of bread from his sandwich and throwing it into the creek. "How did you know to find me here anyway?"

"You always come here this time of day."

His hands stilled before he could throw another crumb of bread. "How did you know?"

"The same way I know that when you are finished eating, you'll dust off your hands and take out your little black book, where you write down any inspiration that comes."

"You mean my prayer book."

"No, I mean your little journal." She'd asked him two summers ago about his writing, but he'd always brushed it aside. She'd respected his privacy since then, but she had burned with curiosity to know what sort of things he recorded. "One of these days, I plan to peek over your shoulder when you aren't looking and get a glimpse of it. Someone should know what you've been scrawling away at all these years."

Miles tipped his head back a little and looked down his nose at her. "I believe you take pleasure in spying on me."

"Observing is the correct word. It's what friends naturally do after a decade or more in each other's company. Speaking of your journal and this tucked-away bench, I'm not certain why you try to hide everything from the others. Secrets in Brookeside are few and far between."

"For you, at least." Miles shifted to one side of the bench and motioned for her to sit beside him.

"My secret wasn't meant to be kept for long." She took the seat, smoothing her skirts in front of her. "What about your secrets?"

"I don't have anything to conceal." He shifted and looked away.

She narrowed her gaze. "You act terribly suspicious for someone who isn't hiding something. Do you have a *real* secret? I mean, besides being a dedicated journal writer?"

"No, no secret." He attempted to scratch his neck, but his cravat prevented it.

"Miles Jackson! You might fool someone else with your Rebel acting but not me." She laughed and shook her head. "At least I know I'm not the only one keeping something from our friends."

Miles speared her with a glare. "Why are you here again? And where is your chaperone? You're growing careless. I know the Rebels aren't strict with this sort of thing when we are together, but our reputations can serve us well. You must try to protect yours better."

She ignored his concern. "You evaded my question, but I will let it lie for now. And I couldn't bring a chaperone, as today is our first lesson."

"A shame you came all this way," Miles said. "I happen to have a meeting with someone."

"Indeed you do. Me."

"I meant a different meeting." Miles lifted one eyebrow. He could raise it dramatically high into a triangular arch, a skill she had never acquired. After all these years, the ridiculous expression still made her smile.

"I checked your calendar on your desk before coming to find you. I penciled my name in for this hour . . . and for next Monday and Wednesday at the same time."

His shoulders shook in a silent laugh, and he rid himself of the rest of his sandwich, the last of it floating down the stream. "You are tenacious, Jemma Fielding, to say the least."

"I have to be. How else will I learn a thing about falling in love? I can barely wrap my head around courtship as it is."

"The last time I gave you lessons, I taught you how to play chess. Do you remember?"

"I beat you in the first game." She grinned. "I was a natural."

Miles smirked. "Exactly. You're a natural in company too. You act like you have never spoken to a man before, but you certainly don't need me or any silly lessons."

"But I do need you." She swiveled so her entire upper body faced him. "Miles, I have flirted before and danced plenty, but this is love we are speaking of. It's big, grand, and incomprehensible. My parents didn't raise me. I had no one demonstrating to me how it is done. Most of the year, it was simply Grandmother and me. I know I have my aunt and uncle and all those happily married in

Brookeside to look up to, but I feel at such a disadvantage. How do I create such an emotion in another person? How do I create it in myself? I have spent too many years focusing on the inconvenience of the idea. I must change the way I see it."

Miles sighed. He was looking at her like she was a lost puppy. "Have you tried poetry?"

She folded her arms. "Poetry is wonderful, but it is mostly about *after* one is in love, not the process. Miles, you will have to humble yourself and start teaching me. In fact, we should start this very minute. I don't plan to waste my afternoon." She tapped her fingers on her arm in an exaggerated motion.

He stared at her for a long moment, but she wouldn't break. The matter was settled. Miles had to be the one to teach her.

He groaned and lifted his hands in the air. "Very well. If I don't give in, you'll start threatening blackmail again."

"I will indeed."

"Where's the mercy in your voice? Sadly, I know you too well to question your sincerity."

She had to bite back her smile. Likely, no one knew her better than he did. Not long after his father died, she'd come to Miles as a young, curious girl and asked him if he believed in heaven. She'd wanted to know about her own parents and wondered if Grandmother was telling her stories about a made-up world just to make her feel better.

Miles hadn't teased her for her silly question, but had patiently explained his view on the afterlife. Jemma had returned with another question and then another and had done the same the following summer when she had visited Brookeside, sometimes saving up her thoughts for months at a time, waiting to tell them to Miles. She couldn't remember many of their conversations now, but somewhere along the line, she'd made him her confidant.

"I can see your smile." He glared. "Do you take great pleasure in making me suffer?"

"This is what friends do for each other."

Miles would give in in the end. He was the kind of person who didn't condemn her for her wild ideas—some of which were not practical for a woman in a man's world. Miles didn't always agree with her, but he listened and offered sound judgment. And more, he was quick to offer his help.

So why was he stalling now? And why was her threat of blackmail so unnerving to him? The idea of Miles and Lisette was ages old, starting when Miles had rescued Lisette from an ice-skating incident at the upper pond.

Everyone had seen shy Lisette bestow a kiss on the surprised Miles's cheek. From that day on, there had been a subtle circle drawn around the two of them. At first, Jemma had thought it nothing, but after mistaking Lisette's journal for her own, Jemma had accidentally discovered her cousin's deep-seated love for Miles. From then, Jemma, too, could see the line connecting them.

As for Miles's devotion, she could see it in simple ways. He'd chastised Mortimer Gibb when he'd teased Lisette, dropped off books for her when she'd caught a persistent cold, and had requested Lisette's first dance at her very first ball. There had been other times as well. Dozens of them.

The day the ice had broken at the upper pond all those years ago, the universe had shifted. Jemma and the rest of Brookeside had known from that moment, Miles and Lisette were meant for each other. The uncomfortable memory had never sat well with Jemma. She thought herself an educated woman who read from the same material as the Oxford men, but she knew nothing of fated hearts and why that moment had left hers untouched and alone.

"Jemma?"

"Hmm?" She looked up at Miles and blinked.

"I said, let's get this over with. I thought you were dying to have this lesson, but apparently, you were woolgathering."

She unfolded her arms and shifted toward him. "I'm all ears."

A mixture of disbelief and distrust lined his features. "Yes, well, move to the very end of the bench."

"What?"

"I don't want you getting the wrong idea while we are here alone together."

She clamped down her laugh and shifted over a few inches. "Better?"

"It will have to suffice. Now, where is your paper? You should write down what I say. It might be more profound than any of my sermons, and I will not be tasked to do it twice."

"I will write the words across my heart, never to be forgotten," she quipped.

His forehead creased. "If only you would." He stood suddenly and walked a few steps toward the creek. He rubbed his hand over his dark brows, clearly contemplating what to begin with. "I won't tell you how to bat your eyelashes or when to simper or tease. If you are looking for lessons in flirtation, you will be quite sorry. I intend to cover subjects of substance."

"But it will help me capture Mr. Bentley's heart?"

"That will be entirely up to your application of the lessons." He peered over his shoulder as if expecting her to argue. When she didn't, his gaze softened and he said, "Well then, let's start with the art of conversation."

Jemma grinned, ready to show how eager she was. "Yes, let's start there. This happens to be my greatest strength."

"Is it?" Miles put his hand on his hip, pushing his jacket back and emphasizing his well-tailored waistcoat that had seen better days.

She frowned at it, and not because Miles did not look well in it but because his question confounded her. "I thought it was."

"Conversation isn't just about asking the right questions and being informed on a variety of interesting subjects."

"What else is there?"

Miles covered his laugh with a cough into his hand. "*Listening*, Jemma. A conversation is an exchange of sharing and listening—an intensely personal dance between two humans who draw past the inhibitions to the heart."

"I listen plenty," Jemma defended. "You don't think I am good at conversation? I am offended."

He clasped his hands behind his back and grinned. "I never said you did not excel at it." He paused and raised a brow once again. "You must not have been listening."

Her scowl deepened, and she retraced the conversation in her head. "Yes, but you implied it."

He shrugged. "Misunderstandings are easy, are they not? They can make a wedge between a couple and prevent love from blossoming or even kill it completely. I've seen it too many times amongst our neighbors, I am sorry to say."

"Not here in Brookeside," Jemma argued. "I know my experience is limited to the summers, but everyone loves everyone here."

He shook his head, his face a little grim. "I wish it were so."

She tilted her head, noticing for the first time an invisible weight on his shoulders. "You really care about the people here, don't you?"

"I know many men in my position do not even claim to be especially religious. Many of them weren't the prized firstborn son with a grand inheritance, and the church was an easy source of income. But it's more than a job to me. It's . . ."

"A calling?" she offered.

He shrugged. "Maybe."

A smile tugged at her lips. "How am I doing with the listening?"

His lips quirked like he was fighting his own smile. "You always were good at conversation."

Jemma snorted, and they both laughed. Miles collapsed onto the bench next to her, much closer than before. His eyes met hers, and his smile suddenly faded. "Well, that ought to keep you until Monday. You were an exemplary student."

She bumped him with her shoulder. "We cannot be done yet. I am certain your parish appreciates a brief sermon, but not me. I'm already seeing conversation in a different light. Tell me what's next."

"Conversation is the first step. Once you get to know . . ." Miles cleared his throat. "Once you get to know *Mr. Bentley* and listen to what his interests are, you can follow it with an act of kindness."

"I like that."

"Good. How about practicing on someone else first?"

"Like you?"

He shook his head much too quickly. "Not me, please. Think of someone you don't understand. The first person who comes to mind."

"The new maid at the Manning House. She walks around with this matted shawl at all hours of the day. I declare, it is swarming with fleas, besides being much too warm for this time of year. I would love an excuse to design a new one for her and have it made up in a practical fabric with an attractive pattern. I have already noted several options in my mind." She mused, quirking a brow. "Maybe the art of conversation will aid my cause."

"Perfect. Get her to talk about herself. Then, based on your conversation, think of something nice to do for her. When you serve someone, you start to think differently about them. It's an amazing thing." His eyes were lit when he finished. His passion for his profession always inspired her.

"Is this the sort of activity you engage in every day?"

He shrugged. "When I can. But this isn't about me. It's about Mr. Bentley." He punctuated each sound of the name.

"You are very right. I shall attempt to apply what I have learned tomorrow night at dinner. You are coming, are you not?"

"To Kensington House?"

"Have you forgotten? I heard Lady Kellen convinced Ian to come. You really ought to join us."

"Yes, I suppose I must."

"Don't sound so enthusiastic."

"I won't, then." He stood and gave a dismissive nod with his head in the direction of the church. "Don't let anyone see you. Someone has to worry about your reputation, even if you do not."

She pushed off the bench and agreed. "Good day to you, Miles." She went a few steps from him before turning abruptly. "I will repay you someday for all your help. You won't regret it."

He said nothing, turning to stare at the creek instead of her. She took one last look at the profile half of Brookeside was in love with. His dark curls hid the top of his ears, and a long lock fell across his forehead. And while his chiseled features were decidedly masculine, he had thicker eyelashes than any woman she knew. She forced her eyes away, as she had trained herself long ago to do. Mr. Bentley might not be as handsome as Miles, but she sincerely hoped she would come to rely on him in a similar way.

CHAPTER 8

MILES SAT AT THE MASSIVE dining table in Kensington House, trying to focus on the ornate candelabras, the bright and wild landscapes from the West Indies adorning the walls, or even the blue-rimmed chinaware. Anything besides Jemma. Her every movement caught his gaze, her words his attention, and her presence his heart. And she was completely oblivious.

As he wanted her to be.

Mr. Bentley said something from his seat at the head of the table, drawing a laugh from Jemma and Ian on the other side of him. Jealousy like Miles had never experienced ruined his appetite and darkened his thoughts. His own mother—a matchmaking accomplice to Lady Kellen—had bragged that very morning about the credit she deserved for helping to choose the perfect man for Jemma.

He loved his mother, but he liked her less after such an aggravating conversation.

"You're not eating."

Miles lifted his gaze to meet Lisette's, who sat on his right. "Pardon?"

Her pale-blue eyes filled with concern. "You're pushing your food around, but I fear you've not even tasted it. Are you unwell?"

Miles masked his feelings and managed a small smile. "I must still be full from my lunch."

Lisette readily accepted his excuse, her eyes softening and her shoulders relaxing. Had she been so very worried about his health?

His fierce jealousy moved aside to make room for simmering guilt. He stabbed a bite of roasted duck and forced it down to set her at ease.

It was a delicate dance between being Lisette's friend and trying not to give the wrong impression. The matrons always seated them together at dinner, so it was especially hard at parties. He cared for her as one did a sister, but he could not feel anything more for her. Still, he wouldn't be unkind either.

Lisette leaned toward him once more, and thankfully, this time, her words were not about him. "Mr. Bentley seems like a wonderful man. Do you not agree?"

It was bad enough to have to eat at the same table as him, but must he talk about him too? "Yes, wonderful." *Wonderfully* vexing.

"I admit I was wary about this," Lisette confided, "but I must give credit to the Matchmaking Society. Once again, they've proven themselves to have excellent taste."

Miles mumbled his agreement. At least someone was pleased about this. Then again, Lisette never saw anything wrong with anyone. She always found a way to see the bright side. If only he could borrow her perspective this time. If only he loved Lisette and not Jemma. "I take it you have forgiven Jemma for not telling you about Mr. Bentley sooner."

Lisette sighed. "How could I not? She's been hurting deeply for months. Oh, I know I mourn Grandmother, too, but it is different for Jemma. She and Grandmother had a special relationship I always envied. I just want her to be happy again."

Miles fingered his napkin, measuring his words. "And you think this is the answer?"

Lisette looked down the table at the intended couple, who were smiling over their shared conversation. "I can't be certain, but it's extremely promising."

Exactly what he was afraid of.

He recognized Jemma's canary-yellow gown of fine silk but noticed it had a new blonde lace trim across the neckline and along the short full sleeves. It was contrasted by robin's-egg-blue netted gloves he knew were lying on her lap until she finished eating. He always noticed what she wore, knowing she loved to be complimented on her trend-setting fashions. She detested sewing herself, but last summer, she had begun exchanging drawings with two modistes overseas, one French and the other American, and her talent had only grown.

Sighing, he looked away . . . again. He hated that he knew this about her. It inevitably served to remind him of his position. He could not provide her the lavish lifestyle she was accustomed to. She was never wasteful, doing over old gowns and donating others to the poor, but she deserved to have every comfort she was used to. With Mr. Bentley in the picture, she would be amply provided for and would likely travel the globe on his arm. He'd say nothing of her gown, not tonight or any other night.

How many times had he swallowed words of praise in an attempt to hide his feelings?

He suddenly wished the marriage over and done with so he could move on with his life. There were so many parish needs for him to focus on, and pining for Jemma was an unproductive use of his time. Almost worse were the lessons on love. But while he might not be worthy of Jemma, at least he could help her feel more of worth. If he couldn't be the one to make her happy, he wanted someone else to do a proper job of it.

After the women left the table, Mr. Manning, Mr. Bentley, Ian, and himself remained at the table.

Miles forced a smile wide enough that he could feel the dents of his dimples. He might be somber by nature, but he wasn't one to sulk. It was his job to be welcoming and embrace everyone into the community, and he took his responsibilities seriously—even if it killed him. "I hope you're enjoying the neighborhood, Mr. Bentley. The rest of us are quite fond of Brookeside."

"It's charming," Mr. Bentley answered.

"Much like the ladies who reside here," Mr. Manning said, raising his brow. Ian's brow went up, too, and they all looked to Mr. Bentley.

"I must admit," Mr. Bentley gave a self-conscious chuckle, "I have not met many others yet, but I am impressed by both Miss Fielding and Miss Manning."

Miles squashed his immediate emotional response. "They are unparalleled," he added, determined to be agreeable.

"So, what are we doing in here?" Mr. Manning asked. "Let us join them post haste so Mr. Bentley might know them better."

Miles crumpled his napkin in his hand. It had been aggravating enough knowing their mothers were scheming against them, but this was further proof that the fathers were not without blame. First, Lord Felcroft had joined forces with his wife to match up Tom, and now, Mr. Manning was acting terribly suspicious.

"By all means." Mr. Bentley stood. "Shall we?"

Miles followed the men into the drawing room, lagging behind while he mentally prepared himself for another grueling hour of practicing patience.

But he'd hardly suspected Jemma to snag his arm at the entrance and yank him to the side as she did now.

He looked at her hand on his arm and ignored the twist in his chest. "Don't tell me you ripped another gown," he said.

She was acting as strange as the first time she'd met Mr. Bentley.

"No, I merely wanted a man's opinion." There was not a trace of her usual confidence in her eyes. "How did I do? Do you think he likes me?"

Miles glanced around desperately for a way to avoid answering, unable to keep himself from noticing the fine room Jemma would someday be the matron of. It was adequately sized, with a tall, masculine fireplace highlighting the main wall. Two high-back chairs were placed opposite it on the other end of the room, with Ian occupying one of them. The others were seated in two indigo-blue sofas flanking the fireplace. Lisette sat beside Mr. Bentley, their discussion conveniently keeping them unaware of Miles and Jemma's conversation.

"Why not ask Mr. Bentley himself?" Miles finally answered. He tried to step around her, but she moved in front of him again.

"I could never be so direct." She glared. "I was simply curious if something was said over port." She glanced at his waistcoat and pointed with a blue-netted finger. "What is this?"

As he had not his box of sweets with him at present, he thought she must be referring to his father's watch he often wore to remember him by. When he looked down, he saw his handkerchief sticking out enough to reveal his initials embroidered in the corner.

"Lisette always stitches laurel leaves around her initials, the same as this one. Did . . . did she gift you it?" Jemma's mouth stretched into a wide, excited grin.

Miles could kick himself for not selecting a different handkerchief to bring.

Jemma gave a hushed squeal. "When did this happen?"

"She gave me a few for Twelfth Night ages ago," he mumbled. "I was not aware I brought this particular one tonight." He had made a point never to bring them anywhere, in fact.

She gave him a sideways glance. "Are you certain you did not hope for her to see it on your person?"

"I had no such hope." Miles shoved the handkerchief deeper into his pocket. The last thing he desired was to give Lisette the wrong impression about his feelings. "You did not see anything either. Let's sit down before the others think you are partial to me and not Mr. Bentley."

She blinked rapidly, and her shoulders drew inward. "They wouldn't think it because they know you are intended for Lisette." She shook herself and straightened again. "I won't say a thing, but please don't hide her gift on my account." Jemma, notorious for breaching propriety where he was concerned, reached over to pull the handkerchief out again. But he could be as unyielding as she in this matter, at least. He reached for the pocket at the same time. He hadn't meant to, but he snatched her hand in his own to stop her.

"What is all the whispering about?" Mrs. Manning called from the sofa. "Come join us, you two."

Miles shifted to hide the fact that he held her hand, when he should have let go. "Jemma . . ."

Mrs. Manning's voice carried over to them. "The young adults in this town are always coming up with ways to improve Brookeside. They are, no doubt, conversing about another project."

She was not completely wrong.

Jemma glanced down at their hands and visibly swallowed. "Yes? What is it?"

His heart thudded in his chest. How he'd dreamed of holding Jemma's hand, and for longer than just a mere assistance into a carriage. The day he'd met Mr. Bentley, she had grabbed his hand for a brief moment, and it had only served to tease him. His hold instinctively tightened on hers now, drawing it closer to his chest. Why had this happened now, when she was more out of his reach than ever?

"Please, Jemma," he said softly, "leave the handkerchief alone." He hadn't meant for the tone of his voice to drop or for his thumb to slide across the back her hand, smooth just below the netted fabric. A rush of warmth traveled up his arm to his chest. No matter how many years being in her company, she always rendered him this way. Touching her only enhanced his reaction.

She bit her bottom lip, her gaze drawing up to meet his. "All right." The words came out in a slow, deliberate whisper. "If you insist."

He drank in her doe-like gaze, wishing to savor her nearness. At long last, he released her. It wouldn't do him any good to hold on to another man's future wife, no matter how tempting she might be.

Jemma exhaled a shaky breath, tucking her hands into the folds of her dress. "I suppose you know best. You've always had a gentle touch with every situation, and I trust you." With a short, unaffected smile, she slipped away from him and strode toward the others, taking a seat beside Lisette.

Gentle.

His gentle touch.

A heavy sigh filtered through him. Would that it were a firm grip, capable of holding on to her. He'd once thought no one capable of such a feat, but it wouldn't be the first time he'd been wrong. Clenching the hand that had held hers moments ago, he moved to an empty chair closest to Mrs. Manning on the sofa and Ian in the tall-back chair beside him.

"More secrets, Miles?" Ian whispered, his gaze both curious and suspicious.

Always careful not to show his true feelings, he waited until the conversation around them muffled his answer. "It appears the Matchmaking Mama's are plotting to marry you off next."

Ian's gaze turned to steel. "What?"

The word drew the attention of the others.

"What . . ." Ian repeated, "an interesting picture on the mantel, Mr. Bentley."

"Ah, thank you for noticing." Mr. Bentley motioned everyone's attention to the painting. "It is an oil depiction of a sunset over Barbados. I am partial to art, if you have not noticed from the dining room. I brought back as many pieces as I could so I might be surrounded by the brilliant colors I found there."

"Do tell us another story about your travels," Jemma pleaded.

Miles nearly glared at her, but Ian's whisper distracted him from his purpose. "Who is the unlucky lady my mother is foisting on me?"

Miles wanted to watch Jemma's reactions, not converse with Ian. Under his breath, he blurted the first name he could think of. "Mrs. Fortescue."

Ian wrinkled his nose. "You're joking."

"For seventy-five, she is not so bad on the eyes. Give her a chance."

Ian snorted, drawing everyone's attention again. He coughed into his hand. "Forgive me, I'm getting a cold." With his overly dry sense of humor, no one questioned him.

Jemma did not even bat an eyelash of concern for Ian's health, for she was too intent on capturing Mr. Bentley's attention. "What were you saying, Mr. Bentley, about being at the Manning House yesterday?"

"Merely, I am sorry to have missed you," Mr. Bentley answered. "A good walk, however, is important for one's health."

"I do love long walks," she said. "But I will be certain to be home during calling hours tomorrow if you are inclined to visit again."

She wasn't being subtle. Could Miles blame her? There was no reason to play coy when her marriage to Mr. Bentley was inevitable. He stole a glance at Lisette, who sat poised beside her cousin. Glowering, he propped his head on his hand and went back and forth between the two women. Lisette was more somber, like himself, practical, and plenty pretty. Why did *she* not make his heart race?

Jemma, on the other hand, acted with certainty, carried a zeal for life about her, and often said and did the unexpected. How many times had he told himself that they were not even compatible?

Along with the differences between the two women, they had similarities enough. Both were loyal, caring, and sympathetic. But only one combination of traits had drawn him in completely from the time they were children. When Jemma had been nine and he not yet thirteen, he had fallen for her for the very first time.

He knew the very day: a warm summer afternoon when he'd thought his life had ended.

With his father dead a year and Miles much too young to work off the mountain of debt left to him, there was no way for his family to keep his newly inherited house. It was time for Miles and his family to say goodbye to Brookeside. The only life he had ever known. The adults gathered in small circles in the garden after Sunday services and whispered about the sorry fortune of his family. Miles and his friends also huddled together, safely hidden behind the church, to have their own discussion of the dreadful news.

Regardless of the circumstances, goodbye would not suffice for Jemma. Even then, she'd visited only in the summers, but no one had minded her and Lisette tagging along with them, not when Jemma's splendid ideas had kept them all entertained. When she'd discovered his news, it had not mattered that she had spent the least amount of time with Miles out of everyone. She'd declared Miles was not leaving Brookeside nor any member of his family. It had been the first time Miles had seen her passion flare to life.

Jemma had climbed up on the stump she'd been sitting on, her small fists tight, and yelled at their small group. "Look at you, sorry lot, giving up on your friend. You should be ashamed of yourselves. Miles is staying, and that is final!" Those words had been the catalyst behind uniting the others to his cause—that and her brilliant idea of instigating a romance between his mother and the new rector.

Initially, everyone had thought her ridiculous. But her enthusiasm and intractable determination had given them hope, and they'd tried anyway. In the end, his mother had remarried a wonderful man, allowing Miles and her to stay in Brookeside. The whole town had seemed to rally around the project. It had been a fair toss up of who had interfered more in the courtship—them or, believe it or not, the matrons of Brookeside.

When summer had ended and the regretful time had come for Jemma to return home with her grandmother, Miles had been as sorry as she. He'd run all the way to the Mannings' house in the rain and hid behind an old twisted tree to watch their carriage pull away. He hadn't wanted her to go. She had given him his life back. But it had been more than gratitude. His adolescent heart had been pricked by the first sensation of love.

Right then, he'd made a decision. He'd lifted his face to the sky, rain drops hitting his skin and chasing down his face, and had vowed to someday marry Jemma Fielding. Neither of them would ever have to leave Brookeside again.

Not two years later, Lisette's near death had complicated everything.

Jemma turned away from Mr. Bentley's enthralling conversation just then and met his intense stare. She screwed up her face in confusion and mouthed. "What?"

He shrugged and straightened.

She frowned and went back to listening to Mr. Bentley, but Miles could not look away so easily.

"You're being obvious," Ian whispered from beside him.

Miles swiveled his gaze. "Am I?" After all these years, were his feelings finally transparent?

Ian put a hand up to shield his words from the others. "We can't both hate the idea of another matchmaking conquest by our mothers. If I have to be supportive—and believe me, it's a real sacrifice—then you do too."

Miles gave a reluctant nod. He'd be supportive and continue to give romance lessons to Jemma, but he didn't have to like it. Everyone had a line, and Mr. Bentley was not even aware he was crossing Miles's. Time, however, would not be something Mr. Bentley robbed him of. They weren't engaged yet, which meant there was nothing wrong with him seeking Jemma out. Or maybe he wouldn't have to seek her out at all. Her silly lessons would do the trick. Though the reason for them did not sit well with him, it was an hour alone with her he would not waste. And then he would do right by her and see her married to Mr. Bentley because at least one of them ought to be happy.

CHAPTER 9

FRIDAY CAME WITH A LOVELY visit from Mr. Bentley. Jemma had hoped he would come. When he mentioned his appreciation for silk and what a rare luxury it was in the West Indies, well, she'd been so excessively thrilled to find they shared a common love for the fabric that she'd spilled her tea down the front of her favorite calico-print gown.

And that had been the end to a visit full of potential. She did not know if she was more upset about her foiled plans or her gown. Part of gaining excitement for the style was wearing it out and about and drawing attention to its uniqueness. She dearly hoped her maid could get the stain out. The dress was certain to be the rage by the next Season, if her charts on fashion trends and notes from a favorite French modiste were correct, so at the very least, the design she'd created would fetch a good price—funds she planned to give to the poor.

Deep down, she knew Mr. Bentley might disapprove if he knew of her business ventures. Indeed, many would frown on her desire to sell or publish her sketches, which was why she employed the false name. But other Rebels had performed far braver acts than this, so wasn't it right for her to use her talents for a good?

Talents she couldn't showcase if she continued to be so clumsy. She was not the sort to nervously bumble about. She was pragmatic—steady! The pressure of making the most of this match was going to be her undoing. Fortunately for her, Mr. Bentley had told

Mrs. Manning he would come again Monday morning to see the new drapes the servants planned to hang later that day in the drawing room. Mrs. Manning could be very insistent when she wanted to be.

The weekend crept by slower than the waxing moon. Jemma passed the time sketching and overthinking every painful interaction with Mr. Bentley. When Monday finally dawned, Jemma was eager to try again. She bent over her dressing table and studied her pallor brought on by a relentless case of nerves, and she pinched her cheeks. Wooing a man was not an easy feat.

"For Grandmother," Jemma reminded herself.

A knock came at her bedchamber door, and then the door opened to reveal Lisette.

"You look lovely today," Lisette said.

"I look ill, but I thank you for lying and saying otherwise."

Lisette laughed and shook her head. She perched on the edge of Jemma's four-poster bed, and Jemma did not have to look in the mirror to know Lisette was examining her. "Are you looking forward to seeing Mr. Bentley again?" she asked.

Jemma pinched her cheeks again for good measure. "I am. He is a good man, don't you think?"

"In my opinion, he is a very good man. His manners are impeccable, he is an excellent host, and he is handsome enough to hold his own when he stands next to you."

Jemma sighed. "I forget, you never could see the worst in a person. But I must agree on your assessment of his character. Do you think him Rebel material?"

Lisette gave a dainty shrug. "Time will tell."

Jemma nodded. "I plan to ask a few more specific questions today. It will be far easier if I can keep from making a fool of myself like I did on Friday at tea."

"No one thought anything of it. Accidents happen."

Jemma shook her head. "They don't happen to me. Not often, at least. I am still mortified. Thank heavens you were there to distract him while I changed."

"I was happy to do so."

Another knock sounded on Jemma's door.

"Come in," Jemma called.

The housekeeper stuck her head inside. "Mr. Bentley is here, waiting in the drawing room."

"We will be down when Miss Fielding is ready," Lisette said. "Please bring up the tea things and some of the leftover cake from dinner."

"I am ready as I'll ever be." Jemma stood and shook out her hands. "Come, Lisette, my destiny awaits." She wouldn't disappoint Grandmother—not after all Grandmother had done in life for Jemma.

Mr. Bentley stood when Jemma and Lisette entered the room before Mrs. Manning. They exchanged pleasantries, and Jemma took a seat next to Mr. Bentley on the sofa, a mere foot from him. She caught a whiff of his cologne—a mix of citrus and soap. It did not make her pulse race, but it wasn't unpleasant either.

"Do you care for politics, Mr. Bentley?" It was not proper drawing room conversation for a lady, but it was high time for her to discover where Mr. Bentley stood.

Mr. Bentley had the grace not to look overly surprised by her question. "I do try to stay apprised of current events and any large-scale matters coming up for vote."

Lisette bit back a smile, and Jemma plowed forward, knowing it would be far more difficult to pursue the topic once Mrs. Manning joined them. "Any particular issues you are passionate about, Mr. Bentley?"

"Religion, morality, education, and a solid military. I also support the complete abolition of the slave trade. We have made decent headway here in England, but the rest of the British empire has a long way to go."

Jemma was glad the tea hadn't arrived yet and her utter surprise did not mean another accident. "How wonderful. How absolutely wonderful." If she had to marry someone, she preferred his mind be similar to hers. In this, at least, they were attuned!

"Pardon?" Mr. Bentley didn't understand her enthusiasm, but most did not.

"We share many commonalities, Mr. Bentley. Not many would rejoice in knowing they shared similar opinions to a woman, but I cannot say the same in reverse."

"You can be at ease, then, because I am always happy to find someone like-minded—male or female."

Mrs. Manning entered then and drew their attention to her new drapes, an eggplant purple with gold tassels. Mr. Bentley remarked how they reminded him of his aunt's drapes, a Lady Billforth who was quite well known for her exquisite decorating. Lady Kellen had mentioned his connections before, but Jemma had not cared too deeply. Mrs. Manning, however, rolled up on her toes with pleasure.

Jemma released a happy sigh under her breath. Everything was going swimmingly.

Until it wasn't.

When she cast her gaze out the far window, a narrow view in width but equal in height and perpendicular to the bay one Mrs. Manning stood beneath, she saw something strange.

Black curls rising above a topiary bush.

"Miles?" Jemma said.

Mr. Bentley turned to her. "Pardon?"

"Mi—My what a coincidence that you are related to Lady Billforth. I hear her rooms are the envy of all of London."

"Then, you have heard of her," Mr. Bentley said. "You will be surprised to know she is the one who selected the furniture in my own drawing room and had it shipped here for me."

"How fascinating." Jemma glanced back to the window, where she no longer saw Miles. She blinked twice. Had she imagined him there?

"If you have never met my aunt, you must come to the house Friday next, for she will be visiting me." He swung his gaze to Lisette and Mrs. Manning. "All of you should come. We will make a party of it."

"A party?" Mrs. Manning stopped petting her drapes and clapped her hands. "What a wonderful idea."

"I didn't think of it before," Mr. Bentley said, "but why not? Perhaps you could all help me come up with a guest list."

"Will there be dancing?" Lisette asked, her gentle eyes hopeful.

"If you could recommend a pianist, I won't be able to say no."

"Mrs. Jackson plays very well," Mrs. Manning offered. "If you approve of the addition to the party. We, of course, adore the family."

"By all means," Mr. Bentley said. "I will depend upon your suggestions. Is she related to our vicar?"

"Yes, she is his mother. Her husband is the rector, so she resides on the border of Brookeside, but we see her quite frequently," Mrs. Manning explained. "I know she will be thrilled to attend the party."

Jemma's eyes strayed to the window again, searching for a glimpse of mysterious black hair. Her eyes widened when the head began to creep up again. What on earth? She could imagine any of the Rebels spying, except for Miles. He might be their finest actor without exerting any effort, but he respected Society's rules more than any of them.

Miles's eyes appeared, confirming it truly was him, and she watched him scan the room, first taking in Mrs. Manning, Lisette, and then Mr. Bentley. When his gaze met hers, his eyes rounded into a rather guilty pair of dark circles before he darted out of view. Of all the idiotic things to do. Well, she wasn't going to let him get away with spying. If he wanted to see Lisette, he needed to be man enough to ring the bell and call on her properly.

She stood without thinking, pulling everyone's gaze her way. "I, uh, feel a sudden headache. Forgive me, I hope you will excuse me." With one last glance at the window, she quit the room, not waiting for anyone to respond.

She shut the drawing room door behind her and tiptoed to the much larger front door. She opened it carefully and slipped outside, closing it with the same care. Hurrying down the steps, she turned just as Miles stepped out from behind another topiary bush. They collided, her face hitting him square in the chest.

CHAPTER 10

"JEMMA?" HIS ARMS WERE AROUND her in an instant, bracing her. "Are you hurt?"

She rubbed her nose. Miles would never forgive himself if he'd broken it, let alone bruised it.

"I . . . I am well. Simply confused by your presence. What are you doing here?"

Miles was generally a careful man. He'd merely been struck by an intense wave of curiosity. Or should he say, jealousy? He dropped his arms awkwardly to his side. At least he had an excuse to offer, weak as it was. "You scheduled a lesson with me today, or did you forget?"

She dropped her hand, revealing a slightly pink nose. "I didn't forget exactly. I had hoped to come see you later." She squirmed. "Oh, all right, I forgot. I'm sorry, Miles. I didn't mean to forget, honestly. I was consumed with the idea of redeeming myself from spilling tea all over my dress when Mr. Bentley visited last."

Miles frowned. "I hope it wasn't hot."

"It was, but not enough to cause any blisters."

He winced. "That isn't like you. He didn't scare you or bother you in any way?"

She absently rubbed one of her arms. "No, it was all my doing. I am a complete ninny from all these nerves."

Was she simply trying too hard? She was too levelheaded for such behavior. "Is your vision changing? No vertigo?"

"Nothing but a little damage to my pride. But do not think my problems are going to distract me from *your* behavior. If you want to see Lisette, why not join us?"

"Have I ever called on Lisette in all these years?" Miles hadn't meant to pose such a question, but it fell from his lips easily. "Outside of family dinners, which, admittedly, are frequent, or matters of health or the duties of my profession, do you see me single her out?" Even if Jemma had no interest in him for herself, couldn't she, of all their friends, recognize there was no room for Lisette in his heart?

"No, but I do not judge you for it. I know you are shy where she is concerned."

"Shy?" He bit his tongue to keep from laughing. Is that what she thought? She wanted him to act honorably and marry Lisette, and he wanted someone to give him permission otherwise.

"Well, yes. I have always wondered if your father had something to do with it too."

"What would Daniel Jackson have to do with my reservations? If anything, the rector would love to officiate at my wedding."

"I did not mean Mr. Daniel Jackson, but Mr. Wilson."

Miles drew back at the mention of his real father.

Jemma had seen what no one else had. It was true his mother had encouraged him to take on his stepfather's surname to elevate his future opportunities. It was also true that he had never felt himself equal to his friends, whose stations were lofty in comparison to his own; however, his station did not keep him from marrying Lisette, but it did keep him from feeling worthy of Jemma.

"My birth and childhood will always influence me." He swallowed hard, forcing his tone to stay light. "Another reason you ought to seek lessons from another person. If I haven't achieved any personal success, I can hardly be an adequate teacher to advise you."

"We are Rebels, Miles. We see the world differently. We see you differently. None of us thinks any less of you because of your birth. In fact, it is quite the opposite. All of us admire you."

She said the last part with such feeling, it amazed him. She had no idea the impact of her words and how they eased the old wound he carried. He had never felt worthy of Jemma Fielding, so now he did not know how to respond.

She must have sensed the conversation was growing too personal, because her gaze flitted around. "As I said, you have much to offer. I do not live here year-round, but I have heard all the stories. You've helped heal many relationships in the town with your clerical advising. As for me, there is no one's advice I respect more, so it *still* has to be you as my teacher."

He shook his head. For a logical woman, she was surprisingly decisive about this absurd notion, but neither could he continue to argue with her about it when he wanted to make the most of their time together "Very well, but only because I enjoy our lively discussions. Did you reach out to your maid, or did you forget that too?"

Jemma grimaced. "I have been under a great deal of stress, but it does not excuse me for not following through. Heaven knows I need the help, what with these wardrobe malfunctions and clumsiness. I want to force this love business along, but I should do it properly, like you suggest. I will do better, I promise. Without a concerted effort, I will never win his affections before we are wed or learn to apply my own heart properly."

"It cannot be so bad. You will gain your steady ground again soon enough. He would be a fool not to like you."

She avoided his gaze. "You have to say that."

He looked away too. "No, I do not. If he is worth pursuing, he won't care a fig about a few accidents."

"I suppose. I wish I could know for certain. You couldn't hear anything through the window, could you?" Her voice was much too curious.

"What?" He whipped his gaze back to hers. With her eyes narrowed like that, he could imagine her thoughts were on the wild end.

"I will only listen in for a moment. After all, if a vicar can do it, an ordinary person like myself shouldn't feel any shame." She darted by him before he could object, weaving through the ornamental shrubbery lining the Manning House.

He followed after her. His very un-vicar-like behavior had not been meant to justify her own unladylike decisions. "Jemma!"

But it was too late. She'd reached the window. Hunched down beneath the ledge, she slowly straightened her back until she could see through the corner. She darted back down and waved him nearer.

Shaking his head, he crept closer. "You can't hear well enough from here. It would be better to listen from the drawing room door."

Her eyes widened. "Why didn't you say so to begin with?"

Crouched beside her, he couldn't help but chuckle at their amusing position. "Because Jemma Fielding is headstrong and doesn't always wait for someone to advise her."

She stuck out her tongue at him, which made him laugh again. She hadn't done that in years, and he suspected the impulsive act of juvenility was to cover her blush. "I might not be thinking straight these days," she muttered.

Oh, he could have told her that the minute she'd walked into the church with her ridiculous confession about marrying a stranger. But underneath her stubborn exterior was a rather tender heart, and he sensed she did not need to hear a list of her mistakes at the moment. "How can I help you?"

She shrugged. "Grandmother let me have my freedom, but she rooted me too. I was so sure about my future. I didn't know she would die or that all my goals would change. Some days, I feel no different from a cottonwood seed adrift on the wind. Meeting Mr. Bentley has at least given me a sense of purpose."

He wished he could tell her a list of alternatives to fill her needs instead of the man on the other side of the window. Cheering her up, though, was Miles's first priority. "I know you, Jemma. Someday, this cottonwood seed will find fertile ground and grow into a strong tree no gust or gale can penetrate."

Her brows rose. "Promise?"

"I promise. Until then, I will help you spy on Mr. Bentley through the drawing room door so you can be at ease."

This time, the corners of her lips rose too. "And then you'll stay and visit with Lisette?"

He hesitated before giving in. "If it pleases you."

Jemma grinned. The simple smile fueled him with satisfaction and made his ridiculous effort to seek her out worthwhile. "What will you and Lisette talk about?"

Just like that, his satisfaction withered away. "Talk? I don't know. Maybe we'll play a game of chess or something."

"Chess?" Jemma shook her head adamantly. "No, that wouldn't do. Lisette doesn't care for it. Besides that's our game. Or did you forget?"

"Our game?" He smirked. "Is that what it means when you force me to play you every summer so you can beat me?"

"Yes."

He laughed. "So I'm never allowed to play with anyone else?"

She wrinkled her nose. "I suppose not. I like being the one who trounces you.

They both laughed. "Come on." He motioned her to follow him. A nagging thought did not allow him to go more than a few feet. What she'd said earlier about her feeling adrift had not settled. He stopped her when they were out of view of the window and could stand again. "One more thing: you know you have friends who would do anything for you, don't you? If you need to speak to anyone or vanquish them soundly at chess, you're not alone. I'm here for you."

She set her hand lightly on his arm, her eyes suddenly glistening. "Thank you, Miles."

"It's not just me. All the Rebels are eager to support you."

She nodded. "I'm quite happy to know we're all back in Brookeside together. I suppose it isn't only Grandmother I mourn but my stability too. At least I know Grandmother lived a full life, and it was her time, but I wish I could be so certain about my own future."

The hurt in her eyes said more than she had. He longed to remove all the heavy burdens she bore. "Change isn't easy, and I'm proud of you for trying to make the most of it."

Her smile seemed just for him. "I needed to hear that."

On a whim, he grabbed her hand and gave it a quick squeeze of reassurance. He didn't linger like he had at Mr. Bentley's dinner party but dropped it and turned away so she would not see his feelings written all over his face. She had no idea how she affected him, and it was getting harder to hide it.

"Er, Miles?"

He shifted back toward her. Her cheeks bloomed into fetching roses. Had she finally felt what he had? His breath suspended. "Yes?"

She cleared her throat. "You . . . you tore your breeches."

"What?" His eyes followed her gaze to his backside. He looked over his shoulder, and sure enough, there was an inch tear along the seam of his seat. When had that happened? His eyes flashed to where they had hovered by the window. How had he not noticed? He quickly angled himself to hide the unsightly rip, his hands going behind his back. Cringing, he muttered, "I suppose I was due for a new pair."

Amusement danced on her features. "Oh? I heard pantaloons as drafty as old houses were all the rage."

He caught her reference to his joke from when she had torn her dress. "Very funny."

She laughed merrily and started walking. "Be glad it was I who discovered you. I happen to believe such folly comes upon the very best of people."

"Is that so?" He was inclined to blame his frugal nature and procrastination in updating his wardrobe.

She nodded and laughed again. "Do let me know if you would like me to sketch you a dashing pair of trousers. Perhaps a blue pinstripe or a nice dust-colored cotton?"

"I don't know if I should be honored or humiliated that you wish to make a dandy of me." At least his embarrassment had made her genuinely happy again. He fell into step with her as they weaved their way through the landscaped perimeter and onto the sidewalk.

Miles drew up short, barely holding in a Bible swear. Jemma, beside him, likewise froze in her step.

"Mr. Bentley," Jemma blurted.

He had just descended the steps, and neither of them had heard him coming.

Mr. Bentley looked from Jemma to Miles, his discomfort likely mirroring their own.

Jemma pointed to Miles. "Miles and I . . . I mean, Mr. Jackson and I were just . . ."

"We were waiting for you," Miles finished, adopting his sincerest expression. "Jemma was hoping to see you to your horse."

Jemma's desperate eyes caught on to his suggestion. "Yes, my . . . my headache is gone, thanks to this fresh air. I would love to walk you to the stables and make up for my hasty departure earlier."

Mr. Bentley glanced toward the topiary bush they had just exited, but some things were better left unexplained. "I, uh, would enjoy your company on my way to the stable." His smile was conflicted, but he extended his arm to Jemma.

Jemma accepted it, and the two of them left Miles standing alone. She did not even look back at him.

He sighed and took a seat on the stone steps of the Manning House, no longer caring an ounce about his confounded trousers and how awkward it would be should someone catch him there. What had he been thinking, coming here today? He should have rejoiced when Jemma had not come for any lessons. Instead, he'd searched her out, uselessly worried that something had happened to keep her away.

What a fool he'd been. What grown man became suspicious after seeing another man's horse in the stable and had to spy through the drawing room window to assure himself?

He'd done a good thing, sending Jemma off with Mr. Bentley. The right thing. So why did each time he saw them together get harder instead of easier? He had never intended to tell Jemma how he felt—never intended to marry her. Even if Lisette were not in the picture, Jemma would never see him as anything other than a good friend. Despite what she'd said about his father, she was in a league of debutantes all her own, and no one deserved her. So nothing about how he felt made any sense.

It seemed Jemma wasn't the only one struggling with change. He rubbed the persistent ache in his chest. Perhaps he needed to have his heart sufficiently broken before he could move on for good. He would savor every last minute with her, and then do the hard thing, and let her go.

CHAPTER 11

FROM A DISTANCE, JEMMA SAW a small group of women milling around the church door. She had a feeling it was not a group of enthusiasts come to discuss the Bible. Her hand went to her hip. Such determined women would encroach on *her* time with Miles. She blinked the thought away as quickly as it had come. She had meant it would shorten her *lesson* time.

No, even that sounded poorly. She was acting jealous when she had no right to do so. She dropped her hand and repented of her selfish thoughts. Vicars performed important responsibilities. It was not right for her to assume these women did not have *real* needs or that hers came first.

Nearing the scene, Jemma drew up short. Was Miles pinned against the door? She stood on her toes. Indeed, he was! His tight smile said plenty about the four women who were far closer than was respectable. One even had the audacity to stroke his hair.

Jemma's lips pinched tight. She took back her remorse. Mr. Romantic's lady entourage was entirely too much, and she wouldn't stand for it. Didn't they know Miles was nearly engaged to Lisette Manning? Everyone in their town expected it. Were they taking advantage of the fact that Miles had not made anything official?

She crowded in with the other women, catching Miles's eye to show her disapproval.

He shrugged helplessly.

Ridiculous man. He was too nice to run them off but clearly was not trying to encourage any of them. And now he was trapped by their cunning. She didn't care to make a scene and have anyone think she was after him, too, but she supposed she *should* help. Casting her eyes to the heavens, she took a resolute breath and leaned toward the closest woman to her, hovering just beyond the others. She was likely a farmer's daughter, similar to Jemma's own age, and in need of a fichu to cover more of her chest. She seemed the type to do anything to attract Miles's attention, which made Jemma far angrier than she deserved to be.

Amid the clamoring for Miles's attention, Jemma whispered into the woman's ear the first thing she could think of. "Did you hear there is a sale at the emporium on ribbon? Mr. Jackson *loves* ribbon."

The woman pulled away from Miles. "He does?"

Not as much as she, but Miles wouldn't mind if she stretched the truth for a good cause. "He uses them to mark his prayer book. Don't you want him to think of you every time he prepares a sermon? Now, I cannot remember the exact price of the sale. Thirty percent off?"

The farmer's daughter's eyes rounded. "I would hate to miss it. And I would get there before the others."

Jemma nodded, grateful she kept apprised of prices on not just fabrics but also all the embellishments. "Better hurry, then." Jemma watched her go. One down, three left. And the best part? She hadn't even come close to making a spectacle of herself. She dusted off her hands, eager to take on a second woman. But who to start with? Jemma knew a little about the two of them: Miss Hardwick was asking Miles to pray for the puppy in her arms, and Miss French wouldn't stop touching his hair, no matter how many times he pulled her arm away. The third possessed a vaguely familiar face tipped beguilingly toward Miles as she begged him to eat her scones. Good heavens. A ribbon sale wouldn't distract these women.

Miss Scones, first. Jemma glanced at the scones made with dates and raisins lying in a basket on the woman's arm, then glanced up at her deceivingly sweet, large eyes behind a pair of spectacles. She was pleading again with Miles.

"They are better than last time, I promise."

"Please, thank your cook, but I must decline." Miles held his hand up to the basket before whirling it to the other side to keep Miss French from reaching his hair again.

Jemma took the moment of distraction to say to Miss Scones, "Mr. Jackson eats too many sweet things." Jemma didn't even bother to whisper over the noisy ladies next to them.

"Nonsense." The woman brushed her aside, annoyance written all over her face.

Jemma leaned toward her once more. "He could use more meat in his diet. I bet women bring him scones all the time anyway."

The other women sent her looks of annoyance amid their attempts to monopolize Miles's attention. Heaven forbid she encroach on their embarrassing petitions. They picked right back up with their incessant talking, but she caught Miss Scones's elbow, pulling her gently back a step and whispering, "Meat would make you stand out from the others." Meat? Had she really just said that?

Miss Scones froze. "Really?"

Jemma shrugged. How would she know if meat appealed as a gift offering? She personally would take the scones. However, she was being honest that it would make her stand out. Either way, the seed was planted and was sprouting before her eyes.

Miss Scones's mouth turned into a deep pout. Her companions had shifted their bodies to push her farther from Miles, their petitions consuming his full attention. She took a long, disappointing glance at her basket and was off, muttering about meat with every step.

Two more to go and Miles was already going to be the lucky recipient of more markers for his favorite verses and meat to balance out his persistent sweet tooth. Jemma took a hard look at Miss Hardwick. She had the biggest hair Jemma had ever seen and the conniving look in her eyes was far more determined than any of the others. She and her little pug would be hard to dissuade, but Miss French would not intimidate her. She had to stop petting Miles's hair. It was exasperating to watch.

"I am happy to pray for your puppy, Miss Hardwick," Miles said. "Miss French, please do stop touching my hair."

"But you promised to gift me a lock of it," Miss French said. "I have been waiting for months."

"I never promised," Miles said more to Jemma than Miss French.

Jemma's eagerness to help waned for a moment. If she were not so eager for her lesson, and a bit disgusted, she might be entertained by all this.

"He can give you a lock later," Miss Hardwick said. "My puppy is sick. Look at him!"

Jemma lifted onto her toes to see the pug, who seemed quite overfed and happily dozing in Miss Hardwick's arms.

Miss French scowled. "But I want what was promised me!"

Running off women was not Jemma's area of expertise, but surely as a Rebel, she could think of some way to help Miles to the bitter end. But if he had really promised this woman his hair, Jemma could be induced to shave it all off to restore Lisette's honor.

"Wait until he gets rid of the lice," Jemma blurted.

Miss French pulled back; revulsion smeared across her face. "Lice?"

"They are not so uncommon, but his is a particularly nasty case. Does it itch badly, Mr. Jackson?" Jemma asked.

Miles glowered at her.

She did not know what possessed her to continue such a charade, but there was no backing down now. She *tsked* her tongue and gave him her best commiserating look. "Poor thing."

Miss Hardwick held her dog a bit closer to her chest, and for the first time, her eyes were not quite so besotted.

"I—I heard of a remedy with turpentine," Miss French said. "I will fetch you some, Mr. Jackson and bring it directly to your home."

"Better try it yourself," Jemma added. "You have already been exposed by touching him so many times. I would refrain from it in the future." Miss Hardwick nodded deeply in agreement.

"I did not think of that," Miss French said, scratching her head and taking a step back.

"Terribly itchy, isn't it?" Jemma asked.

"Miss Fielding," Miles chided.

She had gone too far, but her annoyance with Miss French was all the justification she needed at present. She looked at Miles with as much innocence as she could muster and shrugged.

"I will send for the turpentine," Miss French assured. She hurried away, both hands now scratching under her bonnet.

Jemma did not wait for Miles to take her to task. She put her arm around Miss Hardwick. "What a sweet puppy."

"He's sick," Miss Hardwick repeated, her eyes turning to implore Miles again.

"What he needs is someone to pray for him," Jemma said.

Miss Hardwick gasped. "That is exactly what I have been saying!"

"Mr. Jackson is much too busy, but I am available."

"You?" Miss Hardwick wrinkled her perfect nose. "I would prefer that a vicar do it."

"I can—"

"There are no rites for sick animals," Jemma said, cutting Miles off before he could volunteer. "And I am excessively good at praying. What is your puppy's name?"

"Jackson."

Jemma coughed. Miss Hardwick had named her puppy after Miles? These impertinent women took all sorts of liberties. Jemma regained her breath and gently pulled Miss Hardwick back a step. "Come, we will have a beautiful prayer over Jackson and get him right to bed. He looks terrible, you know. His demeanor is all wrong. You mustn't make him suffer another moment waiting for a man."

Miss Hardwick studied her dog. "His demeanor is wrong? I had thought him excessively sleepy, but I believe you are right."

Lazy, more likely, but Jemma was no doctor. She led Miss Hardwick away, looking back over her shoulder for a brief moment.

Miles slumped against the door, looking like he needed a trip overseas just to forget his morning.

"You're welcome," she mouthed.

He produced a tired but mischievous grin and mouthed back, "Come tomorrow," then pointed toward the side of the church and the path leading to what had become more their bench than his.

Their secret exchange sent an unexpected flutter through her middle. She nodded before turning back to Miss Hardwick, pretending to pay attention to her. It proved difficult when all she could think about was Miles's smile and her reaction to it. He desired to be with her more than those other beautiful women because of their friendship, and yet her body was responding as if it meant more.

Her steps beside Miss Hardwick slowed. It suddenly struck her that her sense of accomplishment for chasing away the others was motivated by her own jealousy and not by her desire to protect Lisette. She slid a fingernail between her teeth, completely tuning out the woman next to her. This wasn't good. Miles had better hurry and marry her cousin to keep his fans at bay—and to remind even her that he was taken.

Miles caught himself smiling on his way home that evening. Several times throughout the afternoon, images of Jemma had flashed in his mind—her face when she had first seen him cornered against the door, the adorable way her eyebrows had flared whenever Miss French had touched his hair, and the genius way she had convinced every woman there to leave him alone. She had a gift.

Even if he had to have a bad case of lice because of it.

He entered his house through the kitchen, curious to see if Mrs. Purcell had dinner prepared. It was early yet, but he had worked up quite an appetite daydreaming about Jemma. The smell of stew simmering over the fire wafted through the air. Mrs. Purcell stood by the pot, her apron on, and her big wooden spoon stirring the carrots and potatoes.

"Good evening, Mrs. Purcell."

Mrs. Purcell doted on him like a second mother. "Yer 'ungry early again, ain't ye?"

"How could I not be? I can smell your divine cooking from a mile away."

"Enough of yer flatterin' words, Mr. Jackson. Go 'elp yerself to a roll. There's butter in the crock."

He snatched a roll off the counter and slathered it with butter.

He was on his second roll when Mrs. Purcell brought him a bowl of stew. "It's rabbit. A Miss Smith 'ad it sent over for ye."

"Miss Smith?"

"A little speckled thing."

He smiled into his fist. This was Jemma's fault. "I will write and thank her."

"Another young miss sent o'er some turpentine. A 'ole gallon o' it. It ain't proper for a vicar t' receive so many presents."

"I will tell them you said so, Mrs. Purcell."

His cook shook her head. "I want no part o' it."

"At least it was rabbit and not the hard scones with dates in them."

Mrs. Purcell scrunched her nose. "Aye. Those uns'll break yer teeth. The Smiths' cook is poor indeed."

Miles chuckled and took a large bite of stew. He had to admit, the rabbit was a nice change from the scones.

"'Aven't ye picked one of these nice young ladies to marry ye yet?"

Miles set down his spoon. "Mrs. Purcell, you must make up your mind. I thought you wanted me to chase them away."

"The right one would chase the others away for ye," Mrs. Purcell said, going back to her pot and dipping her spoon back into it.

"Is that right?" How amusing. The only one he knew with such a talent was Jemma. "If I find a girl capable of such a feat, do you think she would be interested in me?"

Mrs. Purcell laughed. "What a question! 'Ow could she resist ye?"

It didn't matter how—it mattered that she did. Whatever innocent allure that earned him hard scones and turpentine repelled Jemma Fielding. For years, he had been satisfied knowing she had chosen him for one of her dearest friends and confidants. But a friendship no longer seemed enough.

He found himself wondering what being married to Jemma would be like. Usually, he pushed those thoughts away quickly, but they lingered this time. Would she ever sneak into the kitchen with him to eat dinner early? Would she get on well with Mrs. Purcell? Would she visit him regularly at the church to make it clear to the other women that he cared solely for her?

He wished he were not seeing her on the morrow to teach her how to love another man. It would be all too enticing to teach her how to fall in love with him instead. Indeed, if she would show a little interest in him, he would not hold back.

CHAPTER 12

THE NEXT MORNING, JEMMA HOPED to find an uneventful scene at the church. She did not think she was capable of being so creative twice in sending off another entourage, and she did not care to be mean to anyone either. Thankfully, she did not meet a single person on her walk, and the grounds were blessedly empty.

Jemma weaved through the copse of trees just off the dirt path, spotting Miles sitting on the same bench as before, scribbling his thoughts into his little black book.

When Miles noticed her, he snapped his journal shut and set it under his prayer book. Drat. There would be no peeking at his work today. He looked at her with amusement, as if he knew exactly what she had been thinking.

"I see you've made our lessons a priority once more." He stood and smiled.

"And I see you have evaded your many admirers."

"Touché." He motioned for her to sit.

She glanced around once more, although she had been careful to make sure she had not been seen or followed, before taking the hard wooden seat. She wasn't going to ask, but suddenly she blurted, "Did you really promise Miss French a lock of your hair?"

"I made no promise. Some women hear what they want to hear. Speaking of Miss French, I received a gallon of turpentine yesterday to treat my abominably itchy lice."

"Oh dear."

"Not to worry. A miracle happened, and I was cured without a single treatment."

Jemma laughed. "I am happy for you."

"And I am happy you showed up when you did. I was caught unawares." Miles's smile was thanks enough.

In fact, for a moment, she was lost in it and forgot what she was doing. When she remembered, she quickly changed the subject lest he try to thank her again. "I have another reason you will be happy. I completed my homework."

"I had hoped you would say so. I brought a reward if you were a good pupil."

"For me?"

He dug under his books and pulled out a folded newspaper, handing it to her. "I know Mr. Manning isn't always free with his paper. I thought you might enjoy your own copy."

"Would I?" She accepted the paper and unfolded it. "I have been anxious for news of the outside world."

Miles gave a cheeky grin. "Should we start with the gossip column?"

Her cheeks burned, and she folded the paper again so as not to get distracted from her purpose in coming. "For your information, I read that section when I am upset and need to be reminded of how good my life is."

"Then, by all means, save it for a dreary day."

She suppressed a laugh. "I will. Thank you for thinking of me. Most of the adjustments to the Mannings' household have been smooth, but this has been a comfort I've missed."

He didn't preen like some would when giving a good gift. His simple, humble nod matched his personality. It was so subtle, in fact, that she wondered if he knew how grateful she was. It might seem like a small gesture to him, but everyone liked to be thought of and remembered. Not many knew she read the gossip column at all—which was perfectly suitable to her—but Miles had noticed. He often saw what no one else did.

"I suppose I have two things to be grateful to you for," Jemma added. "I also must thank you for saving me from yet another awkward situation with Mr. Bentley."

Miles folded his arms across his chest, his eyes going to the gray-blue clouds on the horizon. "Did you enjoy your walk to the stables?"

"I did. Mostly. To be honest, it was a bit awkward after coming out from behind the bushes with you." She couldn't suppress her giggle. "I don't suppose it looked very good."

Miles gave a short laugh. "No, I doubt it did."

"Well, I thank you just the same. The private moment allowed us to discuss the wedding arrangement properly. We approached it from a business perspective this time—he's eager to begin his new life in England, and we both know my reasons for a wedding. Once my lessons with you are complete, he will surely see potential for more."

Miles shifted.

Was he uncomfortable with her sharing such intimate details? If so, then he had to understand how painful it had been for her to *live* through such a discussion. Especially with a man she barely knew.

"Speaking of lessons," she said, guiding the subject to safer grounds, "you will be quite proud of what I discovered about my maid's shawl. I had to repent of my misjudgments, so you know it is a good story."

He turned to her fully. "Tell me how it went."

"I planned to buy my maid another shawl, if you remember. After asking her about it, I learned it was her deceased mother's." Jemma let her posture droop. "Strange how simply knowing its origin made it no longer offend my sensibilities. I never noticed before, but she has this tender way of wrapping herself in it that reminds me of receiving a hug. The gray shade is a versatile color, too, and perfect for pairing with any gown." When she looked up, she noticed Miles grinning, his dimples like two inverted buttons. Not for the first time, she wanted to reach out and trace the indents of them. "I am glad you find me amusing."

"Sometimes. Well done, Jemma. You had a truly heartwarming experience. Perhaps even better, you forged a connection with another person."

"Thanks to your advice," Jemma added. "I shall endeavor to produce another experience equally beloved between Mr. Bentley and myself."

He nodded. "If you must."

His tone was too bland. She studied him. Something seemed off about his reaction. Come to think of it, it mirrored a few other times when Mr. Bentley's name had come up. "You do like Mr. Bentley, don't you?"

Miles shrugged. "I don't dislike him."

What wasn't he telling her? "You are not warming to him, for some reason. Is there something about him you do not care for?"

"Nothing at all. He is a decent sort of fellow. I find no fault in him." He dropped into the seat beside her, and she wondered if it was so he did not have to look her directly in the eyes.

He was not admitting something. "If nothing is wrong with him, why have you not invited him to ride with you or to join you and the others at Gammon's?" It wasn't really a fine gentleman's club like the ones in London, or so she'd heard, just a private room off the inn, but next to the Dome and Ian's billiard's room, her male friends and the other gentleman about town liked to gather there best. She, of course, was never welcome—despite all the Rebels' loudness about Society's silly rules.

"I did not know I was expected to make Mr. Bentley my chum. Is not being welcoming and friendly sufficient? I am rather busy teaching a certain young lady how to fall in love. My schedule is all tied up at present."

She let her frown fade. "It is certainly sufficient—if you are good at this lesson business. Your first student has yet to make much progress."

Miles objected. "If the young lady in question would stop attaching herself to me, she might actually attract a suitor. At this rate, she'll fall madly in love with the vicar before she has a chance to even dream about Kensington or its fine owner."

Jemma snorted. "Don't flatter yourself."

"Am I? I'm not a bad catch." He straightened and smoothed the lapels of his jacket.

"Can you imagine me a vicar's wife?" She scoffed. "I would be abysmal at it. Thankfully, you're off the table. Taken. Practically engaged. Why else could I sneak off unchaperoned to meet with you? Well, I'll save you the guessing. It's because you're . . . safe."

"Safe?" He shook his head and dropped his hands. "I used to like the word, but coming out of your mouth, it sounds almost insulting."

The man was speaking nonsense now. "Why not apply lesson number one to Lisette? We can both be happily married by the end of the summer." She didn't know why she kept pushing him so hard. It was like she needed him to tell her his plans and how definitive they were.

Miles turned two brooding eyes her way. "Did a Rebel pressure you to change your mind about marriage?"

"No."

"Exactly. They expressed their opinions, as expected. But in the end, they supported you. When or if I ever decide to marry, you will be the first to know. Until then, I am satisfied just as I am."

"But you aren't against marriage?"

"Of course not. I simply am not ready."

Jemma nodded slowly. "I can respect that. I will be delicate in my pressuring you . . . to marry Lisette . . . as soon as humanly possible." His look of exasperation made her laugh again. She snapped her fingers. "Instead of Lisette, why not enact the very same challenge toward Mr. Bentley?"

Miles stared at her. "I am to fall in love with Mr. Bentley now?"

"Heavens no. You need to speak to him more, be kind to him, serve him even."

Miles shook his head. "Let's not get carried away."

"Are you shirking a challenge? That is not like you at all."

"This isn't one of our games of chess."

"I suppose not." She almost wished they were meeting to play chess today and not for a lesson. "Then again, maybe it's not so very different. Are you afraid I will be better at the art of conversation than you are?"

"Impossible."

He was too fun to tease. "A wager, then?"

He raised a brow.

She took it as permission to proceed. "Whoever does the challenge better has to forfeit a kiss."

Miles's cheeks darkened. "You want to kiss me?"

His sheepish expression made her laugh, or maybe it was her own nerves speaking at the image such a thought produced. "No, that's ridiculous. I meant, I kiss Mr. Bentley and you kiss Lisette."

He gave a fierce shake of his head. "Absolutely not."

"It's a harmless wager. After all, we'll be married to the other person someday, so where is the real scandal?"

"You're not kissing Mr. Bentley. You haven't even passed lesson one. You are hardly ready for an intimate moment. You cannot skip over building a relationship and go straight to kissing."

He was so determined that she relented. She had to admit, she enjoyed when he acted so protective of her. He had always been that way. "No wonder Tom dubbed you Mr. Romantic. Very well, you're right. I don't know anything about courtship. I thought to make it a game, but it wouldn't be real, would it?"

"No."

"So, no wager?"

He shook his head. "No wager."

She shifted in her seat to face him better. "Let's have lesson two, then."

He gave a succinct nod, as if a lesson were preferable to the talk of wagers and kissing. "The theme this time is sacrifice. Think of something dear to you that you can give up for a time."

"Is this from your prayer book? I don't see how on earth it will help me fall in love with Mr. Bentley."

"Relationships rely on personal sacrifice. If love is solely self-serving, it chokes the other person. This is merely practice. Then you can make a reasonable concession to support Mr. Bentley's happiness."

"Have you tried this before? Have you given something up for someone else?"

His brown eyes studied her. She saw a hint of sadness and per-haps regret. Whatever he had sacrificed was something momentous.

She was surprised when he said, "I gave up my time working so I can be with you."

His soft words, like the water trickling over the rocks in front of them, tickled her senses. Miles might be her best friend next to Lisette, but he had no idea his effect on women. It was a good thing Jemma had painstakingly built a wall of resistance against his charms to keep him safe for her cousin.

She swallowed and pulled her gaze away. "Very well, I will give up my pin money."

"Will it be a sacrifice?"

She wriggled in her seat. "I had planned to buy a book of sewing patterns."

Miles was trying not to smile, she could tell. "You don't sew."

She scowled. "No, but you don't know everything about me. I have aspirations for an important project. I've spent several months setting everything in order."

Curiosity peaked his brow. "A Rebel project?"

"Isn't that the only kind of project I could possibly desire to undertake?"

"I have a feeling you are going to tell me all about your dealings, despite how secretive you claim them to be." He motioned for her to continue.

"And why not? Someone ought to be privy to my brilliance." Jemma spent the next quarter hour telling Miles all her plans to publish her designs in a fashion magazine under a false name. "I'm waiting to hear back, but my modiste friends have assured me that the drawings will sell."

"I have no doubt they will."

She grinned and told him the next part, how she intended to donate the proceeds to the poor, listing a few charities in London he might be familiar with.

Miles smiled and nodded at all the right parts and even added his opinion on how to improve upon her business plan. His suggestions were always quietly offered but brilliant.

When Jemma began her walk home after their hour was up, she was creating stunning gowns in her head to steal the attention of fashion-hungry debutantes. She spared a thought about how to accomplish her tasks in the next few weeks without her pin money, but she all but forgot her motivation for doing so. In fact, Mr. Bentley seemed the furthest thing from her mind.

CHAPTER 13

JEMMA HADN'T ANYTHING AGAINST RELIGION, but ever since Miles had become the vicar, she had stopped attending services in Brookeside. It had turned from a place of worship into a gathering place for Miles's admirers, and she couldn't stomach the disgusting scene. Today, however, she'd decided to make an exception because Lady Kellen had stopped by for a visit Friday morning and had not so subtly invited her to church, where she might bump into Mr. Bentley.

Since he had mentioned how he supported religion, Jemma had decided she would indeed attend. As a fan of practicality in everything but perhaps fashion—although she would vote some exception there too—Jemma had begun to see the opportunity to go to church as a way of accomplishing her exercises from lessons one and two. She would prove that she could listen and sacrifice.

Seated next to Lisette on the Manning pew, Jemma quietly observed the service. It was as bothersome as ever to see a congregation primarily made up of women and how everyone became excited over everything Miles did and said. However, it was not quite as bad as she remembered. She heard only one or two sighs of longing coming from the row opposite hers.

Rebecca Hardwick, with her too-big hair and hungry eyes, needed a hobby besides husband hunting. Jemma speared her with a glare.

Despite her preoccupation with her annoyances, Jemma found her gaze inevitably carrying again and again to Miles. He was reverent and steady and had the look of a brooding poet. Could she blame anyone for coming to watch him? She really couldn't. Not everyone was immune to Miles Jackson as she was. In truth, it had taken substantial effort to get to that point, but now that she was there, all it took was one look at Lisette next to her to remember her resolutions.

Where was Mr. Bentley? She looked around for him, finally spotting him in the back. When the service ended, Louisa and Paul stopped her for a moment, and by the time she reached Mr. Bentley, he was outside speaking to Lady Kellen in the church's front garden. Jemma hastily moved to join them.

"Miss Fielding," Mr. Bentley said, dipping his head to acknowledge her. "It was a beautiful service, was it not?"

"Very beautiful."

"I haven't found an equal to Mr. Jackson's sermons," Lady Kellen said.

"Yes, he was quite good," Mr. Bentley agreed. "His parishioners seem to care for him a great deal." Mr. Bentley lifted his eyes toward the church, and Jemma followed his line of vision.

Miles stood at the door, surrounded by half a dozen children. Jemma spotted Tom and Cassandra's young Alan with them, his feet bouncing with excitement. It was nice to see him fitting in with the other children and his new family. Miles waved at all the little ones until they formed a decent line.

"What are they doing?" Jemma asked.

"Didn't you know about Mr. Jackson's weekly tradition?" Lady Kellen asked. "If the children tell him one service they've done during the week, they earn a sweet."

"He does this every week?" Jemma put her hand to her heart. Each child beamed up at Miles like he was their hero. After each child exchanged a few words with him, Miles dug a little sweet wrapped in paper out of a purse and gave it to them, and the little one would skip off to their mother.

"Yes. Miss Manning occasionally assists him," Lady Kellen added.

She swallowed. "Truly?" Why did the image of Lisette beside Miles cause a sinking sensation in her middle? Normally such thoughts comforted her and gave her renewed resolve, but this time her body would not cooperate. She wanted to be content with further proof that Lisette and Miles were perfect for each other, but instead, it depressed her. Where was her perfect half?

She remembered her purpose for attending service today and turned back to Mr. Bentley with greater intent than before. He was watching her curiously. What did he see in her? Someone of interest? Or a distracted, desperate woman?

Mr. Bentley's words were careful. "You and Mr. Jackson seem to be quite good friends."

She swallowed. "Childhood friends, nothing more." Had she spoken too quickly?

"I'm merely surprised Mr. Jackson does this frequently and you've never noticed."

She was caught. The last thing she wanted was to explain why she didn't attend church in the summertime. It was better to evade the comment. "Mr. Jackson does a number of kind things, but I don't always pay attention to them. In fact, he's liable to spoil the children's appetite." She glanced back. "The parents must be concerned."

Despite her words of censure, she saw only the sweetness of the moment. No wonder all the women in town were in love with him. The thought made her scowl. What could Miles possibly be thinking? And with Lisette being forced to witness it week after week. No wonder her cousin felt compelled to help on occasion. "Someone ought to caution Mr. Jackson, don't you think?" she asked.

Neither Mr. Bentley nor Lady Kellen could answer before Jemma retreated a few steps and whirled around to walk the remaining distance to Miles. She passed Miss Hardwick, whose open fan did not hide yet another sigh of longing when she looked toward Miles. For heaven's sake! It was a good thing Jemma had decided to attend church today. On a whim, she stepped in the back of the line, since there were all but two boys left.

Miles briefly acknowledged her with a tip of his head before addressing the first boy, a pale redhead. "Ah, Mr. Kenworthy, what good deed did you do this week?"

"I picked wildflowers for my mum."

"How has one so young already learned the secret of pleasing a woman?" Miles winked and drew out a peppermint for the lad. The young Kenworthy thanked Miles and ran off toward his family.

"Mr. Jeeves, what about you? What kindness did you enact?" The black-haired boy rubbed his hands on his too-small trousers. "I played with the baby while Mama napped."

"What a kindness, indeed! Well done, Mr. Jeeves." Another sweet came out of the purse, and the boy barely had it in his hand before it disappeared into his mouth.

Notwithstanding her frustration with the scene Miles was making, Jemma silently laughed into her hand as the Jeeves boy skipped away.

"Miss Fielding? Did you do something exceptionally good this week?"

Jemma cleared her throat. "Yes . . . well, I plan to. I am about to set a man straight. It won't be easy, but it will be for his benefit."

Miles's forehead creased. "Why do I have a feeling that man is going to be me?"

"However did you guess?" Jemma stepped closer so no one passing might overhear. "What are you thinking, doing something as adorable as this?"

His eyes were far too playful. He ought to look chastened, at the very least. "Is it wrong to be adorable?"

"It most certainly is! And you wonder why the women flock to you. Please, Miles, you must exercise self-control."

Miles folded his arms. "You're asking me to stop promoting acts of kindness?"

She could not fault his motives, but honestly, did the man not know the affect he had on women? "In public, yes. You must be more discreet, for Lisette's sake."

"What does she have to do with this?" He frowned, not angry but certainly displeased.

"As if I have to tell you." If Jemma was flustered with heavy sighs from the likes of Rebecca Hardwick, what must Lisette be enduring?

"You can tell me all about it at our next lesson."

"What?"

"I noticed you're still struggling to connect with Mr. Bentley."

She wasn't so pathetic. "I'm not *struggling* with Mr. Bentley."

"Then, why are you here with me instead of over there with him?"

She sputtered, not liking at all how he'd turned this around on her. "I was just talking to . . ." She looked around and realized she no longer knew where Mr. Bentley was. Had he left already? "Oh bother."

"We ought to meet again. Soon. Come tomorrow—our usual spot—and don't be late." He paused, then add, "And I will do my best to leave my adorable self at home." Miles slipped away from the door and moved toward an older gentleman before Jemma could argue.

She folded her arms and grumbled under her breath. If she needed another lesson, it was because of *him*. If things had turned out differently in their childhood, Jemma might not have been so against marriage. She might have paid attention to the natural course of love instead of fighting so hard against it.

CHAPTER 14

MILES DID NOT CARE TO remind Jemma of their purpose for meeting today. She had a newspaper he had brought spread on the bench and was bent over it, her elbow resting on the corner of the paper, her head propped in her hand. He was sitting on the dirt with his back against the bench, his own paper in hand, stealing an occasional glance her way.

The sun warmed the top of his head, and the birds chattered playfully in a nearby thicket close to the creek. Neither the idyllic setting nor the choice in company could be beat. To top it off, no one was around to make a fuss about how incredibly improper their undignified positions were or the fact that they were once again without a chaperone.

He never imagined himself having a day like this. Ordinary in its simplicity and extraordinary in its very existence. He stole another glance at the beautiful woman beside him, and his gaze stuck. He longed to tuck the dark, wavy strand of hair hanging on her cheek behind her ear so she might read better, but for now, he was content just to be near her.

It was . . . perfection.

"It's horrific!" Jemma sat up, her brows furrowed tight. "News is trickling in about the Greek Massacre on the island of Chios. The numbers are staggering: over twenty thousand killed, twice that amount enslaved, and tens of thousands left as refugees."

His stomach tightened at the sheer inhumanity of it all. He had seen some snippets of news covering the Greeks' fight for independence, but the recent headlines were enough to make any civilized person sick. "Horrific is right. It is devastating to learn so many Christians were killed or abused. I hope the Greeks don't give up their fight against the Ottomans. Rights of worship and political representation shouldn't have to come at the cost of death."

Jemma stared at him. "Are the British sending troops to aid them?"

Miles shook his head. "Nothing has been said yet."

"Surely something must be done."

"When there is a strong enough desire to help, a way is provided." He thought of Jemma as a little girl and her willpower to keep him in Brookeside. It was the sort of merciful movement Europe needed to make.

"Let's rally as many as we can to help, Miles."

He grinned, always happy to join a good cause. "Shall we?"

She tapped the paper, and he saw wheels spinning behind her eyes. "I have some personal funds I could donate, and we could encourage our friends to do the same."

"Why not submit some of your fashion designs that truly showcase Greek culture, with your added modern flare, to some magazines?" Miles suggested. "We need as much national sympathy as we can gather."

The passion in her eyes went from a spark to a full glow. "I could still send some to the modiste in London for my other project so I won't sacrifice my cause there but have a more immediate turnaround with the magazines. What a splendid idea."

It was splendid but only because it made her smile widen.

"I have several sketches that would work perfectly," she added. "I cannot wait to get started on a few more." She began folding up the newspaper.

"Don't get carried away, mind you." He wanted to encourage her, dive in beside her in another worthy Rebel cause, but he had to remember she had a great deal on her plate. He couldn't let her wear herself out.

"Why not? It will be a great challenge."

"I agree, but will it be too much?"

She stood and dusted off her dress. "Why would aiding such a righteous cause be too much?"

"With the wedding plans and everything."

"Wedding?" Her eyes dulled. "I had quite forgotten." She nibbled on her bottom lip. "It doesn't bode well if the bride is more excited for her charity work than for her own wedding, does it?"

"Stop fretting. I shall gather support for the Greek cause on your behalf."

The worry on her face lessened. "Spoken like a true Rebel."

Spoken like a man in love, he corrected silently.

"But, Miles, I reserve the right to contribute as many ideas as I can think of."

Before he could agree, he heard his name being called. Both of them looked toward the path leading back to the church. None other than Miss Rebecca Hardwick was walking toward them, her gown too pink for her ruddy complexion and her sausage curls slapping her face with every step. Worse, she had the same determined look in her eyes as a starving person who had finally discovered her next meal.

Miles jumped to his feet and dusted off his backside.

"Should I hide?" Jemma asked, pointing to the small thicket.

"It's a little late," he grumbled, forcing an innocent smile for Miss Hardwick. "Act normal." It seemed his perfect day was coming to a rapid end.

"Oh, Mr. Jackson!" Miss Hardwick waved her closed fan in the air. "I found you."

Jemma backed up so she stood directly beside him. "Should I at least make a run for it?"

He pinched the sleeve of her dress and whispered. "Don't you dare leave me alone." Miss Hardwick had designs on him, and he would not put it beyond her to frame a scandal.

Miss Hardwick came up to the other side of the bench. "You disappeared out of thin air. But I've discovered your hiding place, and I shan't forget it." She pointed her fan at him like a long, chastising finger.

"Good day to you, Miss Hardwick," Jemma said coolly, a timely reminder to Miss Hardwick of her presence.

"Miss Fielding, I did not notice you there."

Miles did not react. Miss Hardwick was a kind, good person, but she had a tendency toward the ridiculous. She had seen Miss Fielding and, for some reason, had chosen to ignore her. Even so, it would do no good to draw Miss Hardwick's attention to his and Jemma's secreted meeting.

"However did the two of you end up all the way out here?" Miss Hardwick's lashes fluttered at such a rapid pace, it made him dizzy.

Miles opened his mouth to say something and looked to Jemma for help.

"I was . . . walking by," Jemma answered.

Miss Hardwick laughed. "Indeed. I had no assumption otherwise. Everyone knows you have no inclination toward romance or marriage, Miss Fielding, so I shan't draw any unnecessary conclusions about this happenstance."

Apparently, Miss Hardwick was unaware of the arrangement with Mr. Bentley. The Matchmaking Mamas could be as discreet as the Rebels, it seemed.

Jemma glowered. "Should I thank you?"

Miles cleared his throat. "Yes, we should both thank Miss Hardwick for not jumping to the wrong conclusion."

"Well, go on, Miss Fielding," Miss Hardwick said with another wave of her fan. "You may continue your walk. Do not let us detain you."

Jemma turned and gave Miles a look. One that said, *"She is insufferable!"*

"I dare not be caught alone with you, Miss Hardwick," Miles added quickly. "You do have your reputation to consider. We had all better part ways."

Miss Hardwick let out a high-pitched whine. "Oh, fiddlesticks. Can I not at least walk you back to the church?"

"No." Miles and Jemma spoke at the same time.

He glanced at Jemma, who looked sheepish.

"I fear it would not be appropriate." He dipped his head and retrieved his newspaper and hat from the end of the bench. "Good day to you both."

He took a few steps before Jemma said, "Oh, Mr. Jackson. I have a message I need to relay to you from Mr. Manning."

"Oh, certainly," he said.

Jemma rushed to his side and stepped in pace with him just as Miss Hardwick realized she had been outed. They heard her huff behind them, but they didn't stop.

"We did not get to our lesson," Jemma whispered.

"What about Wednesday?" He glanced back, but Miss Hardwick had taken a seat on the bench, apparently choosing not to follow them. "I have an appointment at midday, so morning would work better."

"But our spot has been compromised," she hissed.

Our spot. He had called it the same, but it sounded so much better coming from her. "Can you manage to take your horse on a ride without company?"

She nodded without hesitation.

It was terribly un-vicar-like, but planning a clandestine appointment with the woman he was not supposed to be in love with was so perfectly satisfying. "If you can make it, I will be at the upper pond by eight o'clock."

Her eyes sparkled. "I will find a way."

Those words weren't meant to give him hope, but somehow, they did.

Didn't those discerning green eyes of hers see how well she worked with him? No topic was too grave or political. Ideas flowed and were freely discussed. He had offered to help her, but in the end, she had lingered to help him. They were so well matched. An hour in each other's company would never be long enough.

"Then, so shall I," he said, his courage rising. He would find a way—a way for her to see him in a different light. He couldn't keep going like this and pretending that he felt nothing for her.

Jemma dropped her bonnet and gloves on the walnut side table in the Mannings' entrance hall, still annoyed with Miss Hardwick's interruption of her lesson. In truth, she had been so caught up in the idea of gathering funds for the Greek people that she'd forgotten the lesson altogether. But she'd been having a perfect afternoon until Miss Hardwick had arrived. How aggravating it must be to have so many women following one about.

A bouquet of fresh flowers in a vase beside her cast-off bonnet emanated a beautiful scent, a welcome distraction from her thoughts. She bent over to smell them right when the drawing room door opened.

Lisette stepped out. "I thought it must be you. What do you think of the flowers?"

"They smell divine. Did Aunt have them cut from the garden? I didn't realize we had such a variety in bloom already."

"Mr. Bentley brought them by." Lisette crossed the entrance hall and touched the conical bloom of a syringa. "He hired someone to bring them all the way from the hot house in Leeds."

"Leeds? What trouble it must have been. And it means he stopped by again while I was out." Jemma groaned. "How do I keep missing him?"

Lisette leaned back against one end of the side table, careful not to disrupt the flowers. "He grew a little flustered when I reminded him of the hour of your daily walks. He must have been anxious to see you."

Jemma reached for the exposed brass handle on the table drawer, running her finger around the lion head. "Please tell me you kept him company so his time was not completely wasted."

Lisette's smile appeared. "We had a lovely visit, talking all about you."

"Good heavens."

"I highlighted all your best features and talents."

"Always the angel." Jemma put her arm around Lisette and rested her head on her taller cousin's shoulder.

"I find I enjoy thinking about you being married," Lisette said. "We haven't had many gentleman callers here in the last year. Not outside our Rebels friends. I'm all swept up in the idea of romance. It almost makes me believe it's possible for me."

"How could you say such things?" Jemma brought her head up. "Of course you will have romance. You know Miles has been busy establishing himself in the community, but it is only a matter of time."

"Jemma, I asked you last summer not to say such things about Miles and me. It doesn't make it any easier for me."

"Forgive me, but I am merely saying what we are both thinking."

Lisette sighed. "Perhaps once you are wed, I will start dreaming of my own wedding again."

Jemma grinned. "My thought exactly. You will need more time to plan a wedding anyway. I want your special day to be even more grand and special than my own."

Lisette frowned. "What a strange thing to wish for."

"And why not? Doesn't my favorite cousin who has been like a sister to me deserve the very best?"

Lisette's eyes twinkled. "Shall I put you in charge of the whole day?" Her teasing made Jemma forget all about the vexing Miss Hardwick. "Just don't forget to see that the groom arrives. He is a rather important feature."

Miles.

He was the sole groom Lisette would ever refer to. Though she had taken to not saying his name aloud anymore when planning her future.

Jemma opened her mouth to remind Lisette of how perfect she and Miles would be, but the words wouldn't come. It was too hard when Jemma was sneaking off to meet with him. Her lessons with Miles had become coveted time together. Once Jemma married, Lisette could have him all to herself. Jemma just needed him for a little while longer. Then she would see right by Lisette.

She would see the two of them married in the most elegant, perfect wedding one could imagine. It was the least she could do. Lisette had opened her house to Jemma every summer and never begrudged her anything—sharing her friends, her parents, her gowns, and her confidence. Lisette was the kind of person who made the world better just by being alive. She deserved everything she wished for—which wasn't much.

Just Miles.

Jemma could give her that much, right?

She gave Lisette another side hug. "Don't worry, you shall have your handsome groom. No matter what."

Miles wanted Jemma to sacrifice something. She knew one thing that would be harder to give up than money.

CHAPTER 15

WITH HIS JACKET DISCARDED AND his shirtsleeves rolled up to his forearms, Miles perched on the end of the dock at Bellmont Manor's upper pond with his young fishing companion, Tom's son, Alan. Relaxing back on his arms, he let Alan take the lead, watching him hook a worm to the end of his rod. While Alan cast the line, Miles's eyes traveled the length of the pond. How he appreciated the beauty here. It was one of his favorite views in not just Brookeside but all of England. It had always had the ability to clear his mind, which he sorely needed these days.

Vibrant greens and dark swirls of blue covered the canvas only God could have painted. Old oak and yew trees bordered one side of the pond. Among them, a tall willow dangled its flexible branches and teased young boys to swing on its limbs into the sapphire water.

It was the perfect place to talk about love—and the perfect place to avoid it.

Today, he hoped for the prior. And he in no way meant to include Mr. Bentley in the discussion.

A noise distracted him, and he looked over his shoulder to see Jemma ride up. She dismounted and tied her mare to a tree. He wasn't surprised to see her cast off her bonnet with the same ease he had tossed aside his jacket. The pond lent some freedom from propriety's prying eyes.

The light caught on her brown tresses swept up on her head and the long lines of her neck. Just the sight of her sent his thoughts spiraling in all the wrong directions. It would help if her beauty were not superior to the picturesque nature in front of him. Not wanting to be caught staring, he forced himself to look forward again—to think about the pond and only the pond.

The property belonged to the stern Lord Kellen, who was rarely at home, but Ian had no qualms sharing his father's land with his friends. Which meant the Rebels frequented it often in the summer months, along with the Dome, situated an easy walk from the pond. Both had become a secluded corner of the world for them.

The seclusion today would be ideal for their lesson, but he was also relying on the pond's ability to diminish the weight on his mind—the resolution he had made to himself the last time he'd seen Jemma.

Next to him, little Alan adjusted his fishing rod.

"What do you think of this fine fishing spot?" Miles asked.

Alan shrugged. He could talk plenty, but at a mere six years, Alan also had a unique ability to stay quiet—likely from his time at a workhouse—which allowed him to become quite efficient at catching fish. Unfortunately, it also enabled him to sneak away far more often than either Tom or Cassandra appreciated.

Today, however, his silence would be just the thing Miles needed in a chaperone, so he didn't press the boy for more. It wasn't what Lady Kellen would call an acceptable substitute, but Alan would be a sufficient buffer between him and Jemma. It was getting harder and harder to control his feelings around her. Each time he saw her with Mr. Bentley, Miles was more desperate than the time before—a sensation he wished he could drown in the depths of the pond and walk away from.

The clipping of Jemma's half boots on the wooden planks matched the beats of his heart, increasing in sound and pressure as she neared him. He glanced up to meet her green, marbled eyes, bright in the morning sun.

"Good day to you, Miss Fielding," he said to her as if surprised to see her. "Have you come to fish with us?"

"Fish?" She glanced at Alan and caught on to his subtle clue. "Yes, I came to fish." She pushed her skirts to the side and took a seat on the opposite side of Miles, tucking her legs under her dress as she did. He rather liked that after all these years, she still could be at ease in a natural setting, despite the finery of her gowns.

She leaned her head toward his, chasing away any thought he'd had of *him* being at ease. "If I'd known we were fishing, I would have brought my lucky rod."

He pulled his gaze to the slow-rippling water. "You don't have a lucky rod."

"I could have had one made, and it would have out caught yours."

He laughed under his breath. "Impossible. All the other lucky rods you claimed to possess in the past didn't do the trick. We'll see what you can do with an ordinary, luck-free rod, shall we?" He reached for his own rod, lying unused beside him, and handed it to her.

She inspected it carefully. "Does this one catch husbands?"

Miles was beginning to despise the word. "Indeed. The smelly, fishy kind."

"My favorite. I will take a dozen, please."

He gave a short laugh and turned to Alan. "What would Miss Fielding do with a dozen husbands?"

Alan scrunched up his nose and shook his head.

Miles chuckled and placed a worm on the hook at the end of his rod, rinsing his hand in the water when he finished. "Let's start with catching *one*, shall we?"

Jemma cast her line with a smooth flick of her wrist. For a moment, they sat in a comfortable silence, listening to the hum of insects and feeling the alternating cool and warmth on their cheeks while the sun grew higher.

"I've missed this," Jemma breathed.

He nodded. "It's like the old days, is it not? I can see Paul swimming laps, Tom pushing Ian in when he isn't looking, and you and Lisette paddling around in the old rowboat, barely big enough for two."

"I can imagine the very scene. You would have been on the old rope swing, hollering and whooping before you dropped with a splash."

"Now you know why I picked this backdrop for our next lesson. I thought we ought to discuss the concept of work and play."

Jemma grinned. "An odd choice, I daresay, but one I think I will like. But will Mr. Bentley like it? A few weeks have passed, and I've made little progress."

"You will have to trust me."

"After seeing your admirers flock to your sermon on Sunday, I am convinced you know what you are doing. Go ahead, teach away."

He chose to ignore her ridiculous statement about women flocking to him. He had one woman—one—he desired to run to his side, and she came to criticize him in lieu of Lisette or to beg for advice. He'd wanted to be done with these ridiculous lessons, but when given a chance to be with her again, he would cave every time.

Blinking away his dark thoughts, he recited his prepared lesson in a dry, dull voice, refusing to get too excited about the subject matter, for Alan's sake . . . "From what I have observed, a couple tends to do one of two things: work too much or not enough. This is the same for both the poor and the rich. There seems to be a fine balance in which relationships hang on the pendulum. When out of balance, the couple suffers. Frivolity, relaxation, or social engagements, whatever form of play it is, can be tiresome in its excess. It, too, requires the utmost care of balance. Do you understand why diligence in this matter can affect love?"

Her dark lashes lifted as she looked up at him, but it wasn't tears of boredom he saw there. She was paying rapt attention. The silly girl valued his words. He frowned. Did she really appreciate his abstract theories? He'd never spoken them aloud before. His heart stuttered at her impressed expression.

"You've always had a way with words, Miles. You make me think about the ordinary things in a whole new way." She set her hands behind her on the dock and leaned back against them. "Balancing work and play sounds simple enough, but it makes far more sense for a wedded couple. How do I apply it to Mr. Bentley and myself while we are courting?"

As if he would tell her such a thing. "I think the student ought to come up with the application herself."

"I think I already know the answer," Jemma said. "If I am too involved in my Rebel efforts, even letting them occupy my mind with abundance, I won't be making enough room for Mr. Bentley."

Jemma had always been a quick study. "Yes, but not exercising your efforts and talents for a good cause would make you a dull companion." Miles didn't finish his thought, but he wanted to tell her that no matter what, she couldn't give up her time with the Rebels. Him aside, it was her calling as much as his was the church.

Jemma didn't seem to notice his inner struggle. "I quite agree with everything you've said. Mr. Bentley and I will also need leisure time together, like this." She leaned toward Miles. "Thank you for bringing me here and helping me remember better times." She held his gaze a moment too long, and a kind of sweet tension settled in the air around them. She might speak of Mr. Bentley, but her gaze said something else entirely. Her lips tugged at the corners, drawing his eyes to them. Miles wanted nothing more than to lean over and kiss her.

How he wished he knew how she would respond to such a gesture.

How he wanted to find out right now.

"Close your eyes for a moment, Miles," she whispered.

His eyes did the opposite, widening. "Jemma—"

"I mean it. Close your eyes."

She was so intent upon it, he had to obey. For a moment, he forgot about Alan sitting quietly beside him, about Lisette and her hold on his future, and even Mr. Bentley. His eyes closed, and he held perfectly still, though his heart raced, and his next breath stuck inside him.

Nothing happened at first. He heard a rustle and felt her arm brush his. A waft of rose water reached him, the scent nearly undoing him. A small splash sounded, and he briefly wondered if it was the fishing rod.

"You can open them now."

He did, curious and confused. She pointed past her skirts pulled up almost to her knees and toward her feet, now submerged in the water. Her half boots and stockings lay neglected beside her, and her mouth was pulled into a sheepish grin. "I did not want you scolding me about propriety again, but I couldn't help myself."

If only he were half as tempting as the water.

He smirked at his own foolishness. No kiss. No mystery revealed. He didn't wait for her to close her eyes but pulled off his own boots, shoving his toes into the frigid water. He sucked in his breath. "It's freezing!"

Alan giggled beside him, and Miles gave him a wink.

"I was going to warn you," Jemma said, "but you seemed determined."

"I couldn't let you have all the fun."

"Speaking of fun, might you have been having a little too much of it?"

He scratched his head, ruffling his obnoxious curls. "Vicars can't put their feet in water? Do my hairy toes offend you?"

"Are they hairy?" Jemma bent over to see.

He laughed. "Just tell me, Jemma: What am I doing wrong this time?"

"It's Lisette." She seemed to force the name from her mouth and kept her eyes on the water. "You haven't worked very hard to build a relationship with her."

Lisette again? How could she be so blind? Maybe it was Mr. Bentley's presence in town. Maybe it was these dashed romantic lessons. Maybe it was the nearness of Jemma and the ache for one more carefree day. Maybe it was his resolution to finally show her he was not just a vicar. Whatever it was, he blurted the words: "I love Lisette."

Her whole posture went rigid. "You . . . you do?"

"As a *friend*."

She blinked once. Twice. A dozen times. "I, uh, I don't understand what you're saying."

He sank his head into his hands and groaned.

"Miles Jackson!" Jemma's voice grew more flustered. "What are you saying?"

"Jemma, it was never meant to get so out of hand."

"Stop." She pulled her feet from the water and drew herself into standing position. "If you have grown apart, it is all your fault. You've neglected her, and it is high time you take your own advice."

Miles copied her, jumping to his feet. "It's not a matter of effort."

"What effort? I haven't seen much for years."

Her temper was flaring, and she wouldn't see reason until she calmed down, but he couldn't wait. This was his chance to explain himself and rid her of her ridiculous dream—this obsession—she had of him and Lisette marrying. "It's not what you think. Let me explain. I cannot marry Lisette."

Her eyes narrowed to two angry slits, and he almost missed her hands fly to his chest. In a reflex, he grabbed them. "Were you going to push me in?"

"No, but if it shocks some sense into you, I will gladly do it. You cannot make a woman believe you love her, then change your mind."

"Who said I changed my mind?"

She wrestled to free her hands. "Are you or are you not going to marry Lisette?"

Miles dropped his hold on Jemma and blew out a long breath. "I . . . cannot marry her. I never wanted to marry her." He opened his mouth to explain further, but hoping she'd listen was as logical as letting his guard down.

Jemma pushed him, and this time, he was not ready for it. Somehow, her small amount of weight gained just the right momentum, sending him sprawling backward into the water. Nothing cleared a man's head as fast as a shockingly cold bath.

If only one's heart were so easily wiped clean.

CHAPTER 16

JEMMA STEPPED TO THE EDGE of the dock, remorse sweeping over her as Miles's head came up out of the water. She should never have lost her temper, despite how justified she might have felt. They weren't adolescents anymore. She couldn't push someone into a pond. Especially not a vicar!

Calm, gentle Miles was gone, and angry, wronged Miles now gripped the dock with his strong, athletic arms to draw himself out of the water.

She took a step back as he found his footing again. Miles glared and ran a hand through his wet curls, slicking them back. Without taking his eyes off her, his lips in a stern line, he unbuttoned his drenched waistcoat and threw it onto the dock.

Jemma's heart hiccuped.

His translucent shirt clung to his firm chest, and his hands went to his hips. His eyes, dark and brooding, narrowed further, and he took a purposeful step toward her.

She took two steps backward to match his stride. "Miles . . ."

"Jemma."

How could she explain why she couldn't listen to his explanation? Why some things just had to be, regardless of feelings. "Miles, I . . ." The heel of her bare foot caught between the planks of wood, and she stumbled. Two wet arms caught her.

She looked into Miles's eyes, softened by his worry for her. Her pulse ricocheted in her chest, hummed in her ears, and sent heat waves through her veins. She wasn't supposed to be in his arms. It wasn't safe for her.

"Jemma, I . . ." Miles paused and blinked, as if swallowing back the words he wanted to say.

Reflexively, she reached for his wet shirt, but her fingers barely brushed it when he righted her. He was too quick to drop his hands, leaving her cold where the wetness seeped into her gown. She was safer now, but his nearness had confused her—taunted her even.

Shouldn't anger be her only emotion?

Miles looked over her shoulder, searching past her. "Where is Alan?" He pivoted around her. "Alan?"

Jemma hadn't even noticed Alan's disappearance. It wouldn't be the first time Tom's son had run off, but this was on their watch.

"Did he fall in the water?" They had learned last September that Alan was a natural swimmer, but the pond appeared empty.

Miles scanned every inch of the area to make certain. "He loves to swim, but I don't see any sign of him, nor did I hear any splash." He shoved his feet into his boots, leaving his waistcoat and jacket by the fishing things. He wasted no time darting away, his steps clipping down the dock at a sprint. She shoved her feet through her own stockings and half boots and followed after Miles.

Miles's voice was more frantic now. "Alan! Alan, please come out if you're hiding."

Ian rode up on his horse just as Jemma reached the grass. "Did I miss an invitation for swimming?" He chuckled at the sight of Miles still soaked through.

Ian maneuvered his horse up alongside Jemma's under the tall oak.

"Fishing, actually." Miles cleared his throat. "An unfortunate incident ensued, but not the most important at the moment. Alan has disappeared."

"Again?"

"Could he have run home?" Jemma came up beside Miles, folding her arms over her chest. She could restrain her myriad feelings long enough to find Alan.

"It's a good three miles or more." Ian's horse danced, feeling the indecision of his rider. "I didn't notice anything on my ride, and if he knows the road home, we should have crossed paths."

"He might be hiding close by, then." Miles ran his hand through his wet hair again and scoured the bushes along the pond with his gaze.

Jemma drummed her fingers on her arm, wishing she knew of a way to draw the boy out. Suddenly, an unbidden memory came to her of Alan standing in line for a sweet from Miles. "You don't happen to have any sweets hidden in your waistcoat pockets, do you?"

Miles's eyes swung to meet hers, and he grinned. "If they did not wash away in the pond."

A few moments later, Ian was off his horse, and all three of them were calling out bribes to Alan and promising he wouldn't get in trouble.

It didn't take a minute before Alan dropped down from an oak tree branch by Jemma's mare. "You promise you won't tell Mama Cassie?"

It was the first time Jemma had heard Alan call Cassandra *Mama*. Jemma was so happy to learn he was embracing his new family that much of her ire softened. "Of course not, Alan. Why would you hide from us? We don't want you to be unhappy."

"I don't like when people fight."

Jemma dragged her eyes to Miles, who refused to meet her gaze.

Ian, however, raised his brow. "Is that how Mr. Jackson ended up soaking wet?"

Alan nodded. "They were talking about love and getting married."

"Were they now?" Ian swung his gaze to the two of them, and Jemma hoped she looked the least guilty.

"Come on, Alan," Ian said, mounting his horse. "I'll find you something extra delicious at Bellmont Manor and see that you are brought home."

Miles helped Alan climb up in front of Ian. Jemma heard Miles whisper to Ian, "Perhaps I should take him . . ."

"And leave me to Jemma's wrath?" Ian shook his head.

"I heard that!" Jemma's hands fell to her hips.

"Do play nice, both of you," Ian said. "This smells strongly of matchmaking mischief, and I want to be as far from it as possible."

"Coward," Jemma said, and not under her breath either. Ian's smile widened. He kicked his horse, and he and Alan rode away.

With Ian's horse gone, she went to untie her own. She moved her mare over to a stump she often used as a mounting block.

"Jemma, we should talk." Miles's voice was soft, pleading.

"I should like that," Jemma said. "Once you get your head on straight, we shall have a lovely little chat. Do let me know when it happens."

"Jemma, you haven't let me explain."

"Explain how you plan to break my cousin's heart?" She shook her head. "My own heart is heavy enough without adding this to everything. I'm sorry, Miles, but I need you to reconsider." She kicked her mount and sent the mare flying away from the upper pond, gathering speed as she went.

Rubbish lessons.

She would have to learn how to capture Mr. Bentley's affection and stir up her own all by herself. Mr. Romantic should change his name to Mr. Happiness Killer.

Poor Lisette.

When Jemma reached a safe distance from the upper pond, she reined in her mare. Her chest catching and tears forming. But it wasn't for Lisette that she cried. It was for her own miserable heart. A heart that had nearly betrayed her moments ago in Miles's arms— the same reason she had to push him into the water.

When he had said he couldn't marry Lisette, for one brief moment, she had hoped it to be true.

She was a wretched person and an even worse friend.

She urged her mount to run faster. No. She wasn't going to think of Miles in any other way than as her confidant and adviser. She would go to Mr. Bentley's house for his party come Friday night and dance and play court to him.

Miles was meant for Lisette, and everyone knew it.

Everyone, that was, except for the tiniest corner of her being. The wind whipped against her gown and blew through her hair, but it did not blow away the tormenting truth. Despite years of convincing herself otherwise, a sliver of her heart believed Miles had always been meant for her.

CHAPTER 17

MILES CLENCHED THE INVITATION TO Mr. Bentley's party being held on the morrow tightly in his fist, crumpling the better half of it. After the incident at the pond the day before, he planned to politely refuse the invite and spend the evening reading. He had no sooner decided this when the older Mrs. Sheldon stopped at the church to drop off a few things to add to his charity baskets.

He tucked the invitation aside and accepted the items piled in her footman's arms. "Thank you so much, Mrs. Sheldon. Your donations are always appreciated."

"I love helping when I can," she said. Pausing at the church door, she added, "Paul and Louisa are looking forward to the party tomorrow night at Mr. Bentley's house. You will be there, of course, won't you?"

"Actually, I have had a long week and plan to sit this one out."

Mrs. Sheldon was rather thin and frail, but her grip on Miles's arm was surprisingly firm. "You cannot miss the party. What if you offend Mr. Bentley?"

He didn't want to offend anyone, which was why it would be better to keep his uncontrolled thoughts to himself at home. He bid goodbye to Mrs. Sheldon and began sorting through the items she had left him.

Not an hour later, Lady Kellen breezed through the church doors. She had come with a few prayer books to donate to the Sunday school they hoped to start for the children. The extra materials were greatly appreciated.

"Use them well, Mr. Jackson. I will see you tomorrow at Mr. Bentley's party."

It felt dishonest not to say anything. "I am not certain yet if I will be available." As soon as he'd said it, he hoped she would not press his decision.

She was a tall woman who carried herself with some unseen power. Her response was a quelling look that made him straighten. Then she said, "As the vicar, you must make it a priority to support Mr. Bentley. It is your duty to make him feel welcome."

Duty? He was tired of duty. "I will make it a priority to . . . consider it." It was the best he could do.

Lady Kellen gave him another strong look and left him to his business. Well, he was not going to press his luck by sitting around the church. Who knew what matron would stop by to harass him next? He saddled his mare, mounted, and rode all the way to visit Mr. Reed—a recent young widower. If anything was going to clear his mind, it would be time serving someone whose lot was worse off than his own.

A few hours later, Miles left with a lighter heart. Mr. Reed was in mourning, but his perspective was inspiring. On Miles's ride home, he happened to pass his family's carriage on the lane.

His mother put her arm on the window and leaned her head out. Her dark hair, a mirror of Miles's, was framed in an elegant bonnet she had likely fashioned herself. "I was just passing by on my way home from town. I wanted to make certain you had received your invitation to Mr. Bentley's party tomorrow."

Not the party again. "Yes, Mama, I received it."

"And?"

And? What did the matrons of this town want from him? "And I plan to read a good mystery in my wingback chair, make toast by the fire, and sip melted chocolate instead." Or maybe he'd forgo the mystery and spend the evening with his favorite pen, corralling his feelings into the safe confines of paper—a much happier place than reality.

Her frown could have matched his own. "But you always burn your toast. Wouldn't the party's fare be better?"

His horse danced, likely sensing Miles's desire to keep riding. "They won't have melted chocolate, and I am in the mood for nothing else."

"Oh, botheration. You like your chocolate much too bitter anyway."

He smiled and responded gently. "I will add a drop of honey to it and think of you."

The suggestion did not inspire her warmth. "Miles, you must come. I insist, and you know I do not insist very often."

He bit his tongue. What mother did not *insist* often? He sighed. "Very well. I do not know why everyone thinks I need to attend, but do not expect me to stay long."

Immediately, his mother's grin was victorious. He knew the smile too well, for he had lost plenty of arguments to her. But pleasing his mother was often easier than dissuading her. Waving goodbye, he urged his horse forward. Once out of sight of the carriage, he took his hat off and swatted his leg with it.

How fortunate he was to have life smile upon him again today. The matrons of Brookeside were such a joy to interact with. Who needed a reprieve when he could spend his weekend watching Jemma dance with Mr. Bentley? It was such a sweet image, it would likely haunt his dreams.

Lisette and Jemma decided to get ready for the party together in Lisette's bedchamber. Jemma picked out Lisette's gown and fussed over her. "Can you look any more angelic?"

Lisette laughed under her breath. "It isn't a fancy ball in London, but it is nice to have something to look forward to."

"I like a big ball on occasion, but a party of close friends is far preferable to me." Jemma handed a pearl comb to the maid to place in Lisette's hair. "What do you think? I adore it."

"I like it," Lisette said. "But I do think you are fussing entirely too much."

"Me? Not at all. I know you are excited to dance tonight."

"Do you think our friends will take pity on me and be my partner?"

"Pity?" Jemma blew out an exasperated breath. "All the single men will be chasing you for the opportunity."

Lisette giggled. "However will I fend them off long enough to dance?"

The two of them laughed. When it was Jemma's turn to have her hair done, they chatted about what food would be served and if Tom would reenact the ballroom scandal and kiss Cassandra in public again.

When they finished, Jemma stood at the mirror next to Lisette. "I think you ought to wear Grandmother's lace shawl tonight."

Lisette's brow puckered. "But it is your favorite."

"I know, but it will compliment this dress so well." She wanted Lisette to feel like a diamond of the first water. Perhaps then the guilt simmering inside Jemma would fade. If she tried hard enough, everything could still fall into place as planned. One day of confusion was a minor setback. Tonight, nothing would tempt or sway her heart.

CHAPTER 18

MILES GLARED AT THE BACK of their host's head—not a practice he usually condoned but not one he could help either. Mr. Bentley, unaware of the visual daggers pointed his way, led the austere Lady Billforth across his drawing room to introduce her to another of his many dinner guests. All the Rebels were in attendance, along with the entire Society of Matchmaking Mamas. A few other townspeople were smattered throughout the room, too, but until Jemma made her entrance, Miles kept his gaze riveted on Mr. Bentley.

How he wished he could hate the man. He almost did after he heard Mr. Bentley had sent his carriage for Jemma and the Manning family. Did he have to be so upstanding? They had their own carriage, so why send his? There could be but one reason: Mr. Bentley desired to make a clear statement of claim on Jemma Fielding.

Miles gave a childish huff.

"Are you overheated, Mr. Jackson?"

Miles turned to find Lady Felcroft, Tom's mother, observing him amid the chatter in the room. He had not even noticed her sit on the same sofa as him. He set his jaw and shook his head. "I am perfectly well. How do you do, Lady Felcroft?"

"Splendid." The baroness studied him for a moment, his answer apparently not satisfying enough. She did not have the same regal, commanding presence as Lady Kellen, but Miles thought her quite elegant all the same. Then again, anyone who mothered his friend Tom couldn't be too pretentious.

Miles cleared his throat. "How is young Master Alan?" Her suspicious features softened into a smile. "He is a real joy. I love having a child about the house again."

"Alan is a special young man."

"He can be a bit restless, but he is always polite. I daresay, his heart is bigger than he is."

A commotion sounded at the door, and the last guests arrived. Mr. and Mrs. Manning entered first, followed by Jemma and Lisette arm in arm. Before Miles could so much as inch forward on the couch, Mr. Bentley was at Jemma's side, with Lady Billforth in tow.

"Don't they look well together?" Lady Felcroft asked.

"Hmm?" Miles muttered. "Oh, yes, I suppose." He had eyes only for Jemma. She was beautiful in her pink muslin. The wider neck line emphasized her creamy skin, while the pink brought out the color in her cheeks. He had no desire to study Mr. Bentley or how well he and Jemma looked as a couple, but he could study Jemma all night.

His mother came and took a seat on the other side of him, her dark hair pulled into an elegant coiffure and her high cheekbones rosy from the warmth of the room. His glimpse of her in the carriage had been similar to all their meetings these days—never long enough for much conversation. Even though the parsonage was not far from the rectory, both of them were very busy.

"Good evening, Mother. I wondered when you would come greet your oldest son."

"Oh, Miles," she said, not even hearing him. "Look at them." He followed her gaze to Jemma and Mr. Bentley. "What a handsome pair they make." Her small squeal of pleasure sickened him. How could his own mother betray him? She never should have agreed to support the latest so-called match.

Miles squeezed his hands together in his lap, popping a knuckle or two in the process. He had come to the party because of three nosy, persistent matrons. So, must they now torture him by spending every breath gloating about their triumphs? The frustration brewing inside him pushed him to his feet. "Excuse me."

The Rebels surrounded him before he could make it far, everyone except Jemma, who still stood in conversation with Mr. Bentley. They took no notice of Miles's inner turmoil, naturally coming together in a room as they always did and including him in their circle.

"Mr. Bentley seems like a friendly chap," Tom said, his wife, Cassandra, on his arm. "It was kind of him to invite a few strangers to his welcome party."

"And he and Jemma seem to get on well," Louisa added, her signature smile a little too bright.

Miles gritted his teeth. Lucky him. More conversation in which Mr. Bentley and Jemma were the central topic. Was he the only one noticing the way Jemma wrung her hands together? He took no pleasure in seeing her so uncomfortable. She was trying too hard to force something that wasn't there to begin with.

"Miles," Paul said as if hearing his inner pleas for a change in subject, "I do believe I saw you when I was out riding today. I wanted to greet you, but you were just stopping at Mr. Reed's."

"Yes, you saw correctly."

"How is he? I was sorry to hear his wife died."

"He is devastated, as you can imagine. He and his wife shared great affection for each other." It was heavy to think about it for too long. Would if he could borrow Mr. Reed's inner strength to drive away his jealousy.

"At least he had happiness for a time," Lisette said. "Everyone deserves that." Her gaze met his, and her soft-spoken words permeated through him.

Everyone? It wasn't the way of things. Happiness was an attitude, and marriage was too often an act of convenience. As a result, one chose to be happy with whatever lot one was given.

He wanted to believe Lisette over Society's stance.

He was still thinking on her words when dinner was announced. It was far more formal than he'd expected, the couples entering the dining room by rank and sitting in assigned seats with name cards set around the table.

Mr. Bentley mentioned in passing his gratitude for Lady Kellen's assistance with the placements. Knowing this, Miles frowned when he saw his name card. He was seated between Cassandra and Jemma. Lisette sat farther down, at the end of the table. It wasn't like Lady Kellen to get something wrong. She had a motive for everything.

He waited while the footman held out Jemma's chair for her to sit before slipping into his own seat. The air beside him rippled with tension. It meant one thing: Jemma hadn't forgiven him yet. She proved his gut right when she studiously ignored him through the first course.

"Jemma," he whispered, putting his glass to his lips. "You cannot ignore me forever."

Her back went rigid. She chewed her food with slow deliberation. When she swallowed, she finally answered, "Yes, I can."

He had a sudden urge to goad her until she smiled. "Does that mean you won't dance with me tonight? I was hoping to ask you for the first set." He was an idiot bent on suffering, but the invitation had to be made. He couldn't let her stay mad at him.

"I cannot. I was going to save that dance for—" Her bright-green eyes met his, and she visibly swallowed.

It took him a moment to process what would have been the rest of her answer. "I didn't think about Mr. Bentley. A later dance would be better."

She gave a short nod and turned back to her food. She did not seem pleased with accepting him at all, but she had also not seemed capable of refusing. Where Lisette was quick to forgive, Jemma often took coaxing. That she hadn't guilted him a little longer had to be a good sign. Maybe she had thought on his answer at the pond, and her heart had softened on the matter.

When dinner ended, the footmen pushed the furniture up to the walls in the drawing room to clear the floor for dancing. His mother took a seat at the pianoforte, her fingers trilling out the first notes.

The couples began to pair up. Mr. Bentley claimed Jemma's hand, and they lined up with the others.

Miles committed himself to being patient—to being long-suffering. But something about confessing his feelings about Lisette to Jemma had weakened him. Seeing Jemma and Mr. Bentley's smiles bending toward each other was too much. He couldn't stand to see them so near each other, their gazes locked in practice for the rest of their mortality together. Miles turned away, but it was not soon enough. Inside him, a sharp blade formed by years of longing now ran jagged with disappointment as it ripped its way through his heart.

Any small chance he'd had with Jemma had passed long ago.

Raw and bleeding inside, he surmised one thing as he stared blankly at the wall: he had to leave Brookeside. Soon. But fleeing this room was his first priority. His feet moved before he could think twice. In his haste, he stumbled around Lord and Lady Felcroft and mumbled an apology.

Once through the door and in the corridor, he blindly walked until he found an empty room. The library. The safest haven in the house. Sinking onto a chair by the fire, he resisted the urge to throw his fist into the stone mantel. Anger didn't suit him. It never did him any favors or changed any situation for the better.

He would go to his sister and brother-in-law in Shropshire until a position could be found for him. Throwing his head back into the cushion, he groaned. How it would pain him to leave his parish. He loved all of them. He loved Brookeside. His family was here. His friends.

But he couldn't live seeing Jemma as *Mrs.* Bentley forevermore. How could he bear it? He'd turn down her silly lessons and . . .

The lessons.

His brow furrowed. Those two little words circulated in his mind like a nondescript answer. The lessons were his last opportunity to be with Jemma. Dare he take advantage of them before he was gone forever? The very idea seemed immoral. She was practically engaged.

Unless she wasn't.

He sat up in his seat, his mind whirling. He loved Jemma, there was no doubt about it. Could he fight for her? Could he risk Lisette's heart to recover his own? This question had teased him a thousand times, but this time, it stayed at the forefront of his mind, marinating and burning into his thoughts. He heard in his mind Lisette's words telling him everyone deserved to be happy.

What if his own happiness mattered as much as the happiness he dearly wanted for his friends? He felt loathsome and selfish to even consider it. He'd devoted his time to caring for others and bringing them joy. Didn't Lisette deserve to find someone who loved her like he loved Jemma? His eyes widened with the revelation.

Life was more than just keeping others happy. He saw now how merely pleasing others was a careful kind of love that brought a surface level of happiness to him and those around him. It didn't require him to be vulnerable and lulled him into thinking he was being selfless.

In protecting everyone by keeping his feelings to himself, he could hurt himself—but he could also hurt everyone else too. He couldn't eliminate anyone's opportunity for growth, much like he could not take away those experiences for himself. If he loved his friends, he would want them to develop tenacity, character, and the kind of joy that didn't always accompany a smile.

He would always want to serve everyone and care for them, but those things were only the beginning. True love meant wanting more than happiness. It encompassed so much more—and he understood now why love was the root of joy. He wanted to love and be loved, and he wanted for all his friends to have the same.

So, was he brave enough to chase what he knew was right and good? The path had an unclear ending and was fraught with living obstacles—people he cared for.

He couldn't think too far ahead, or it overwhelmed him. There were two lessons left. Two opportunities to convince Jemma to marry him instead. Miles grasped the hope in his mind, tightening his resolve around it. Mr. Romantic was about to become the best teacher Jemma Fielding had ever had.

CHAPTER 19

JEMMA COULDN'T HELP WORRYING OVER Miles's words again: *I cannot marry Lisette.* They circled around in her head more times than she spun around the dance floor with Mr. Bentley. She had suppressed them, trying to pretend them away, but being in the same house as Miles flung them back in her face with full force.

What did he mean by it exactly? He couldn't be serious. Why couldn't he commit to Lisette? Jemma should have asked the reason when they were together at the pond. Maybe then she could concentrate on making conversation with Mr. Bentley.

But she'd let her temper flare instead, refusing to say more than was absolutely necessary to Miles. She regretted her behavior. The song ended, signaling another lost opportunity to win over Mr. Bentley—to convince her own heart toward his. He escorted her to Mrs. Manning's side, exchanging her hand for Lisette's. At least her cousin would dance tonight—a comfort worth noting. Mrs. Manning acknowledged it all with a smile of approval but returned to her conversation with Louisa—something about butterflies.

Instead of joining in, Jemma stepped back to the wall and took a glance around the room. Where had Miles disappeared to? He wasn't a great fan of dancing, but when he was inclined to do so, he executed the motions with more feeling than precision. Not that she'd paid him particular notice; he simply didn't dance often, so when he did, he was hard to miss.

She shook her head, clearing a sudden image of him taking her hands in his in the dance line. The spins from her previous set had left her brain addled. If she couldn't think about Miles properly, then she should have refused dancing with him when he had asked at dinner. She *would* pull herself together when the time came.

Her eyes flitted about the room again. Would Miles return, or had he forgotten about his invitation and gone home? And why did either idea leave her so unsettled?

Those who weren't dancing were chatting and laughing together. All those in attendance were close friends, and they'd brought Mr. Bentley into their circles like one of their own. Jemma was pleased, truly. She wanted her future husband to belong here. But her pleasure diminished to a mere fragment of gratitude since Miles's disappearance was all she could think about.

She danced with a reluctant Ian for the next set, laughing at his look of discomfort. He was a good man and the best leader of the Rebels, but he clearly preferred billiards or games to anything resembling courtship. Dancing fell neatly in the courtship realm, which meant he detested it. Amused as she was, she kept taking distracted looks toward the door.

Until Miles finally slipped back inside.

Her heart flip-flopped.

She maintained her steps, though his presence startled her. It was a relief, surely. Now she could have a civilized conversation with him and settle the argument between them before he left for the night. They would have to dance first, of course.

A sudden, unbidden thrill grew inside her at the thought.

It was the music. The mood of the night. A fleeting, fanciful whim. Absolutely nothing more.

Suppressing the rapid fire of feelings fighting for supremacy was maddening, but she would conquer it. She purposefully kept her gaze on Ian's until the final note of the pianoforte.

Ian bowed to her and extended his arm.

"I'll take your place, if the lady agrees," Miles said, suddenly beside Ian.

Jemma swallowed. The time of reckoning had come. "The lady agrees."

Ian stepped aside, allowing Miles to replace him. Miles pushed his dark hair back with a quick swipe of his hand. He seemed nervous.

Why was *he* nervous? She was the one battling so many confusing emotions. "I thought you had left," she breathed.

"How could I leave without dancing with you?"

His voice, soft as a caress, sent another flood of feeling through her. "I . . . I did not think it so important to you."

"I find this dance especially significant." He stepped nearer, much closer than the others lining up on either side of them. "Since I missed the last opportunity to expound a lesson upon you, I thought a short bonus session appropriate."

She glanced at the others to see if they had heard, but no one seemed concerned. *Her resolve.* Where was her *resolve*? Her gaze flitted back to him, but her eyes remained on his cravat tied modestly around his slender neck. "What sort of lesson?"

"The power of eye connection."

A string of soprano notes trilled out the beginning of Mozart's *Ländler*—a slow waltz. Jemma, unable to look at Miles despite the topic of their lesson, accepted his arm. The small group of dancers promenaded about the room. Tom and Cassandra were in front of them and Mr. and Mrs. Manning behind them, but Jemma had no sense of who the other couples were. The waltz had been popular since she had been out in Society, but never had it felt so confining. So intimate. So unnerving.

Her eyes caught on Mrs. Jackson's at the piano for a fleeting moment. Was it curiosity she saw there? If only the Matchmaking Mamas knew the frantic state of Jemma's heart.

"Shall we begin?" The alluring whisper near her ear sent her pulse racing. "Retain eye connection where possible, but do not say a single word. Allow your thoughts and feelings to rise to the surface and communicate through sight alone. They say the way to see a man's soul is through his eyes."

She gulped.

Lifting her gaze to meet his took all her courage. She didn't want him to see into her soul. There were secrets hiding within that she could not reveal. With a tug of her hand, he turned her body to face him. He set his hand on her waist and gently pulled her closer. She did the same with her own hands, lifting one above her head as he did. In the window of their arms, she finally met his gaze.

What she saw in him, however, made her momentarily forget her carefully crafted walls. Swirled in amber and onyx was the Miles she had known forever—a man she could trust. Useless to resist, she became his student, searching the depths beyond the Miles she knew and seeing more than she had ever seen before.

His eyes were gentle, as always, but far more intent, accentuating the fine smile lines in the corners. Beyond the surface lay a startling truth. Longing. Heartache. Unyielding determination. One thing was very clear. The subject of his attention was no one but her.

She blinked, unbelieving, too caught up in the moment. But his gaze, his steady, enveloping gaze pulled her in once more, completely and utterly capturing her own. No matter the dance steps or the dizzying spins, her eyes couldn't stray for long. The truth was, she wanted to read his soul. She craved to know it backward and forward. Fear alone made her hesitate. Unnerved in one breath, the next she was pulled in by the comfort she always relied on from him.

A light filtered through his caressing gaze, full of warmth and startling affection. With an exhale of breath, she let her feet drift closer to him. His hand tightened on her waist. She longed to close the gap completely. His eyes were so welcoming—so adoring. They held her as surely as his arms and shattered her cold resistance.

Mr. Romantic was an excellent teacher. The communication happening between them was extremely educational. Her favorite subject, in fact. The entire dance was an impossible dream she hoped to never wake from. The music pulled at her heartstrings, resurrecting buried longings with every note until its sweet but bitter end.

Miles stepped back.

She was supposed to look away now. She screamed Lisette's name in her mind. Told herself to look for Mr. Bentley. Even thought of Grandmother. But her yearning for Miles had awakened.

It was Miles who broke the connection first, three distinct emotions crossing his face: pleasure, pain, and . . . reluctance. He walked away without a word, disappearing through the drawing room door.

The rest of the night passed in a haze. Jemma barely registered the goodbyes, the carriage ride home, the walk to her room, or her donning her nightgown.

She sat at her dressing table, staring into the mirror, wondering what she'd seen in Miles's eyes—wondering what he'd seen in hers.

Lisette came in humming a tune from a quadrille she had danced, waking Jemma from her fog. "Did you not think the party simply lovely?"

Jemma uttered the first response she could think of. "Yes, Mr. Bentley was an excellent host." Mr. Bentley . . . Had she even thanked him when they had parted? What a terrible guest she had been. And friend, she might add. Had Lisette witnessed her dance with Miles?

By the way Lisette was humming, it could not be possible. She was much too happy.

She wouldn't be happy at all if she knew Jemma was thinking *romantic* thoughts about Miles. How she longed to be back in his stirring embrace and for him to gaze at her with his entire soul night after night for forever. She held back the deep moan threatening to escape. She could not be so disloyal! She wouldn't!

Lisette picked up the brush on the dressing table and started ministering to Jemma's hair in gentle, smooth strokes. "I thought it so kind of Mr. Bentley to include all our friends. He really is so thoughtful."

He was. There was nothing in his person that she might criticize. "He deserves better," she mumbled.

"Nonsense. Once you have spent more time in each other's company, you will see how well suited you are." More happy humming.

The sound was so sweet . . . so cheerful. How could she diminish Lisette's happiness for her own? She turned in her seat and, on impulse, grabbed Lisette's free hand. "Thank you for believing in me. I am committed to knowing Mr. Bentley better, just as you said."

Lisette gave a quiet laugh. "Good."

"You believe me, don't you?" Jemma asked. "Now it is your turn to be cared for." She pulled Lisette into the seat in her place and took over brushing her cousin's silky blonde ringlets. "Once I sort out my own problems, we will begin turning you into a bride."

Jemma clenched her jaw, determined to bury her feelings for Miles. It would be harder this time, infinitely so. But she'd done it before, and nothing could stop her from doing it again. A dance was the perfect place to confuse one's heart, but all dances came to an end. One night of weakness need not define her future nor her friends'.

Miles was meant for Lisette. Somehow, she had to convince him.

She took a shaky breath. And then she had to convince herself again too.

CHAPTER 20

SURROUNDED BY HIS FRIENDS AT Gammon's, Miles set his arms on the table in front of him and let his eyes trail past the heavy maroon drapes to the street outside. He couldn't say when he had ceased paying attention to the amiable chatter around him, but his mind drifted back to Jemma and to Mr. Bentley's party. To their dance.

It had been no mere movement to music. With his emotions raw, he'd wanted nothing more than to confess everything. He'd said it all in his gaze. Somewhere between figures two and four of their waltz, their friendship had shifted.

She cared. He knew she did. He'd seen it in her eyes and felt her lean into him. But feeling and wanting were not the same.

And he feared he wanted more than she did.

"Miles Jackson."

He looked up. "Pardon?"

Paul shook his head. "I asked you twice what you thought of inviting Mr. Bentley to participate in the cricket match."

"What cricket match?" Miles straightened in his seat. "I love cricket. Why has no one said anything to me about it?"

"We were just telling you." Tom's grin widened. "You must have been daydreaming about something . . . or perhaps, someone?"

Ian raised his eyes to the ceiling. "We don't need any more matchmakers, Tom. Miles, pay attention. We've been issued a challenge by the Gents in Bradford. Tom's agreed to hold the match at

Rivenwood since the side yard is the ideal size and flatness of ground. With only two weeks to prepare, recruitment is our top priority. Lucky us, Mr. Bentley played on the Oxford team a few years back and will be quite the Corinthian on the field."

Mr. Bentley? He would be a sportsman on top of all his other glowing assets. Miles blew out a long breath.

"We also have the four of us," Ian continued, "the Hater twins, and James Udall if his wife holds off having her baby. It's a shame it's a men's league and we cannot let Jemma and Lisette play. They both are excellent batsmen."

"Only because I taught them everything I know," Tom said, his hands going to the lapels of his jacket like some proud father.

Miles shook his head. "I believe it is because Jemma has a competitive spirit and Lisette has a fear of letting her team down. But we will have to rely on the rest of the Rebels this time."

"Don't forget Mr. Reed," Paul added, "if Miles thinks the man can rally his spirits. It might be a good distraction from his loss."

Paul's idea had merit. "I will ask him," Miles said. "Where does that put our team?"

"If everyone agrees to play," Ian said, "we will still require two more players to make eleven." He held out his hand and began listing on his fingers. "We will need a spare player or two, a scorer, and one of the two umpires. Not just any chap will do. I will only accept the elite of Brookeside on our team. He must be active in body and sharp in mind. I won't abide any lazy, sluggish players. And don't recommend a man if he is the sensitive sort. I refuse squeamish players who cannot take a bump or dirty their clothes."

Miles thought for a moment. "My younger brother's summer break from University has begun, and we expect him home in the next few days."

"Splendid! Kent is just the sort of man we are looking for," Ian said, slapping the table.

"My father would be an excellent umpire, but I think a nonrelative would be more fair." Tom gave a mischievous smile. "So long as he is a fan of Brookeside, of course."

They all chuckled and raised their glasses with cheers of, "Here, here!"

"Mortimer Gibbons could score for us," Paul suggested.

"Excellent," Ian concluded. "Be on the lookout for two more men. The Rebels of Brookeside must uphold their honor."

After a few more minutes of planning out the details, Tom and Paul excused themselves out the private exit separate from Gammon's Inn—both men eager to return to their wives. Miles envied them.

Ian nudged Miles with his foot. "What was that earlier? You were in a whole different world."

He shrugged. "I must be tired from all the dancing last night."

"From what I recall, you danced only once and left directly after." Ian leaned his tall body over the table and hunched over on his elbows. "Something strange was going on with you. I thought something was off at dinner, but it most definitely was during your one and only dance. Tell me I was imagining the immense tension radiating from you and Jemma."

"You were imagining it," he repeated, his voice even.

"I thought so, too, at first." Ian narrowed his gaze. "And then you walked out without a word to anyone. The Miles I know is too mannerly to not even thank the host or bid goodbye to his friends. What happened during that dance? When I was with Jemma, she was perfectly fine. Afterward, she was not herself at all. Do you have something to tell me, Mr. Romantic?"

Miles shrugged. "She liked dancing with me more than you?"

Ian gave a short laugh. "Apparently."

"No confessions today, Ian." If he was ever going to admit his feelings vocally, it would be to Jemma first and foremost.

"Something odd is going on here." Ian rubbed his jaw in a slow, deliberate manner. "I cannot put my finger on it, but I don't like it. Are you trying to persuade her against Mr. Bentley? Or is it worse?

A love triangle? No, surely not." He dragged out his words, his steely gaze punctuating his point. "Can you imagine? Such a dreaded scenario would lead to certain pain and devastation of friendship." Ian searched Miles for an answer, but the power of eye connection worked only when one let their guard down, and Miles was not about to do that.

Ian finally sat back and released a sigh. "If you won't tell me anything, I can only make inferences based on observation. I could be wrong . . . I hope I'm wrong. But I have to warn you. If I am noticing your odd behavior, who else is? Someone is liable to get hurt, Miles, and I am afraid that someone will be you. Because if it isn't you getting hurt, then it will be Jemma or Lisette, and I cannot allow that."

Miles nodded, knowing Ian's words were out of protection for their friends and not because he cared any less for him. "Everything will work out as it is meant to."

Whether he was left with a broken heart or not—he would know soon enough. There was not much time left until the six-week period ended and Jemma's engagement was announced. Would that it were his name attached to hers when that day came.

CHAPTER 21

JEMMA RETURNED FROM HER DAILY walk, having taken longer than normal to purge her thoughts with alone time and fresh air. Lisette met her in the corridor up the stairs.

"There you are, Jemma! You really have the most wretched timing," Lisette grabbed her hand and pulled her back down the stairs.

"Is something wrong?"

"You will see." She did not stop until they were both in the drawing room. There, on the tea table, was a basket tied in ribbon. "It's a gift from Mr. Bentley. I am sorry you missed him."

"What sort of gift is it?" Jemma picked up one of several jars inside.

"Spices from the Bahamas as a thank-you for our support of his house-warming party."

The jar in her hand was labeled pimento. She held it to her nose and took in the strong peppery scent. "How very kind of him. Did he stay long?"

"Over an hour. I did think you would be back sooner, but he did not seem to mind."

Jemma sighed. "The man will be made a saint for all his patience with me. Thank you for entertaining him . . . again."

Lisette shook her head. "You would have done the same for me. Did you enjoy your walk?"

"It was just what I needed, thank you." She set the jar back inside, her mind spinning. She couldn't keep missing Mr. Bentley. She needed progress, not time to wallow in her problems. "I guess it wasn't all I needed. In lieu of my commitment to give Mr. Bentley more of my time, I suppose I will have to invite him over again."

Lisette laughed. "Are we to have our own party?"

"No, I need something simple, with fewer guests." And most definitely not with Miles. She made a mental list of summer activities, stopping on the perfect one. It was the perfect balance of work and play—just as Miles had taught her. "I shall invite him to our annual strawberry-picking contest! I often walk by the patch, and it's brimming with ripe fruit." The Mannings had a large patch and held a picking contest every June but generally kept the activity in the family.

"I can see him enjoying that."

"You can?" She found she was holding her breath.

"He told us he loves plants after overseeing his plantations. Come, let's go ask Mama what she thinks."

Thankfully, both Mr. and Mrs. Manning were all too excited to add Mr. Bentley to the event. Mrs. Manning had even said it was right and proper to include him since he would be a member of the family anyway. They sent a note over to request his presence the following day, and it was returned not two hours later with an affirmative.

The weather the next day was picturesque, with enough cloud cover to make the temperature pleasant. Jemma dressed in a sturdier gown but one that also showed off her flair for style. Mr. Bentley smiled at her when he arrived, and they all filed out to the garden. With pails and baskets in hand, Mr. Manning staked out sections of the patch.

It was the perfect day to think of Mr. Bentley and only Mr. Bentley.

"There are only two rules," Mr. Manning announced. "One, the winner picks the most strawberries in a half hours' time. Two, no stealing from anyone else's pail."

"Easy enough," Mr. Bentley said, discarding his jacket and rolling up his shirtsleeves.

When all were ready in position, Mr. Manning yelled time, and they shot forward, frantically searching the plants for the ripe, red berries. The best part wasn't the picking. It was the half hour of exaggerated stories from Mr. Manning. Most were of past competitions he and his brothers had competed in. By the end, they were tired from laughing, groaning of aching backs, and congratulating each other on only one spilled pail—and it wasn't even Jemma's.

Mrs. Manning was declared the winner, and they all settled onto a blanket to sample the berries and drink cool lemonade. With Mr. Bentley seated nearest her, this was Jemma's chance to engage him in a more private conversation. She wished she hadn't spent so many years exerting her independence and trying to prove she did not need a husband or marriage. It would have benefited her now if she'd prepared herself properly.

She cleared her throat. "Mr. Bentley, what sort of pastimes do you enjoy?"

"Interesting you should ask. I happen to be an avid fan of cricket. It's been a few years since I've had a chance to play, but your friends have invited me to join a team. There is to be a match next week at Tom Harwood's estate."

"I hadn't heard," Jemma said, growing excited at the idea of a match in Brookeside. "I adore cricket. I make a good short slip, you know, and am a fair hand with the bat."

"You?"

The disbelief in his eyes made her choke back her words. "As a young, *very young*, girl. There are no women's teams here, so I, uh, was a good substitute when not enough players could be found." She laughed sheepishly. Not everyone thought it appropriate for grown women to play cricket. She had managed to keep from causing any accidents, but now her tongue was making blunders. Reaching for her lemonade, she took a long drink.

He shifted, clearly uncomfortable. "What sort of pastimes do you prefer besides cricket?"

She opened her mouth to tell him, but no words came out. She had to give him a proper pastime, not a Rebel one. It would be better to ease him into her bluestocking ways. Most men would not find her charities a favorable attribute. "I like to draw," she finally said.

He seemed relieved by her answer. "I have always wished for such a skill. Do you prefer nature or people as your subject?"

"Clothes, actually." She winced.

"Clothes?"

"I like to predict upcoming fashions and sometimes even create my own." She pointed to the cape-like collar buttoned at her neck and draped just over the top of her shoulders. "The French wear their pelerine with tight ruffles around the neck, but I adapted the design for a looser ruffle around the neck and a fringe at the hem."

She had no expectation of him knowing about the intricacies of women's fashion, but it was important to her. He gave a slight smile and nodded in feigned interest before reaching for another strawberry.

Her shoulders dropped. This wasn't going well at all. Mr. Bentley wasn't trying to find her lacking, she knew he wasn't. Even so, their personalities were not melding together. Feeling frustrated and quite desperate, she recalled Miles's most recent lesson. The bonus one that had worked quite well on her.

It was time for sparks to fly. She squeezed her hands together tightly in her lap and cleared her throat. "What shade of blue would you say your eyes are?"

Mr. Bentley looked up, his eyes wide. "Uh . . . I have not thought on it before."

She purposefully leaned forward, intent on falling into his gaze and staying there as long as it took. His blue eyes were indeed an interesting shade darker on the edge and quite light at the center. Why had she never noticed them before? "They are quite a nice color, Mr. Bentley." She studied them longer than necessary, searching for his soul, as Miles had instructed.

While he came across as a man of experience, his eyes were surprisingly innocent. They were also honorable and kind. She waited for the sparks. She waited to fall. She would wait all day if she had to.

Mr. Bentley wiped at his face. "Do I have strawberry juice all over me?"

Jemma did not see anything. "No, not at all."

"But you keep staring at me."

She forced a grin, albeit a lopsided one. "I know. Is it not wonderful?"

"I, uh . . ."

"Oh, I do not mind if you stare at me in return. You might even see . . . something." She tilted her head, trying to assume her best angle.

"Why? Did you get something in your eye?"

She batted her lashes, not because she wanted to look pretty but out of frustration. The man was not getting it. But if Miles could turn eye connection into an intimate moment, the principle must work for others. "Never mind, my eyes are fine." She tilted her head at a different angle. "Look to your heart's content, Mr. Bentley. We have all afternoon."

In fact, they had a lifetime.

Mr. Bentley blinked a few times, the tops of his ears reddening. He turned away suddenly. "I think I might pick a few more strawberries." He climbed to his feet and took long strides toward the patch.

Her jaw slackened. Had she just scared him away? A confident, grown man? How could they possibly get married if he could not endure her looking at him? She pushed aside her frustrations, refusing to let this be a sign of failure. Besides, the afternoon was still young.

She jumped to her feet and chased after him.

But try as she may, the next few hours passed without her being able to salvage a friendly mood between them. If Jemma came too close, Mr. Bentley acted like she might bite. And if it would have helped, she might have tried. Her desperation turned into annoyance. She even took eye connection to a whole new level, attempting to pin him in one place with her glare.

Lisette took note of Mr. Bentley's avoidance and Jemma's agitation and attempted to make herself a middleman, but the atmosphere felt entirely too awkward. What had Jemma done wrong?

With Miles, everything was natural. Love was as simple as breathing.

After Mr. Bentley left, Jemma took a walk, having missed her earlier exercise and feeling desperate for a moment alone. Her half boots crunched against the rocky road while her hand trailed against the smooth stone half wall running along the perimeter. Her thoughts were circling faster than the crows above the field beside her. The sound of a horse galloping nearer drew her attention. She looked up.

Miles?

Her heart pounded. A few moments later, she knew for certain. When he had nearly reached her, she fumbled with her hands, not certain how to act. The vision of their dance together stole away all her rational thought and sent her pulse racing fiercely through her body. Miles slowed his mount and alighted before she could regain her presence of mind.

"Jemma, I did not think to meet you on the road today." His smile faded. "But you are not well. What is it?"

There was not a trace of awkwardness in his manners. Had he not seen the secret in her eyes that night? Did he not know? And hadn't he said plenty in his own gaze? "I am well . . . truly."

"I am happy to hear it." His whole presence exuded confidence. More so than she had seen in him the last month. His smile returned. "Are you coming or going?"

"Actually, I was about to turn around."

"May I walk with you for a bit?"

Why did such a question send fire to her cheeks? "Please."

Miles nodded, and they fell into step. "I am just on my way back from a visit with Mr. Reed."

"I see." She blinked. Such a normal topic. Had she dreamed it all? She must have, for he was acting much too calm. Then, had nothing changed between them? It could be as if they'd never danced.

She was relieved and oddly hurt. "How is Mr. Reed? I was sorry to hear about his wife."

"He is soldiering through, I daresay. He even agreed to play in the cricket match against Bradford."

"I only just heard of this match. I am happy to hear Mr. Reed will come out for it."

"It will be good for him." Miles slowed his pace. "What about you? Are you ready to tell me what happened? Did you make another bungle with Mr. Bentley?"

She gave an airy laugh. "How did you guess?"

"I could never have guessed before this past month. Making bungles is not something typical for Jemma Fielding."

His eyes drew her in like they had done the night of the dance. She put her hand to her forehead and rubbed it for a moment. "I've never felt this kind of pressure before. I cannot even be myself." Nor could she control herself, it seemed.

"Hmm." Miles strung out the monotone note, thinking aloud. Had he always looked so dashing while pondering something? "We ought to think of something to distract you. How about some kissing until an idea strikes?"

Her heart stopped just before her feet. "You . . . you want to kiss me?" How could he say something of such great magnitude so nonchalantly? As if everything did not hinge upon such an action! Her pulse raced through her veins again, stealing her breath with it.

"I, uh . . ." He paused and pulled a small tin box from his waistcoat pocket. "I think you misheard." He popped open the box. "Kissing *comfit*?"

She let out a high-pitched, strangled laugh. "A comfit, you say? Good heavens." She plucked the bite-sized purple sweet from his hand, grateful to have something else to look at. "I did not know anyone still called them *kissing* comfits." Before he could answer, she shoved the treat into her mouth, willing it to cool her scorched cheeks.

Miles chuckled. "If it was good enough for Shakespeare, it's good enough for me."

"You writers must share a sort of kinship, it seems." A sweet plum flavor suffused over her tongue. "Regardless of its name, I must admit, it is delicious." She glanced up and regretted it. She sucked on the small confection for all it was worth, not so much to savor the sweetness around the coriander-seed center but to keep her mind off the way Miles moved his mouth around his own comfit.

Had she really believed he wanted to kiss her? Knowing her weakness toward him lately, her mind might have simply heard what it wanted to hear. Thankfully, her errant thoughts ended when Miles abruptly snapped his fingers.

"I have it. You need a diversion. Some Rebel fun."

Fun? Her? "I'm intrigued." And it wasn't just because his eyes were alight and she had to know why. "Do I get to keep score in the cricket match?"

"Unfortunately, we have found someone to take on the task already. I do hope you will come cheer us on instead."

His hopeful look melted her heart. "I wouldn't miss watching the Rebels beat those big-headed Bradford boys."

"That's the spirit." Miles laughed, not at all shocked by her strong words. His prominent dimples creased his cheeks and drew her eyes to his mouth. It wasn't a sweetmeat that came to mind either. She shifted so her bonnet blocked her view of him and, in return, his view of yet another blush.

Clearing her throat, she said, "I am not certain how being an audience for the game will require any *Rebel* fun."

"Ah," Miles said. "My idea for diversion has nothing to do with cricket. I have some charity baskets to deliver tomorrow. Why not join me? Afterward, we can visit a few more affluent families to gather funds for our Greek campaign."

"Truly?" She had donated gowns for charity before but never delivered any item personally. But a Rebel cause was something she was familiar with. A cause to champion was more soothing to her dampened spirits than even reading ridiculous tidbits in the gossip columns. "I am not certain I can be helpful with the baskets, but I know I could beg our neighbors for donations."

"I believe you will find both tasks enjoyable. The two are not so dissimilar."

Perhaps not for him. It was part of his profession to help them. "I have always preferred keeping my anonymity or serving people who do not know me personally. I will be recognized here. Will they think me self-aggrandizing?"

"They will think you are a good and kind person, just like I do. But I won't force you. If you are not comfortable with the idea, we can make other arrangements."

She was much more comfortable saying no, but part of her wanted to take on the difficult task and prove she was capable of it. "I will come."

He smiled. "Why don't you bring Lisette and maybe even Mrs. Manning, if they are agreeable to our project. These visits must be done properly, with adequate chaperones. We must tamper your Rebel spirit for independence for the betterment of the Greek people."

She laughed and agreed, feeling lighter than she had all day. "Thank you for cheering me up, Miles." He had come at the exact moment she'd needed him.

"You are very welcome. By the time we are finished, you will be able to face *Mr. Bentley* with confidence."

Face Mr. Bentley? Her smile froze. How had she forgotten him so quickly? Standing next to Miles, his alluring dimples teasing her, had distracted her completely.

Miles had emphasized the man's name for a reason. Was he testing her? She focused her attention on the road directly ahead, forcing thoughts of Lisette and greater commitments to be diligent. She *would* discipline her mind.

But it was growing harder by the day. Exhaustingly so.

And Miles's presence was not helping.

CHAPTER 22

MILES WAS QUITE PROUD OF his carriage. They were expensive, and for a single man, it was a luxury. Employing enough servants for driving it as well as owning a second horse, however, were not privileges he enjoyed. He did have Sean Beagle—a footman who acted as a groomsman. Sean wasn't very good at either position, but he agreed to drive the carriage so Miles might escort the ladies on his visits.

The trip was much bumpier than normal and a great deal faster. To Miles's chagrin, Sean was a mite liberal with the whip, but the women pretended not to notice, chattering on about how excited they were to be helping him.

"I am especially looking forward to gathering funds afterward for the Chios massacre," Lisette said. "I am removed from the happenings in the world and had no idea."

Jemma looked out the small carriage window as if she could see the faraway island. "I get upset every time I think about it. So many people brutally killed—even the children. The survivors deserve far more."

"I agree, but even a small act of kindness can bring comfort." Lisette met Miles's gaze. "Thank you for letting us join you, Mr. Jackson."

The use of his surname sounded strange coming from Lisette, but Mrs. Manning beside him was a stickler for propriety, so he understood the necessity. "You're very welcome."

Lisette grinned at him. He waited, as he always did, for her sweet smile to do something to his heart, but like past times, it did not move beyond feelings of friendship.

He glanced at Jemma, who was still gazing out the window, and immediately, a familiar ache in his chest pulled at him. The body and mind were finicky things.

After Mr. Bentley's party, Miles had agonized over how to outwardly react around Jemma—the only thing he could control. On their walk, being near her had only made him surer of his intentions. He had tried to gauge her feelings for him. They had to both want a relationship for his efforts to make any headway. And though he'd sensed she cared during their dance, for some reason, she'd pretended otherwise on their walk. He wouldn't force her to accept him. So, reining in his growing emotions, he silently agreed to bide his time. For now, at least.

Until he could convince her heart otherwise.

The carriage rocked to a stop at the Reeds' cottage first. Mr. Reed was a gentleman of no great means, but he had enough to meet his basic necessities. His girls, on the other hand, had a greater need. They were in want of cheer. Only the day before, a timely donation of two cloth dolls was left on the church doorstep. They were pretty things and in excellent condition.

Miles had seen it happen before in his position as vicar. When someone had need, someone else in the parish seemed divinely led to help. More often than not, it was a small gesture—a warm meal or a visit—just the thing to offer comfort to the downtrodden. Every once in a while, the gesture of kindness came from an unknown party—an earthly angel intent to serve without recognition. Miles wished he could have thanked many generous souls over the years, and this was one of those times.

He reached for the basket of dolls on the carriage floor, admiring the delicately carved wooden features one last time before covering them with a bread cloth. He had a mind to have Jemma deliver them.

When they were all descended from the carriage, he handed her the basket.

"I thought a gentleman always carried everything for the lady," she teased.

"Not this time. You get to make the first delivery."

Jemma looked at Lisette and Mrs. Manning for help.

"Lisette can be next," Miles added. "She has brought some stockings she knitted, which the Johnson family will greatly appreciate."

"Go ahead, dear," Mrs. Manning encouraged.

Miles could see Jemma's mind spinning a false tale. Lisette had *made* an offering to give. She would make the perfect vicar's wife. Miles hadn't planned the outing for this purpose, but that morning, the idea had come strong and clear. He needed to show Jemma that her gifts had a purpose in the vicarage too—and they need not be the kind one could put in a basket. Sometimes the greatest gift came from the heart, and Jemma had more heart than anyone he knew.

The ladies gathered into Mr. Reed's drawing room—a modest but well cared for space—while his daughters were summoned from the nursery. Miles ended up seated between Jemma and Lisette, and Mrs. Manning took the open chair next to Mr. Reed, using the opportunity to invite him to dinner. She had finally convinced him when the nursemaid brought in two dark-haired children around five or six years of age, their faces much too solemn for their size. One was just an inch or so taller than the other, but otherwise, they could be mistaken for twins.

Miles lightly tapped Jemma on the arm. "Are you ready?"

She studied the children, unmoving. "Do you think I looked this sad when my parents died?"

Miles froze. Had he unintentionally opened an old wound? Why had he not realized the possibility sooner? He would give the dolls to the children and hurry Jemma away—

Jemma sprang forward, basket in hand, before he could intervene. She went straight to the children and knelt in front of them.

"Good morning. My name is Miss Fielding. Do you know I have searched all morning for two raven-haired girls to give a present to?"

Her voice was so intent, he held his breath.

The sisters shook their heads, the youngest putting her two middle fingers in her mouth.

Jemma continued. "There is only one way to find out if you two are the right ones I am searching for. Have you been very good lately?"

The older one shook her head no.

"It cannot be," Jemma said. "You see, my nose itches when someone is good, and it is itching mightily right now." She wiggled her nose and scratched it.

The youngest Reed girl giggled, and Miles found himself grinning too.

"And because you two have been very good, you may have a present." She extended the cloth-covered basket.

Neither girl moved to accept it.

Jemma set the basket in front of them and shifted away, giving them room to explore it themselves.

The youngest made the first move, tugging at the bread cloth and pulling it away to expose the dolls.

The older girl gasped and snatched one of the dolls from inside, quickly followed by her sister. Soon, they were on the floor playing, with Jemma narrating a pretend tea party.

Miles gave a wry smile. She was a natural at this. After all his experience, he knew he never could have won the girls over as quickly and effectively as Jemma.

They left the Reed house with two happy daughters and a relieved and grateful father. A sense of humble satisfaction permeated the air on their walk to the carriage. While the ladies settled in the conveyance, Miles gave Sean strict instructions to drive slower on their return. Then he climbed inside himself and sank into the seat beside Mrs. Manning again and across from Jemma.

Jemma smiled at him. "Is it always this rewarding?"

"Not always in the moment," Miles answered. "Some deliveries are outright rejected, while others are simply unappreciated. It's never convenient or easy, but giving is the only service compensated from the heart. It is a payment far more valuable than any other I have received." The carriage hit a rock and jolted them. He grimaced, suddenly wishing for a little less heart and a little more money. How he would like to invest in a proper driver.

After the last of the charity baskets were delivered, including the stockings and jars of broth to a sick widow, the foursome stopped by four families' homes, asking for donations to aid the Greek in their time of need. They were far more fruitful in their errands than they'd expected. News of the terrible slaughter by the Turks was spreading quickly and gaining much sympathy.

They were all exhausted when they reached Manning House, Jemma and Lisette leaning on each other, arms linked.

Miles walked them all to the door and expressed his gratitude for their assistance. "I hope I didn't wear anyone out. It was a longer day than I expected."

Mrs. Manning patted his cheek as though she were his own mother. "You are the best vicar Brookside has ever had—along with your father, of course." She smiled warmly, letting herself inside first. He had a feeling Mrs. Manning would give the same compliment to any vicar, but he appreciated it all the same.

Lisette released Jemma's arm and stopped in front of him. Jemma glanced between them, bit her lip, and gave him a small smile in parting. She disappeared inside, leaving him alone with Lisette.

He didn't wait for her to speak first, worried that if they tarried too long, it would cement further ideas in Jemma's mind. "Thank you for gifting the stockings, Lisette. I know they were greatly appreciated."

"You're welcome." Her smile drooped. "Miles, I have a question for you, and it has nothing to do with today."

He nodded, encouraging her to speak.

"We are good friends, are we not?"

His hands stilled on his breeches. "Yes."

"Nothing has happened to make our friendship change?" Her slender, fair brows arched in the middle.

Guilt, regret, and sadness flooded him at once. Had he neglected her in his carefulness to not give her the wrong idea? It was a fine line and one he'd conscientiously tread for years now. "Nothing has changed." He hoped she saw the sincerity in his eyes.

Her smile grew only a fraction. "I am pleased to hear it."

"I am happy to reassure you whenever you need a reminder." He wasn't in the same hurry to leave now, but she stepped back and said goodbye. He tipped his head in farewell and watched her go inside.

"Well done, Miles." He took his hat off and hit it against his leg. Affections were not meant to be toyed with. He had tried his best to protect Lisette from himself and himself from Jemma, but it hadn't been enough. Irritated, he raked his hand through his hair, mussing it to match the mess of his love life, then stalked to the carriage.

He had his foot on the step of his carriage when the door of Manning House shut behind him. He dropped back down and turned to see who had exited.

Jemma?

She picked up her skirts, hurried down the steps, and jogged to meet him. "I thought you'd left." Her chest heaved, and she caught her breath. "I had to thank you again. Today fed my soul. I needed to forget myself, and for one day, I did. Thank you, Miles."

He smoothed his hair, suddenly self-conscious of the disarray atop his head.

"The wind must have picked up." Jemma pushed a curl off his forehead. Her touch sent his skin tingling. Their hands brushed in the process, and they both quickly pulled back. She hid hers in the folds of her skirt, and he dropped his awkwardly to his side.

"I'm glad today helped," he started, returning his hat to his head. "If you think another lesson would help, I have thought of a few more ideas." Ideas that could finally win him her heart.

Her expression turned sheepish. "I am not sure a dozen lessons would help me. Mr. Bentley might be stuck with a marriage of convenience."

Miles's hands involuntarily tightened into fists. Mr. Bentley would have to fight him for such a privilege. He forced his muscles to relax before responding. "Day after tomorrow, let's try the bench again." He wanted to plead for her not to give up. Not on the lessons but on him.

She was slow to answer, ducking her head as she did. "I will be there."

Even with the reluctance in her stance, her agreement gave him a whisper of hope. Another lesson meant another opportunity to be with her. Unless . . . unless she started to develop feelings for Mr. Bentley. Miles wouldn't want to take that from her. But didn't she deserve to have a choice between them? If she wouldn't let him tell her how he felt, he would show her. He would tread carefully, examining her feelings with every move. It might just be the most important lesson he had left to give.

CHAPTER 23

JEMMA HADN'T MEANT TO BE careful in her selection of gowns on the day she was to meet Miles. It just happened. She chose her new sea-green dress with the wide neckline, hoping the color would bring out her eyes. The slender gold chain she donned on a whim, much like the splash of rose water to her throat. She added a pale-pink bandeau around her head and sighed. "What am I doing?"

She studied her reflection in the mirror, and her fingers began to tremble. She was nervous to spend time with Miles again. Excited, too, if she were honest.

Lisette knocked and let herself in. "I thought I would accompany you on your walk today, if you would like a companion." She stepped farther into the room. "I feel the need to stretch my legs and take in some sunshine."

Jemma's hand gripped the edge of her dressing table. Any other day would be acceptable, but not today. It wasn't like she could confess that she was seeing Miles—not with her feeling the way she was lately. Her guilt would be all over her face. It could be that way even now. Lisette would feel betrayed . . .

Or maybe this was the perfect opportunity to tell her cousin everything. Jemma could invite Lisette to join them to see that it was all harmless and for a good cause. And that neither her nor Miles was at all confused. "Actually—"

"Good morning, girls." Mrs. Manning stopped in the doorway behind Lisette, cutting of Jemma's response. "I have a short visit planned this afternoon to see Lady Felcroft around nuncheon. Would you two like to come and visit with Cassandra?"

"What a lovely idea," Lisette said.

Jemma chewed on the inside of her cheek. "I had some things I wanted to see to today. Go ahead without me."

"Are you certain?" Lisette's forehead puckered.

"Send Cassie my love. Tell her I will see her next week at the cricket match."

They agreed, and Lisette followed her mother out.

Jemma groaned and let her face fall into her hands. Nothing felt right anymore. If Grandmother had known how difficult her last wish would prove to be, she was sure Grandmother would have taken it all back. The life of a rich spinster sounded much simpler than chasing love—or running from it.

When the time came, Jemma let herself out and walked the road to the church. She beat Miles to the bench, so she took a seat and waited for him. The slow trickle of water down the hill into the creek made a pleasant dripping sound, soothing her nerves. She pictured Mr. Bentley's face and repeated his name like a personal creed, ensuring she would not forget her purpose for their lesson.

She heard Miles's soft footfalls before she saw him. She turned and lifted her hand in a slow wave.

He lifted his hand in a wave of his own. "I hope you did not wait too long. Mrs. Fortescue needed to speak to me."

"Is she well?"

Miles grimaced. And was that a blush? "She is considering courtship, actually."

"I suppose it is never too late, even for a widow of her age, to find love or companionship." Jemma paused, piecing together Miles's discomfort with Mrs. Fortescue's reason for coming. "You're jesting! She came because she hopes to court you?"

"I plan to speak to Lady Kellen about arranging a match for her."

Jemma giggled. "Brilliant."

"For her situation, it might be. For the man she pursues, perhaps not." He took a seat beside her. "But it is a discussion for another day. I know you are limited in time before your family grows suspicious. Shall we begin our lesson?"

She swallowed. Was it her, or was he sitting closer than normal? She could not remember what normal even was anymore. She caught his scent, and her lips started to smile all on their own.

"I'll take your smile as a yes. Our next lesson is on the power of touch."

Jemma choked on dry air. Coughing into her hand, she sputtered, "T-touch?"

Miles's grin was almost roguish. "Touch," he repeated. "The ability to physically feel the emotion so often trapped inside us."

"Is it necessary?"

"Absolutely." He reached over and picked up her hand. She wanted to act unaffected, but she was very much the opposite. "Do you mind if I remove your glove?"

She bit her bottom lip but nodded. With his other hand, he tugged at the kid glove, the fabric sliding off. Every inch of her trembled, and she willed her body to be still. With the glove out of the way, he took her hand in his and tightened his grip into a gentle hug around her fingers. It was similar to the heart-pounding moment when he'd tucked her hand in his and hadn't let go the night they'd eaten dinner at the Kensingtons'. But no one was under duress now, and the privacy of the moment made the connection all the more intimate.

With her skin bare against his own palm, she suddenly could not remember the name of the man she was supposed to be thinking about. In fact, she could hardly think at all.

"See, it is not so painful?" Miles's grin was soft now, more sincere.

"Not at all."

His thumb drew a slow circle on the back of her hand, sending shivers up her arms. "Even the smallest touch can feel intimate when given and received with equal intent and desire. Do you agree?"

She lifted her gaze to meet his, those brown eyes asking far more than the question on his lips. It was difficult to process anything besides the feel of her hand in his, but something he'd said struck her. "Are you saying I cannot create a moment unless the other person feels something too?"

"As much as you think I am an expert on the subject, I am not, Jemma. The only thing I know for certain is from my own experience."

If he was basing his lesson off this moment, could his feelings mirror hers? Was this the sort of moment he was speaking of?

"What about kissing?" she blurted. Every time the word came up in conversation, palpable energy pervaded the mood between them, but she had to know. Eventually, she must kiss Mr. What's His Name, and the idea was not entirely appealing. She longed to hear Miles's opinion.

He smiled as if she had just broached his favorite topic. "What about kissing?"

The teasing in his eyes was nearly her undoing. "I brought it up during a previous lesson, and you had strong feelings about it."

"Yes, but then you were ready to kiss a stranger." His leaned back and studied her. "Our Society has two general camps: the rakes and the prudes. I prefer you remain a prude . . . at least where Mr. Bentley is concerned." He muttered the last part under his breath.

She barely suppressed a giggle, warming to the topic—or maybe to him. "And is this excessively prim Jemma allowed to kiss before she is wed?"

Miles's eyes sparked. "Some say it is not advisable to kiss before marriage, but I think there are circumstances where it might be appropriate."

"I have always thought a kiss a measure of physical pleasure, not real devotion."

His brow rose, all pointed in the middle, as though she had spoken blasphemy. "How can you judge if you have never been kissed yourself?"

"I just know." She shrugged, smiling at his indignation. When his thumb moved against her skin again, it made her want to lean into him. Kissing couldn't be as sweet and pure as hand holding. This was heaven. She never wanted Miles to let go.

"Your statement on kissing is fairly ignorant—not at all like the Jemma I know, who is passionate about exposing the truth."

"Yes, but couldn't I kiss someone and feel wonderful whether it was for the right reasons or not?"

Miles was not quick to answer. She liked that about him. He pondered a matter, not just debated it. "Let me ask you this," he finally said. "Wouldn't kissing someone who trusted your heart and you theirs be different from kissing just for sport?"

"I suppose so," Jemma answered. "The intent would be different."

Miles nodded once. "It would be with their feelings and care in mind. No one would be taking advantage of the other person. Instead of a trite kiss, it would be a beautiful expression of love."

His words painted an image so sweet it nearly cracked years of resolve. Tears suddenly pricked her eyes as a realization hit her. It was *his* kiss she desired, not Mr. Bentley's—who she seemed to forget completely at times like this. It had always been Miles she'd wanted to have by her side. Why couldn't it have been her all those years ago who had fallen through the ice? Why couldn't Miles have saved her?

She sniffed, blinking to clear her eyes before Miles could notice and doing her best to seal those determined cracks with greater determination. "It is a good thing I will not be married for some weeks. My talents at romance are sorely lacking. You should have seen what sort of power my eye connection had over Mr. Bentley. I sent him running."

Miles threaded his fingers through hers. "Romance does not take talent; it takes love."

"I don't know how to force those feelings."

"Who said anything about force?" He leaned close. Wonderfully close.

A nervous laugh bubbled out. "I meant *learn*. But perhaps a vicar should not be the one to teach such things."

"You mean, someone might be shocked to find I am meeting a young lady in secret and holding her hand?"

She should have let go of said hand ages ago and run home. Even now, her disobedient fingers remained safely ensconced in his. She looked everywhere but at him. "At least we are not kissing."

His voice came steady and sure and entirely too convincing. "But then you might always hold the opinion that kisses are irrelevant and inconsequential physical gestures. What sort of teacher of romance would I be if I let you believe that?"

She looked at him again, for she could not help it, her eyes going straight to his mouth. "Miles, I . . ."

Miles leaned closer, his voice husky. "They say a connection with a kiss is something indescribable—a sort of bond between two people for those sweet, tender moments."

She swallowed, her chin lifting of its own accord. "Who says that?"

He reached up and tucked a ringlet behind her ear. "Mr. Romantic. Who else? It's exactly what I imagine it would be like kissing you."

Her heart pounded in the most delicious way. He lowered his head, and she tipped her own back to meet his. She wanted him to kiss her. To hold her.

To *marry* her.

Those words sent her dreams crashing back into reality, and she yanked her hand away from Miles's, his lips a breath away from her own.

She practically leaped off the bench. This lesson was getting wildly out of hand. A chill swept through the air, but she could finally breathe again. "It is not like we can practice . . . that." She could no longer even say the word. She took a step backward for good measure. "If what you say is true and a kiss bonds two people, then what could happen between the two of us? If you were right, . . . then . . . then the two of us would be in a precarious position." She had to leave. She took a step toward the path, but Miles captured her wrist.

"Jemma, wait, please. Let's talk about this." Like molasses, deep and sweet, his voice pulled at her.

"Talk?" Jemma gave a depreciating laugh. "You talk a great deal about feelings, Mr. Jackson. I wouldn't want you to give someone the wrong idea." She needed a fan. Where was hers when she needed it? "I would prefer that you talk less right now and . . . and . . ."

"And?" He stood, placing himself much too close to her. "Kiss you?"

She shook her head, desperate to be rid of him but desperate to never leave him at the same time.

"I can see in your eyes that you are considering this. There can be more than friendship between us. You never needed a matchmaker."

"And do you see the fear and panic in my eyes too? I am the one who is nearly *engaged*. You are to marry Lisette!" She would cry if she did not leave now.

Reluctance flashed through his eyes before he released his hold on her, leaving her skin cold. "Don't we have a say in our own happiness?"

His question lingered between them. "Our greatest chance for happiness is if I listen to the matchmakers and you marry Lisette as planned."

"That plan was made *for* us."

"You're confused. This is what you want." She put her hands to her cheeks, willing them to soak up the heat radiating there from all the emotion whirling inside. She dropped them uselessly to her side. "Listen to me, Miles. I am no expert on love, that much is obvious, but I do know a little about life. Happiness is fleeting and temporary and often comes with a price. Grandmother was lucky to have had more. I was a fool to think I could have the same. But you . . . you and Lisette have a chance for the real thing."

His voice was calm, opposite of her own. "I already told you I cannot marry her. I think you know why."

"No, no, no. Our feelings are jumbled from spending too much time together. Chaperones are the protectors of hearts. I was wrong to discredit them."

Miles stared at her. The disappointment in his eyes sent pain through her chest and twisted her stomach into a knot. She hugged her middle to combat the fierce ache, hating that there was no better solution.

"Jemma," he whispered. "I'm in love with you."

She shook her head. "I have to leave."

He stared hard. "Is this checkmate, then?" He took a step back. "It's your move."

He was letting her win again. He'd always let her win. And this time, he was doing it by leaving the decision completely up to her own heart. But nothing would change today. It couldn't. She moved around him but only made it a few steps before turning back. "Please, Miles, don't let this ruin our friendship." Then she turned away again, tears choking her. She could not let him see how hard it was for her to leave him.

CHAPTER 24

Miles threw himself on his lumpy sofa and covered his face with his arm. He stayed in a similar position for hours, regretting his choices one minute and regretting nothing the next. Though she had rejected him, at least she could not doubt his feelings. His secret was out.

For years, he had battled to hide his affection and for good reason. He firmly believed there was a time to swallow a desire if it would not grow into the path one wanted. Why follow a road leading to a dead end? He had imagined confessing a thousand times, but it had always pointed to the same miserable destination—heartache.

Everything had changed, however, that day in the church with Jemma's sudden decision to marry. And now look at him. He was in the very place he had feared being in. At least Lisette had been spared thus far. Well, wallowing around for all eternity was not going to be his fate. He needed to do something useful before he went mad.

His mind latched onto an idea, and he sat up in a rush. The room spun, and he clutched his head until the dizziness passed. Jemma *had* wanted him to talk less and act more. She might actually be proud of him for what he was about to do, if she ever forgave him. Moving to his secretaire desk, he sat and pulled out his writing box.

He would not renew his feelings to Jemma but put his efforts toward something she would approve of. He intended to write a letter to every person he knew for this secret project. He'd learned long ago that Rebel work had the capability of distracting him better than anything else. He dipped his pen in ink and breathed, "For Jemma."

One sheet of paper after another, he scrawled his request. Long into the night, he wrote until his fingers ached. Thoughts of Jemma compelled him to keep going. Twice, he rose to stretch his stiff muscles before sitting and writing again, refusing to think again on his bleak future. In the early hours of the morning, he picked up the remaining nub of his candle and took himself to bed.

There was nothing more exhausting than a broken heart. That was the last thought he had before sleep overtook him.

〄

Jemma pushed aside the sketch of the gown she had been working on. She had sent out a few to magazines but had yet to hear back. She ought to send more to London to the dressmaker she knew there, but concentrating was madness.

Miles had wanted to kiss her.

He *loved* her.

Heat flooded through every limb, infusing her with incomprehensible happiness and utter terror at the same time. Despite the cold fireplace, the room was suddenly overbearingly hot. She propelled herself out of her chair toward her bedroom window. Fumbling with the latch, she pushed it open, throwing her head through the opening. "It's not real!" she squealed.

"What?" came a distant voice.

Her eyes darted about only to see the gardener working a shovel into the ground directly below her. His gray clothing blended directly into the stone wall. And he had heard her girlish scream of delight mixed heavily with denial.

"What's not real?" he asked again.

She looked around for something—anything to comment on. "The flowers . . . are not real. They are too beautiful. Well done, Mr. Hansen."

He gave her a strange look and nodded. "Thank you, miss."

She pulled her head back inside her room and took several steps backward. She had gone from an intelligent, logical woman to a hysteric fool. Miles was completely to blame. He wasn't supposed to care for her. Not in that way. Her heart leaped with elation in one breath and plummeted in despair in the next. It was everything she'd secretly dreamed of and her worst nightmare too.

She covered her face with her hands. She had narrowly kept herself from kissing him. She groaned. How could she fix this? Miles had to hate her now, and if Lisette ever found out, she would despise her too. She wanted to put aside her promise to see Lisette happily married and take Miles for herself.

"It is selfish!" she announced to the empty room, dropping her hands to her hips. How could she break Lisette's heart—her own best friend?

A true friend would bind up her feelings. She had done it once, swearing off love entirely, so certainly she could do it again. What was the point of being born with such willful resolve if she did not use it?

A knock sounded at the door.

Jemma whirled toward it. "Come in."

Mrs. Manning stepped inside. "I assumed Lisette would be in here. I thought I heard voices."

"Just me." She produced a sheepish smile.

"Even better. There was something I wanted to ask you privately." She pushed her drooping coiffure up, but it fell directly back down to its odd angle when she released it.

"Go ahead."

"Frankly, I am worried about you. You came home from your walk yesterday with puffy eyes and tearstained cheeks. Is there anything amiss? I do not want you to feel trapped in this house or in your soon-to-be engagement."

Jemma had managed to hide most of her emotions from the Mannings, but yesterday's encounter with Miles had left her undone.

"I might not be perfectly happy, but I am getting there. And it is all thanks to you and Lisette and this family," she added quickly.

"So . . . everything is well with Mr. Bentley?"

Jemma swallowed. "As well as can be imagined." She hadn't meant to sound hesitant, but her tone betrayed her. "It's just not how I expected it to be. I have much to learn, it seems."

Mrs. Manning came fully into the room and tucked Jemma into a hug. "Dear girl. Even the most capable humans have much to learn in this life. Remember not to settle for the easy road. Not when the harder path takes us toward a greater happiness." Mrs. Manning pulled back and gave Jemma an affectionate smile. "We love you, Jemma. And we will support you in whatever you decide." She released her and quietly left the room. Mrs. Manning's advice lingered long after her departure.

Even the most capable humans have much to learn.

Miles. He was her teacher . . . In fact, he was all of Brookeside's spiritual instructor. But even he did not know everything. Maybe he needed lessons of his own. She would take the harder path toward Mr. Bentley so they could all be happier. It would be up to her to remind Miles of why he had fallen for Lisette and not Jemma all those years ago. His feelings for her cousin were likely hidden by insecurities. Miles had willingly helped Jemma in her time of need. Could she help him in return?

Jemma rushed back to her desk, pushing aside her sketches and pulling out a fresh sheet of paper.

Dear Miles,
      Lesson one . . .

CHAPTER 25

MILES LEANED BACK IN HIS chair, having spent a couple of hours going through clerical business at the church, and slid his penknife into a letter just delivered to him. Once the sealing wafer broke, he unfolded the paper, his eyes naturally dropping to the bottom to see the sender's name.

Jemma?

What was she doing, sending him letters? He could think of a number of people who would not approve, which meant the contents were likely important enough for her to risk her reputation. He quickly sat up in his seat, and his gaze tore to the top.

> *Dear Miles,*
>> *Lesson one for Mr. Romantic: remember the past.*

Lesson one? Had Jemma decided it was time to switch roles from student to teacher?

>> *Since it has been made clear that you no longer remember falling in love for the first time, I thought I would take it upon myself to remind you of the account.*

Miles blinked. This is what she had written to him about? And who said he didn't remember? He humored her and read the tale through. The story of the ice breaking and him saving Lisette was slightly different told from Jemma's perspective, but the main details were the same.

He set the letter down and stared at it. Jemma was a fixer. She saw a problem and had to address it. Apparently, his feelings for her were such a dire problem that she had to remedy them immediately. He tipped his head back on his seat and stared at the old church ceiling, crumbling in places. Just like his pathetic heart.

Sitting up again, he ran a hand over his jaw and pulled out his own sheet of paper to record his response. When he finished, he stared at the finished product. He didn't want to get Jemma in trouble by sending it to the house. He would have to hold on to it until he saw her again. Who knew when it would be since she had clearly not forgiven him for trying to kiss her.

Despite her resistance, he knew she cared in her own way. He sensed it when she looked at him, when she let him hold her hand, and when she confided in him her fears and worries. Love either existed, or it did not. His devotion to her was real and tangible, like the air he breathed, but it wasn't that simple for her. Mr. Bentley had crept into the picture, and Lisette was already its center. Perhaps Jemma did not know her own heart.

Perhaps she did not truly know his either. If she thought a lesson on romance could sway his feelings, let her try. She would fail.

He had lost the choice to fight or feel. His heart had awakened, and it wouldn't sleep again.

❧

Miles had not expected an opportunity to deliver his letter to Jemma to come so soon or for it to be because of an unfortunate circumstance.

"Lisette is sick?" Miles met Tom's and Cassandra's solemn gaze after church services.

"I stopped by Manning House yesterday for some strawberry starts, and Mrs. Manning told me." Cassandra had her arm tucked into Tom's. "They think she caught an illness during their charity visits. She has a fever, but the doctor said she is faring well."

From their charity visits? The widow Talbridge had had a fever too. It was Miles's fault for taking the ladies with him to see her. "I will ride over this afternoon to see if there have been any changes."

"We thought you would want to know." Tom squeezed his shoulder in parting, and the couple made their way to Lord Felcroft's carriage.

As soon as Miles gave out his bag of sweets to the eager children and said goodbye to the last parishioner, he mounted his horse and rode to Manning House. By the time he arrived, the air had grown heavy and the sky had darkened with a thick layer of ominous clouds. He pushed away any concerns about the weather along with his uncomfortable thoughts of speaking with Jemma again. This would force them to see each other on neutral ground—as friends once more. If it were even possible.

The butler let Miles into the drawing room to wait for anyone who could attend to him. Miles wasn't in the mood to sit, so he studied the garden painting above the mantel and the knickknacks from the Mannings' travels. Nothing seemed to keep his attention. Not with Jemma somewhere in the house and Lisette ill.

Mrs. Manning greeted him from the doorway. "It is always a pleasure to have you visit, Mr. Jackson."

Miles stepped away from the mantel and toward her. "Mrs. Harwood said Lisette has a fever. Is she any better today?" He searched Mrs. Manning's face, but besides a few fatigue lines around her fair eyes, she seemed relatively cheerful.

"After three days, she is finally up from her bed. She requires more rest, but the doctor assures us it is a fairly mild case."

"I am relieved to hear it." Fevers were unpredictable in their longevity and power.

Mrs. Manning patted him on the arm. "Lisette will be so happy to know you have come to see how she is doing. She is anxious to be back on her feet. I am afraid she is tired of being tucked away from everything."

"May I sit with her for a time?"

Mrs. Manning hesitated. "A generous thought, Mr. Jackson, but we would not want our vicar catching an illness."

"Please, I feel responsible. After all, I chose the locations of our charity visits. The least I can do is provide a distraction for an hour or so."

Mrs. Manning finally let slip a smile. "How very kind of you. Let me show you to my sitting room."

Miles had been upstairs only once in the Manning House, many years ago, during a game of hide-and-seek. Nothing was terribly familiar except for the general layout, a sort of box design with the corridor forming an angular circle. Mrs. Manning's sitting room was around the first bend on the right.

Mrs. Manning knocked on the door and stuck her head inside. "Dearest, you have a visitor." After a moment, Mrs. Manning motioned him inside, leaving the door ajar. "I'll return to sit with you in a trice." Jemma stood from a chair beside Lisette, and his attention was immediately arrested by her wide, green eyes. She looked well. Thank heavens. He nodded a greeting to her.

Jemma seemed neither happy nor unhappy to see him, but there was no warmth for him either.

"Please, sit here. I will take my leave." She collected her lace shawl cast aside on the chair, one that reminded him of the late Mrs. Fielding, and quickly stepped around him. He caught her brief scent of roses, but it dissipated all too soon.

He hated how she felt the need to flee from his presence, but he did not let any emotion show on his face. Now was not the time to think about Jemma. He slid into her vacated seat, a maid hovering nearby, and took in Lisette's pale complexion. Her flaxen hair was pulled into a loose bun at her neck, and strands hung limp by her cheeks. She wore a collared dressing gown with a blanket across her lap.

She gave him a tired smile. "You did not have to come, Miles. I am not dying, as you can see."

"I am relieved to see it. You will forgive me for taking you to see the widow Talbridge? I feel terrible that you caught her illness."

"Is she faring better?"

"How like you to worry about someone else when you yourself are unwell. She did not attend services today, but her neighbor said she is on the mend."

"Good news, considering her health has been poor for so long. How were services today?"

"Very dull, indeed, without the Manning family."

Lisette laughed—not a full laugh like Jemma's but soft and lyrical. "Don't be absurd, Miles. We all know the Mannings do their best to fade into the background."

"Then you can imagine how we suffered without our usual background. A lack of consistency is always problematic."

Lisette laughed again.

He told her some of the good deeds the children reported to him, drawing more amusement from her. An hour passed quickly, and Miles was glad he had come. Lisette had always been a good friend, even if at times he felt the necessity to avoid her.

He wished her well and slipped from the room. He had planned to leave forthwith, but when he reached the bottom of the staircase, he peeked inside the drawing room in hopes of catching a glimpse of Jemma. Empty. He made his way toward the library.

The door was open. There she was, curled up on the lone sofa, a blanket stretched over her legs and a newspaper in her hands.

He leaned against the doorframe, content to watch her without her knowing for a moment. "Any news on the island of Chios?"

The newspaper came down until he could see the top of her head and her green eyes, but no more. "More casualties discovered. More slaves taken."

"Sorry news, indeed."

The newspaper came down a little more so only her chin was hidden.

"May I come in?"

That she didn't stand or make any pretenses testified of how comfortable they had grown in each other's company. Her hesitation, unfortunately, said differently. After a half minute, she swung her legs to the floor and shifted to the corner of the sofa.

He took it as an invitation to enter, but he stopped when he reached the sofa. Had she been resting because she was becoming sick? "Have you been unwell at all?"

She shook her head.

"You are still speaking to me though?"

She cleared her throat. "I believe my long walks and all the fresh air have helped my constitution."

He sighed inwardly with relief. She was healthy and speaking to him. He set his hand on the sofa's back, fingering the smooth wooden trim. "I have been thinking a great deal about our last conversation. I want to apologize for crossing any lines. You have my support in whatever you choose. If it is Mr. Bentley, then I wish you all the happiness in the world."

There, he'd said it. Even if he did not quite feel it yet.

Time stretched in the silence between them, making a minute feel far longer than it was.

"Thank you, Miles." Her shoulders seemed to visibly relax. "I'm sorry too. For being awkward. I didn't want to be this way. I just am."

He had been told he was an excellent actor from all their Rebel escapades over the years, so he borrowed Tom's easy grin, pretending he was more collected than he felt. "You were a bit awkward."

She gave a short laugh. "Thank you for noticing."

He pulled out his folded letter from his waistcoat pocket and dropped it on the sofa. He made certain she saw it before dipping his head in a silent parting. He was not eager to leave her, but the disconsolate air around them.

As soon as he had mounted his horse once more, the rain began. It beat against the brim of his hat and ran down his jacket. He didn't feel a thing, even though he knew it had to be soaking him through. There was too much on his mind. He couldn't go back to suppressing his feelings for Jemma, but neither would he press them on her. There was too much history between them to do otherwise. He was a Rebel, but not on matters of the heart.

CHAPTER 26

WHEN LISETTE ASKED TO ACCOMPANY Jemma on her walk Monday morning, Jemma could not refuse her. "You may come but only if it is a short distance with plenty of stops to rest."

Lisette agreed. "I do not want to overtire myself, believe me. It would only mean more naps."

"You must be heartily sick of your bed."

"Yes, and grateful for fresh air."

The morning was crisp and the shadows cool, all traces of the flash storm from the day before gone. They took the long way around the perimeter of the estate before heading toward the road. The sparrows flitted about, chirping their greetings to them and making Lisette sigh with pleasure.

"The weather is perfect for a walk, is it not?" Jemma asked.

"Actually, I was thinking about how nice it was for Miles and Mr. Bentley to visit me while I was sick." Lisette pushed a large rock out of the way with her boot.

"Mr. Bentley has proven himself to be quite a gentleman." It took some effort not to talk of Miles and to focus on Mr. Bentley instead, but Jemma forced herself to expound. "I want you to know I was the picture of a lady and did not say or do anything capable of censure. You will never believe this, but I did not want to run from the room when he was with me, and I believe, neither did he."

Lisette's soft laugh caught on a breeze, muffling it. "I am happy to hear it. I am always pleased to see Mr. Bentley, but I admit I enjoyed Miles's visit particularly."

Jemma swallowed. "Oh?"

"It has been a while since I have felt close to him."

Jemma's stomach clenched. This was what she had wanted, but envisioning it did not settle well. Miles had listened to her wishes, despite his cryptic note. The words rang in her mind: *May I correct one mistake in your accounting? I did not fall in love for the first time that day on the ice.*

She shook her head to block out his puzzling words. He had already begun to transition his feelings back to Lisette since she had done everything to reject him, so it did not matter. And yet, no sense of satisfaction bubbled up inside Jemma; instead, her eyes pricked with tears. "We should turn around now."

"We haven't made it very far."

She kept her voice steady. "You promised, remember?"

"Very well." Lisette groaned, turning about. "You truly appreciate the change of scenery and the beauty of nature when you cannot have it, but tomorrow, it will still be here."

Jemma kept her head averted; her watery eyes trained on the field dotted with sheep on the side of the road. "And you will have even more energy to enjoy it if you are careful today."

They both had need of being careful.

Lisette smiled, oblivious to the pain Jemma felt. "You are very right."

Jemma was happy to see the color back in Lisette's cheeks and her strength returning, just like she *would* be happy to see Lisette with Miles. Though the thought was far more forced than ever before. Her willpower had to last only a little longer before her engagement was announced. Mrs. Manning thought that after the cricket match would be best, while everyone was gathered. Once it was official, everything would fall into place, including her and Miles's misplaced feelings.

Tuesday and Wednesday, it rained again, leaving the ground soggy and damp Thursday morning. Jemma was about to forgo her walk when Mrs. Manning came into her bedchamber, carrying a small basket.

"Good morning, Jemma. I am so glad I caught you before you left on your walk. Could you deliver this to the church for me for Mr. Jackson? I believe you walk that direction on occasion."

She did walk the route fairly regularly. But deliver something to Miles? With some hesitation, she peered into the basket to see at least a dozen chocolate biscuits the size of walnuts. They were stamped with a pretty heart and dusted with sugar—obviously made with particular care. Mrs. Manning carefully folded a tea towel over the top.

Jemma chewed on her lip. She had hoped to avoid Miles until the cricket match. If she visited him now, it might give him the wrong idea. "Actually, I—"

"I was so pleased by his visit to Lisette," Mrs. Manning cut her off. "Mr. Jackson does so much for the community and, yet, on his busiest day, came here to see to Lisette's welfare. Of course, I did want Lisette to deliver this, but I do not want her out in this damp air, and I have a meeting with my musical club today."

After all the Matchmaking Mamas had done for Jemma, the delivery of biscuits was the least she could do in return. Especially if they were said to be from Lisette. Besides, Miles deserved to have them, even if Jemma was reluctant to see him. The Mannings' cook was one of the best she knew, and Miles had such a liking for sweets.

"I would be happy to take it to him." She said it without enthusiasm, knowing she would likely regret her decision.

"Thank you, dear." Mrs. Manning handed her the basket and left the room.

Jemma stared at the basket before setting it on her writing desk. If she was going to see Miles, it would do good to safeguard her heart first. Her intentions had to be clear to the both of them. In fact, this would be a good chance to send him another written lesson. She pulled open the desk drawer and fingered the stiff, folded letter he had dropped on the library sofa several days before. She didn't have to open it to know what it said. The words hadn't left her alone since she had read them earlier.

I did not fall in love for the first time that day on the ice.

No signature or a single detail more. He knew her curiosity would drive her mad, but she would not ask for clarification. He was baiting her, she was sure. But why? No, it did not matter. She was to blame for insisting on Miles's coaching her through her courtship.

She shut the drawer with too much force, the sharpness of wood against wood reverberating in her ears. Determined to forget a few puzzling words and even more complicated feelings, she picked up her pen and began composing her response.

Lesson two: the importance of chaperones and the evils of eye connection.

When she finished, she had to sneak one of Miles's chocolate biscuits to give her strength. The outside was crispy, the inside chewy and soft. One might not suffice, but she could procrastinate no longer. Donning her sturdiest pair of half boots and a lightweight spencer trimmed with ruffles, she trekked through the mud to the church. When she arrived, voices came from the side of the building, drawing her in that direction. She turned the corner only to pull back so she wouldn't be seen.

Peering around the corner, she observed Miss Hardwick playing with the honey ringlets by her face. "Are they really talking about Mr. Jackson all the way in London?"

The woman next to Miss Hardwick shared similar coloring but with larger features. She squeaked with disbelief. "Then, no one in Brookeside knows he published a book? His poems and ideas are all the rage in the circles I know."

Jemma gasped, quickly covering her mouth to silence it. Miles Jackson published a book! Why had he never told anyone? Why had he never told her?

"How long has he been married?" the unknown woman asked.

"Married?" Miss Hardwick laughed. "Cousin, Mr. Jackson is a bachelor."

"Oh? Even better!"

Jemma frowned. She could barely stomach Miss Hardwick's exuberant affection for Miles. Must she endure an equally enamored cousin?

"I am surprised to learn this," the cousin said. "Mr. Jackson has such a beautiful view on relationships. One would naturally expect he had an abundance of experience and years of marriage. But come to think of it, there was a selection about heartache. Was he thwarted in love? Did his fiancé die?"

Miss Hardwick laughed again. "You are reading into what is not there. They are fictional poems with plain truths in their themes. Does that not satisfy you?"

Her cousin shook her head. "I should still like to meet Mr. Jackson. I will never believe a bachelor can be any expert on love unless I speak to him for myself."

"And you shall," Miss Hardwick assured. "Mama will invite him to dine with us next week. She is very regular with her company. Besides, I would not be surprised if Mr. Jackson were soon engaged and able to satisfy all your concerns."

Jemma's heart unconsciously stuttered.

"Engaged? Truly?" Miss Hardwick's cousin bent an ear forward. "Do tell."

Miss Hardwick flipped the long ringlet from her chignon over her shoulder. "I have set my sights on him, Cousin. It is only a matter of time until he is engaged to me."

Jemma winced, even knowing there was not a single reason to be jealous of Miss Hardwick and her nonsense. Poor Miles though. His secret project had become famous. Knowing him, he would not be happy to know he had been found out. Selfishly, she was disappointed that she had not discovered the news before Miss Hardwick, and from Miles's own mouth. All this time, he'd been scribbling away at poetry? Inspirational poetry, at that. And some obviously about love. Why had he never shared even one with her?

More depressed in spirit than before, Jemma let herself into the church. She waited a good half hour, but there was no sign of Miles. She could leave the biscuits. She *should* leave the biscuits. But now that she knew about his book, she wanted nothing more than to ask him about it.

She finally gave up after chewing off the top of one of her fingernails. It was better if she did not converse with him for some time, even if it hurt to not know his secrets. She forced herself to exit the church. The ladies were well and gone, thank heavens. Jemma's eyes traced the path to the bench, and a sudden longing pulled at her. Miles wouldn't be there. It wasn't even the lunch hour. Her feet had a mind of their own, because they began the short trek down the path toward the copse of trees and the hidden stream.

The waterfall was fuller today after all the rainfall, and it drew her gaze. The bubbling sound filled her ears and soul. Nowhere on earth looked more beautiful than this did right now. Sentimentality hadn't always colored her view of things. Maybe it was because she knew she would have to stop coming here, and deep inside, she wished otherwise.

Inevitably, her gaze went to the bench. It was empty, just as she had imagined. How lonely it looked without Miles sitting on it. She set down the basket of biscuits on one end where she generally sat, and went and perched on other end instead—the side Miles generally occupied. Her hand absently fell to the wood beside her, but no one picked it up and held it close. Even so, sitting where Miles did made her feel closer to him, in a way.

Her fingers ran along the rough grain. In coming days, would Miles bring Lisette here to share his luncheon? Would all his and

Jemma's memories here be forgotten? Such thoughts were torture to her, despite all her efforts to discipline herself.

She scooted to the very edge of the bench, shifting her weight to one hip so she might look at the seat as if Miles were still there. "Don't even think of desecrating our memories. Marry who you want, but this spot is ours."

"Is it now?"

Jemma startled and fell off the bench, her backside landing hard in damp soil. She did not care to look up, but the humiliation was inevitable. "How long have you been there?" She pulled her gaze behind her and into the trees. Miles stood with his hands clasped behind his back and his somber eyes on her.

"Long enough to know you've begun talking to yourself."

"I was not talking to myself. I was talking to . . . someone else." She ran her hands down her skirts. It did not look good for her.

"Seeing how you were stroking the bench where I sit, I am inclined to believe you were speaking to me."

Her entire face burned.

His steps were slow and deliberate, and all too soon, he was by her side with his hand outstretched.

She stared at it. She had missed that hand.

With a brave and, perchance, foolish breath, she took it and let him pull her to her feet.

He didn't let go.

But then again, neither did she.

His hand was warm. Very warm. His eyes dull and his cheeks ruddy. She frowned. "Miles, are you well?"

He raised his brow. "Why are you here? I have no more lessons to teach you."

"I wish it were the truth. Apparently, you have much to teach everyone." She slipped her hand from his and stepped back, stumbling on a tree root. Miles's hand came up to catch her, but she waved it off. "I, er, brought you some biscuits from Mrs. Manning, but you were not at the church. Miss Hardwick was, however, and I overheard her talking to her cousin about a book you published."

Miles eyes grew from almond shaped to as round as chestnuts. "How did they know?"

She walked sideways to spare Miles the worst of her dress. This had not been the most graceful month of her life. She again took a seat on the bench, effectively hiding her dirty backside. This time, she sat closer to the biscuits and far away from the edge. "Your book is a favorite of many, it seems. A shame you did not share it with your closest friends."

"You are angry with me?"

"No." She stared at him. She could stare at him forever. "I understand."

"You do?"

"Certainly. I know you value your privacy. I might also be slightly jealous that so many others have read it and I have not."

He studied her. "It's about love and relationships."

She swallowed. "A topic you are passionate about." Did she really say that? Her cheeks burned. "I, of course, know little about the topic, which is why I need a copy, I suppose. What is love anyway? I daresay, I will never understand it."

"Love?" Miles walked to the bench, sinking into his normal place, facing the stream with eyes glassed over. "It's a natural emotion. Some would even say they wish they had greater power to suppress it."

Something was definitely off about his color and the tone of his voice. "You are not well, Miles."

He laughed bitterly. "For once, you see me plainly."

Her brow pinched. "Should you return inside? Perhaps lie down?"

He didn't answer.

She was by his side in an instant, throwing out all her reservations about touching him and setting her hand to his head. "Miles, you're burning with fever! We need to call a doctor and get you home to bed."

"No doctor."

"Tom, then. Or Paul or Ian?"

In one short motion, his head fell on her shoulder. "I will not trouble them."

Her pulse raced, and she wanted nothing more than to smooth his curls with her hand and be the one to comfort him. "Why can you not trouble them? I cannot carry you to your horse."

"Can't you try?"

She looked down to see a glimpse of a grin. She sputtered a laugh. "Certainly not."

She should pull away, but he was ill . . .

"Would you carry Mr. Bentley?"

"You're being absurd."

"I suppose I am." He lifted his head up and stood. "Can you manage to keep your seat on the bench if I leave you? I would hate for you to ruin another pretty dress."

She stood, too, no longer caring about the damage to the back of her gown. "I promise not to fall twice." She wished such a statement applied to her love life as much as her clumsiness. "Now, go home, Miles Jackson. I will send the others to look in on you." On a whim, she tucked her letter into his hand and stepped back. She pointed to the path. "Go."

He did not reply, his gait tired as he walked back up the path. She whispered a prayer for his health. She wanted to rush to his side and let him lean into her, but she resisted. Part of binding up her heart meant letting someone else be the one to tend him. She stabbed her fingernails into the palms of her hands. It was much harder in real life than in her head.

CHAPTER 27

MILES SLEPT ALL FRIDAY AND woke in the evening, feeling much improved. It was not quite dinner, but he was starving. He threw a quilted banyan his mother had made him on over his shirt and breeches, the loose robe coming to his knees, and went in search of food.

Mrs. Purcell sent up a familiar basket of chocolate biscuits—likely the same ones Jemma had tried to give him—and a steaming bowl of white soup. He picked up a heart-stamped biscuit and slipped one into his mouth, savoring the sweetness.

Unavoidably, his thoughts chased after his last encounter with Jemma, his memory sharpening with renewed clarity. Everything had been a little hazy until now. He was not often sick, but he did not recall any illness impairing his judgment.

He put another biscuit into his mouth. At least his taste was in order, even if his senses were not. Had he really laid his head on Jemma's shoulder? He cringed. No wonder she had been concerned enough to make the other male Rebels call on him. Though he was not certain if they were more worried about his health or about the cricket match.

Thankfully, he would not disappoint them on either count. He was feeling more himself already, and the game wasn't for another three days. He moved the bowl closer to him and ate the hearty soup. He had just finished when the door burst open and his brother, Kent, entered the drawing room. He was a younger version of Miles, with coiled hair a shade lighter and matching long legs, but his grin leaned more toward mischievousness.

"Don't get up." Kent strolled to the table. "A little bird . . . actually a big bird with rather broad shoulders and a teasing grin, told me you were sick."

"Tom?" Miles pushed his empty bowl away.

"How did you guess?"

"Lucky, I suppose." Miles put out his hand, and Kent pumped it up and down. "It's good to see you. You look taller."

"It is because I am standing and you're sitting." Kent pulled out a chair and sat himself. His hands came up behind his head, and his long legs crossed at the ankle. "I had barely arrived in town when I was sent post haste to your side with a special message."

"Let me make another guess." Miles folded his hands on the table. "You were sent to remind me how serious beating the boys from Bradford in cricket is to this town and how I had better be well by Monday."

Kent's brow lifted. "I'm impressed. Do you often receive such perfect revelation as a vicar?"

Miles chuckled. "It isn't heavenly knowledge; it's Brookeside pride. Not to worry. No fever would stop me from standing with my team."

"I always did like a martyr's last speech."

Miles chuckled. "Then, you will be disappointed to know I am feeling better."

"Disappointed? I like our best batsman to be healthy more than I care for a martyr's last speech."

"That's the spirit."

"Now I've warmed up your mood," Kent said, "it's a good time to tell you I am staying here until the end of the match."

"Because it is closer to Tom's estate, or because you are worried about me?" Miles knew the answer, but he had to tease Kent anyway.

"Both." Kent reached over and patted Miles's cheek. Miles swatted at his hand but was not deeply irritated. Kent would be the perfect distraction to prevent Miles from thinking overmuch about Jemma.

After instructing his housekeeper to make up a bed for Kent, Miles was tired again. When he slipped into his own room, he discovered a folded letter on the ground. Instantly, he remembered the missive Jemma had placed in his hand in the copse of trees outside the church. It must have fallen from his waistcoat when he had undressed for bed upon his return.

He snatched it off the ground and broke the seal with his fingers. He knew it would be no confession of love, but like a glutton for punishment, he unfolded it and read the words.

Required chaperones? Forbidden eye connection?

His chances for winning over Jemma's heart grew slimmer by the second. Especially since the *perils* of alone time were steep indeed. However, only a complete fool would see this as a total loss. She had admitted to one thing. The truth was plainly written between the lines: he had affected her. Why else would she be preaching chaperones and this nonsense about how gazing into a woman's eyes could ensnare the wrong heart?

Hitting the letter against his hand, he knew he was stuck. Her six weeks would be up at the end of the cricket match. Time was running out. Jemma was just stubborn enough to go along with the Matchmaking Mamas and marry Mr. Bentley.

The lucky man.

With less restraint than he ought to have, he penned a reply at his desk. It wasn't poetic or even clever, but it would do. He would wait until he could deliver it personally the morning of the match.

The weekend passed quickly, and when Monday morning dawned, Miles had his full strength back. Kent's conversation and the anticipation for the match temporarily took over Miles's troubled mind. Even his staff was anxious for the match and planned to come cheer for the Brookeside team. Miles was determined not to think about Jemma and enjoy himself. If no opportunity presented itself to deliver his letter, he would not create one. The day was about bonding with his team and enjoying a sport—a leisure he did not often have.

On the ride to Tom's estate, Kent pulled his horse up next to Miles's. "How many days do you think the match will last?"

Miles shrugged. "I've heard the Bradford boys have put together an impressive team, but we are an active bunch and nothing to sniff at. I'd wager it lasts two or three days."

Kent pulled his hat down lower. "Tom predicted an even match. I've never played the full five-day limit. I love the sport, but who can last that long? It's beyond the pale."

Five days was long for even the most dedicated cricket player. "The Brookeside team won't let you quit. Chin up, Kent. We'll clobber them before it is drawn out too much."

They arrived early to Tom's estate, but so did many others. By quarter after eight, a large crowd surrounded the mowed field. A chalk line traced the oval boundary and the pitch where the batsmen and bowlers would play. A hum of excitement buzzed through their growing audience.

When his family arrived, he waved. Behind them, he spotted Jemma and Lisette walking over with the Mannings to take their place under a tent with Lord and Lady Felcroft, Cassandra, the Sheldons, and Lady Kellen. He looked away, purposefully putting his arm around Mr. Reed to wish his teammate luck.

"The Bradford Gents are strong and quick," Mr. Reed said, studying their opponents.

Miles watched for a moment and found himself agreeing. "Don't worry, Reed, we have our own strengths."

"Oh, Mr. Jackson!"

Miles squeezed his eyes shut. He knew the high-pitched voice better than he wanted to. When he turned, he was surprised to see not just Miss Hardwick but also four or five other young ladies, each with a token offering in hand. Miss Hardwick put herself ahead of the others and held out a basket of baked goods tied with a ribbon. He thanked them all while desperately searching for a place of retreat. Paul stepped up and politely explained that the spectators had to stay back. Having perceptive friends was reason enough for rejoicing.

Was it too much to hope Jemma had not seen his entourage? Miles wanted to look over to the white tent to see her response, and it took great discipline to avoid her. If only Ian were not so intimidating, the women might flock after him instead.

The game began precisely at nine, putting any thoughts of Jemma from his mind. Brookside won the coin toss and chose to play as the in-party, with Ian as the first striker and Kent preparing to run. Miles stood with the rest of his teammates, ready to bat when his turn came.

The bowler on the Bradford team opposite Ian signaled to his player and threw a roundarm bowl and sent the ball soaring. The ball bounced and went wide. The player delivered the second bowl straight, and Ian swung. His bat connected with the ball, and it flew toward the outfield, just shy of the boundary.

The Brookeside team jumped with excitement, and cheers rippled through the crowd. Brookeside made three runs before the ball was returned to the wicket keeper. Miles watched proudly as Mortimer Gibbons, the scorekeeper, made three notches in his long, hazel stick. After the first over, Kent was up. He hit the ball on the first bowl, and a fielder caught it. A disappointing out.

Their luck was back and forth for the rest of the inning. Just as the second inning ended, it was noon, and a break was called. The sky was overcast but the weather warm and a touch humid. Lady Felcroft served cold lemonade, meat, finger sandwiches, and cake to both teams.

Out of the corner of his eye, Miles noticed Jemma and Lisette making their way toward the Brookeside team. His lips turned up in anticipation, but he squelched such thoughts immediately. Jemma would be coming to congratulate Mr. Bentley on his fine catch in the last inning.

Sure enough, the women spoke with Mr. Bentley first. Dressed down to his shirtsleeves, the man had an advantage with his broad shoulders. Miles had always had a lean and long, narrow frame. It had never bothered him until this minute.

Tom interrupted his thoughts with his usual ridiculousness. "We're all kissing the ball for good luck."

He tossed the leather ball, and Miles caught it. "You bet a pretty penny on the game, didn't you?" Miles asked.

"Easy money," Tom said with a wink.

Miles grimaced at the ball. "Who kissed it last?"

"Pretend it was a woman."

Done. He pecked the ball with Jemma in mind. The sweaty leather would be nothing like her sweet lips, but in the name of the sport, he endured it. He tossed it back. "I want my cut of your winnings for that."

Tom's gaze slid away from him, and his whole countenance brightened. "Aw, there is my beautiful wife come to congratulate her husband on his fine bowling skills. Excuse me." Tom pulled his wife to him and shamelessly kissed her on the mouth.

Miles shook his head.

"I thought you approved of such demonstrations of affection," came his favorite contralto voice from behind him. Not only had she come to speak to him, but she had also brought up his favorite topic to discuss with her.

He turned slowly, his mouth pulling at the corners with amusement. Jemma wore a wide-brimmed, simply adorned bonnet, accentuating the loose tendrils framing her face. Her daffodil-colored gown stood out among the others, with puffed sleeves bunched once at her elbow and again to her forearm. Brown gloves matched the brown bows at her shoulders and the small, brown print dotting the rest of the gown. No one else was like her, and he wouldn't change a thing.

He overcame the momentary distraction of seeing her. "You misunderstand. I shook my head out of envy, not disapproval. I am happy for Tom and Cassandra. They complete each other."

Her cheeks colored, making her all the more beautiful to him. "You are fortunate to have so many young ladies vying for your hand to choose from."

So, she had seen his flock of admirers. Those ladies did not even know him—or see the real him. He had no interest in any of them. Besides, not one of them was Jemma. If only he could help her understand. If she gave him a chance . . .

She stepped back. "I only wanted to commend your batting this morning—one *friend* to another. You played well, as always. Excuse me."

Her rushed words almost made him forget the letter hiding in his pocket. "Jemma, wait."

She faced him again, her entire person hesitant.

He stepped close to avoid others from seeing the exchange. "I thought we were not going to be awkward around each other. It seems there is more than one thing we need to practice." He looked over his shoulder as he slipped the folded paper into her hand. He wanted to weave his fingers through hers and kiss her palm, but as soon as he felt her fingers grip the missive, he stepped past her and walked away.

He wished he could see her face when she read his words, but indiscretion was more appropriate. Weaving through the crowd of people, he barely restrained his grin. Sharing a secret together was exactly what he shouldn't be doing. Desperate times required a bit of boldness. But with his letter delivered, it was time to forget her again.

CHAPTER 28

JEMMA WATCHED MILES WALK AWAY from her, his shirt sleeves rolled to his elbows, giving a fine display of his muscled forearms, and his coal-colored curls tousled. Fingers tingling, she hid the letter in the folds of her skirt. She shouldn't read it. Not now. Not with Mr. Bentley only ten feet away.

It wouldn't do. Her willpower was as weak as ever. If she hurried and slipped away, she could read it before the next inning began. She took a step toward Rivenwood.

Lisette gave a tug on her arm. "Come, Jemma. Louisa, Cassandra, and I are all going to make a fuss over Ian and embarrass him thoroughly."

Jemma laughed at the idea, both relieved that she had not been caught with the letter and disappointed that it would have to wait. She wrapped her arm around Lisette's. "This I must be a part of."

Not twenty minutes later, they found themselves back in the tent for the third inning.

"How many overs are there again?" Lisette asked, taking her seat on one of the chairs Lord Felcroft had brought out for their group. Most of the crowd sat on blankets or in the grass. "Was it seventy? It has been too long since I have watched a match."

"Ninety overs a day, if you can imagine. We have another three hours, at least." Long enough for Jemma to be sufficiently tortured. For someone who loved the game, she had a letter burning in her reticule, driving her to distraction. Instead of sitting, she stood, leaning against the back of her chair. How could she endure another minute without reading Miles's letter? "Come to think of it," she said suddenly, "I will take a quick walk to stretch my legs before I sit again."

"Do hurry," Lisette said. "I believe Mr. Bentley is going in as the second batsman."

"I will." Jemma did not have to be told twice. She grabbed her reticule and weaved around the blankets. She hid herself a short distance away, behind a group of men standing and conversing.

She unfolded the paper, her hands shaking and read: *You may try, but no chaperone could keep you from looking at me.*

Jemma gasped. Of all the conceited, ridiculous things to say . . .

She swallowed down her insult when she read the next line, and her heart set to pounding. *As for me, I have no desire to look anywhere else.*

An abundance of warmth flooded her limbs and chest.

That man. Did he not comprehend the meaning of her lessons? He was worse than a cricket ball falling just within the boundaries edge, teasing the crowd to no end. This would not do. She ripped the paper in half, leaving his words intact. She folded his letter back up and tucked it into her reticule, digging out a nub of a pencil she knew lay at the bottom from the last time she'd sketched out of doors. With the remaining blank piece, she scribbled her response. Just one line.

Lesson Three: Stop confusing unassuming women!

She did not like Miles's newfound devil-may-care attitude. She folded her note up and searched for a little boy who could act as a messenger. There was no reason to wait to put Miles in his place, and it was not hard to find a young boy who accepted her coin and was off to do her bidding.

She folded her arms, watching him go. Her frustration only built. What did Miles mean by saying she couldn't look away from him?

Did he think her so weak? He was not thirty feet away from her, and she hadn't even stolen a glance his way.

Ah, Mr. Bentley was up to bat.

She watched him miss an easy throw. "Protect the wicket, Mr. Bentley!" she called to him. He was a good bowler, but batting was not his strong point—no matter if he had played at Oxford.

Had her letter been delivered yet? Before realizing what she was doing, she glanced at Miles. He had her missive open in his hand, and he looked up at the exact moment, their eyes meeting.

Alarmed, she tore away her gaze. But not before she'd seen his impertinent, affirming grin. A small, humiliating whine escaped as she tore back through the crowd toward the tent. She'd wanted to put him in his place, not prove he was right!

Once back with her family and friends and seated next to Lisette, she could not concentrate to watch the rest of Mr. Bentley's turn. In fact, the next two overs passed in a haze. This was not normal for her at all. The bowler changed, and a ruddy, large man with thick, strong arms stepped up to the pitch, digging his foot into the sawdust. With one fast pitch after the next, he bowled out the next two batsmen.

"Did they hold this man back as a surprise?" Lord Felcroft asked in wonder. "Someone had better get some runs off him, or we will lose indeed."

Miles was next up as striker.

Jemma's finger went to her mouth, her nail catching between her teeth. "Come on, Miles," she whispered to herself. "You can do it." For all his fallacious romantic nonsense, she wanted him to soundly beat the Bradford bowler.

The large man's first bowl hit Miles in the leg.

The crowd yelled their opinions to the umpires, who stalled in their call. They stood apart from the other players in their jackets, cocked hats, and long bats in their hands.

"It's a run!" several called.

"It's an out if I ever saw one," someone next to Jemma yelled back.

"You're wrong!" she cried back to the man. "It's a run, fair and square!"

When the umpire called the hit a run, the ruddy bowler stomped his foot in rage.

"Is he really sulking?" Jemma asked no one in particular. She dropped back against her seat with a humph.

Lisette laughed. "I forget how competitive you are, but you cannot be worried about Miles. He is an excellent batsman."

"I am not worried," Jemma said, suddenly flustered. "I merely wanted the call to be just."

Lisette humored her with a smile.

It is true!

The next three overs scored them another two runs.

"Well done, Miles!" she called. Her voice blended with the other cheers, specifically Lisette's next to her.

A sudden realization dawned on Jemma. She had notably cheered louder for Miles than for any of the other players. Would her cousin notice? Miles's letter was right. She couldn't look away from him, despite all her efforts otherwise.

Not a half hour later, a little boy tapped her on the arm. "Miss Fielding?"

Her eyes widened, noting another missive in his hand.

The others were caught up in their clapping, so she quickly accepted the folded paper, now a fourth of its original size. She turned her body and read it quickly.

> *I have no intention of confusing you. Just say the word, and I will tell you exactly how I feel. Unless, of course, you desire me to show you.*

Her fingers fumbled on her reticule as she shoved the note inside. Her heart raced while her feelings weighed heavily in her chest. His words were everything she wanted to hear—and all wrong too. How could she, in good conscience, announce her engagement if she could not fully commit to Mr. Bentley? What was this pull Mr.

Romantic had to him that even she, the most headstrong woman she knew, could not resist? She was doomed!

Her lessons had been an utter failure. She stole a glimpse of Lisette's profile. Sweet, angel Lisette—who never asked anything of anyone and stood by Jemma through thick and thin. She tightened her fists and fought the worry hovering around her. No more lessons. No more letters. No more friendship. The only way to train her heart toward Mr. Bentley and to fulfill her promise to Grandmother was to cut off Miles completely.

CHAPTER 29

MILES AND HIS BROTHER DRESSED for their second day of cricket. The first day had ended in a draw. While Brookeside was up a few runs, neither team had bowled the other out twice.

However, it wasn't cricket on Miles's mind. An uneasy feeling had settled over him from the moment he had awoken. He shook it off now as best he could. Nerves were always a part of any sportsman's event. It couldn't be anything else.

When he and Kent reached Tom's estate, the strange feeling in Miles's gut only increased. Was someone ill? Had he left unfinished business at the church? The only thing that made any sense was his concern for Jemma.

Should he seek her out and set things right between them? A few words exchanged in a handful of letters was not as effective as a single conversation. Knowing her, she was probably angry with him instead of flattered. This had to be it. His frankness had no doubt provoked her.

It was a shame she couldn't read any responses from the letters he'd sent to all his friends—many of them chaps from his school days, while others were acquaintances who had come and gone through Brookeside over the years. Her ire might lessen if she did. His surprise, however, wasn't meant to win her heart but to bring her happiness. Now he hoped it would also soften her enough that there could be peace between them again. Such hopes depended on the timeliness of the post, though, and would not do him any good today.

If he could speak to her for even a moment, it would surely set him at ease for the game. As soon as the Mannings' carriage arrived, he set down his practice bat and excused himself. He came upon his family gathered on a blanket near the Felcroft tent. After shaking his stepfather's hand and kissing his mother on the cheek, he slipped behind their other friends and made his way to the Mannings.

Jemma took one look at him, and her mouth hardened into a fine line. He thought she might be frustrated with him, but this was worse than he'd predicted. She drew Lady Kellen into a conversation, preventing him from speaking to her.

Even angry, she was beautiful. Dressed in a dark orange few could wear as well as she and a straw bonnet with feathers pluming from the back, she was eye-catching. Mr. Manning noticed him, and soon Miles was standing by Lisette and asking after her and her family.

After a few minutes, he returned to his team. The feeling of unease only increased, and no matter how much attention he paid to the match, he couldn't shake it.

When the inning ended, the Brookeside team took to the field. Paul stepped in as the next bowler, a quick hand at it, and Mr. Reed as the wicket keeper. Miles jogged to the outfield with Ian, each of them taking opposite sides. He didn't trust himself any closer since he needed to clear his head to focus.

All the same, he sought out Jemma, knowing she was too far away to realize he was looking for her, but discovered she was no longer in the tent. He glanced around, searching for a glimpse of orange, and finally found her by the score keeper, not terribly far from him. He caught her voice. A cheer—a cheer for Mr. Bentley.

Miles huffed in disgust and forced his mind back on the game. Nothing came his way for several overs. After the next batsman, he would rotate closer to the pitch.

The ruddy-faced bowler with the thick arms from the day before stepped in front of the wicket for his turn at bat. Paul bowled a clean, underarm throw, and the batsman swung hard. The ball connected with a resounding whack and soared toward the boundary. Miles would never make it in time to catch it, but he started running to retrieve the ball wherever it landed.

Only it didn't land. A woman walking along the far side of the field, far from the crowd, was struck in the back of the head before she crumpled to the ground in a heap of *orange*.

Jemma?

Miles's run turned into an all-out sprint. She was too still. *Move. Please. Move.* He slid to her side only moments later. Her eyes were closed when he scooped up her upper body, turning her so his arm carefully cradled her head. "Jemma, can you hear me?" Was she even breathing? "Hold on, love." His hand went to her throat, searching for a pulse. Nothing. His very soul could feel hers slipping away from this world. "Please, open your eyes." Oh, why wasn't she opening her eyes?

A dry sob caught in his throat, his fingers fumbling for any sign of life. He needed to feel life. Her life. Forgetting her pulse, his eyes fell on her lips. She had to know she couldn't give up. He brought his head down and kissed her, his mouth as desperate as the rest of him. There was no thought of the why or the how behind his actions, just the need to be close and to communicate to her soul the only way he knew how.

His kiss was neither short nor long, but against her warm mouth, he felt her breath on his upper lip—the taste of a miracle. He pulled back, his heart pounding, and her eyes fluttered open.

"Jemma?" he gasped, relief searing through the ache in his chest.

Her eyes dulled and rolled back, closing once more.

"Stay with me, love. Stay with me." He started thinking logically. The wound. He should check the wound. His hand searched for her bonnet pins, tugging at the two he found. By the time he freed them, Ian dropped to his side.

"How is she?" Ian's breath heaved.

"Her eyes opened for a moment." As gently as possible, Miles dug his fingers through her hair until he found the large goose egg and a wet, sticky spot. Without looking, he knew it was blood. Heaven help her. "Give me your cravat."

Ian ripped it from his throat as more of their teammates reached their side, flanking around her. Miles took the cravat from Ian and pressed it to her head wound.

"Vixen?" Tom cried, pushing closer. "Tell me she was just knocked cold."

"It looks to be that way," Ian said, "but she is bleeding."

"What can I do?" Mr. Bentley bumbled, bouncing up and down on his toes and running his hands through his hair. "Someone tell me how I can help."

"Start by calming down," Paul ordered. "And give her room to breathe."

"Right, be calm."

Miles glanced up at the man he had painted as far too perfect in his head. Mr. Bentley was mumbling under his breath, his eyes impossibly wide. Miles was struck with compassion for him. The man was anxious for Jemma but had no claim on her to do anything about it. Miles had no claim either, despite his long history, fierce friendship, and deep-seated love for her. It was a helplessness that couldn't be measured.

"We need to get her back to the house," Ian instructed.

Miles nodded, putting gentle pressure on the cravat. His touch was steady, but underneath his skin, he was shaking to his core. He couldn't lose Jemma—wouldn't lose her. But he was scared. More scared than he had ever been in his life. He forced himself to breathe evenly. If she woke again, he wanted her to see his full confidence in her ability to recover. "Ian, take one side of her, and I will take the other so we do not jostle her head too much."

"I see a carriage nearby. Bring her there instead." Paul pointed to the nearest conveyance, the horses still hitched to it. "We can get her to the house faster in there than going through the crowd."

Miles agreed, and he maneuvered his hand, now covered in blood, to beneath her knees, then stood with her in his arms.

Mr. Bentley took one look at the blood on Miles's hand and now Jemma's dress and fainted.

"I've got him," Mr. Reed said, crouching beside Mr. Bentley. "Take care of Miss Fielding."

Mr. Reed, in his own grieving, was perhaps the most qualified to help. No one had a calmer demeanor out of all of them.

With Ian to assist, they made it to the carriage quickly. It did not matter if a Bradford guest owned it or a Brookeside local, the driver jumped to help. Ian took Jemma while Miles climbed inside. Then Miles turned and took her back in his arms and settled carefully onto a rather short bench. Ian jumped inside and dropped onto the opposite seat—the two of them far too tall for the narrow carriage.

Paul stopped Tom from climbing in along with them. "I will ride for the doctor. Will you tell the Mannings?"

Tom straightened. "Of course. I will bring them directly to the house." He leaned into the carriage. "Miles, Ian, take Jemma to one of the guest rooms upstairs. The housekeeper can gather bandages. Keep Jemma comfortable until we can get there."

Miles gave a nod, and the door was shut behind them. The carriage rocked, and they were on their way. He reached for Jemma's hand just as he heard his name.

"Miles?"

The near whisper stole his breath. Her eyes were barely open, and her mouth pulled tight with pain.

"I'm here." He released her hand and smoothed the disheveled hair from her cheek.

"My head . . ."

"We've sent for the doctor," Ian said, hunching toward them. "Try not to move too much, no matter how intolerable it is being in Miles's arms."

Her eyes fluttered closed again, but her moment of coherence gave Miles needed hope. It felt like hours before they had her in the house and in a bed upstairs. He moved awkwardly to the side as Lisette, Tom, and Cassandra barreled into the room.

"I'll fetch her a nightgown," Cassandra said.

Lisette scooped up Jemma's hand, tears streaming down her face. "I never should have let you take so many walks alone."

Mr. and Mrs. Manning came in next, just before Lord and Lady Felcroft. Mrs. Manning was crying profusely, holding on to her husband's side. Lord and Lady Felcroft were both a little pale.

"How bad is it?" Mr. Manning asked.

Miles was used to comforting people during trying circumstances, but he couldn't quite find his voice. He looked to Ian for help, a rock in times of emotion.

"She has woken a few times, but we will know more when the doctor arrives."

"We should let her rest," Lord Felcroft said. "Tom, I sent Alan up to the nursery, but perhaps we should take the men to the library while the women tend to Miss Fielding?"

Cassandra returned with the nightgown. "I think it would be best. Louisa and the Sheldons will be here soon too."

"I will see to them, dear," Lady Felcroft said to her daughter-in-law. Mrs. Manning bent to remove Jemma's shoes and stockings while Miles and the men filed from the room. They made their way down the stairs and into the library.

Miles had never felt displaced in a library before, but he did now, and it had nothing to do with the grandness of the space. A room full of texts to learn from generally filled him with comfort, but it was not so now. The books taunted him. There would be no lasting words for him to journal and put on the shelf. The greatest story of his life could end before it ever began. He dragged his feet to a corner of the room—the closest thing to being alone—and sank into a chair, where he buried his head in his hands.

"Miles, are you well?"

He recognized Tom's voice, but it took a moment to find his own to answer. "Barely." He dropped his hands and sighed, releasing every possible ounce of despair from his lungs that he could. Why had Tom and Ian followed him? The room was large enough for them all to find their own quiet space. Their parents were on the other side, happy to visit if they felt inclined to do so.

Ian lifted one brow and tilted his head a fraction. "I do hope your mood is because of Jemma's health and not because of a mistake you regret."

Miles blanched. Was it because of him that she had needed to take a walk by herself? He had not thought of that . . .

"Mistake?" Tom scoffed. "Be reasonable, *Mother Hen*. Don't you think you are being a little too protective? Miles was not the one who struck Jemma, and even the Bradford Gent couldn't be blamed for an honest accident."

Ian's eyes didn't leave Miles's. "It isn't the head wound I am referring to. I was the second to Jemma's side, but from my position coming across the field, I swear I saw something rather shocking."

Miles blinked, unable to hold the penetrating gaze pinning him in place. "Who wouldn't be shocked? Jemma could have been killed."

"The accident warranted a natural response of its own, but this was something else entirely. A reaction only a man in love would make." Ian paused, his voice turning regretful. "Does our saintly Mr. Romantic have a confession to make?"

Confession? The blood drained from his face.

"From protective to accusatory. Mother Hen isn't playing very nice today." Tom folded his arms across his broad chest. "Are you inferring that Miles hugged her to his chest while he lifted her off the ground like a gentleman?" He sputtered a laugh. "How dare he!"

Miles winced at Tom's attempt at humor.

Ian folded his arms too. "This was more than hugging or even hair stroking. It's shocking enough for you to kiss your wife in a ballroom, but no one was married out on that corner of the field."

Tom coughed. "Mother Hen, did you hit your head too? Surely the chaos of the moment made you imagine it. There is no tendre between them."

Ian glowered. "I can hardly believe it either. Miles? Would you care to defend yourself?"

A disconsolate air filled the spaces between them. Miles swallowed back the bile forming in his throat. "I don't know what you want me to say."

"Say it was a friendly response in a moment of panic," Tom suggested. "It couldn't be anything else, so Ian and the rest of us will believe you."

Ian's laugh was dry. "He cannot say what isn't true. Miles has too much integrity to lie to us. Besides, this was not the kind of kiss one would give his grandmother, which means the consequences are grave indeed. There is a crowd outside, in case anyone has forgotten. I don't think even Paul, our genius barrister, could present Miles's side in a favorable light," Ian said. "I'm not sure he could convince me either. Jemma's reputation is at risk as much as Lisette's future."

Tom grabbed one of Miles's shoulders. "Don't listen to him. We will laugh about this soon enough. We all know Lisette has your heart."

Paul burst into the library and announced to the room, "Good news. Dr. Giles was in attendance at the match and is with Jemma now."

The men gave a collective sigh of relief, and Mr. Manning even dipped his head and prayed his thanks. Relief flooded Miles but only momentarily. They still had yet to hear the prognosis, and he had yet to explain to his friends.

Paul jogged to their side and crowded into their small circle, and everyone shifted to give him the space he preferred on either side of him. "Dr. Giles took a moment with Mr. Bentley to assure us of his health. He is conscious now and on his way home, with Mr. Reed escorting him. After he has rested, he will call on Jem . . . Wait, did I miss something?"

Miles stood, his emotional strength all but diminished. "I kissed Jemma."

Paul's eyes widened. "Because you were afraid for her life?"

Miles nodded.

Paul chuckled under his breath. "For a second there, I thought you were confessing something."

"I am." Miles winced as he observed their reactions. Ian, who had seen the signs a little sooner than the others, was less shocked and more displeased. Tom's mouth worked, but no sound came out—not even a joke. Paul looked as if his solicitor had just presented him an impossible case.

Paul was the first to find his voice, though it was as solemn as ever. "There will be repercussions, but nothing the Rebels cannot weather with some creative thinking. Who saw it happen?"

Miles scratched his head. "I was a little preoccupied worrying over Jemma's life. Ian here is the only witness I am aware of."

"We can all hope I am the only one," Ian grumbled. "If news spreads, more than just our friend group will be hurt."

Miles's stomach sank. He had not meant to break the gentleman's code of honor, but neither could he deny his feelings for Jemma any longer. But to hurt her reputation—that was something he could not abide. "I know you are disappointed in me and probably angry, but unless another witness is found, could we not put this discussion on hold until Jemma's life is stable? Please."

One by one, they nodded. Ian was the most reluctant, but even he had to see the wisdom in it. With taut nerves, they would reach no positive resolution. Miles was putting off the inevitable, but he could face it better once he knew Jemma's life was out of danger.

"There you are." Miles's mother pushed her small form into their circle, her arm going around his waist. "Don't you worry for a minute. What Miss Fielding lacks in size is made up for in spirit. She will fight through this."

His mother's comfort reached him but did not fully take hold. There was too much regret of wasted time nagging at his heart. All the should haves and shouldn't haves weighed heavily on him. And now his friends' feelings added to it. He put his arm around his mother's shoulders and leaned into her embrace. Would she despise him, too, once she found out how he had inadvertently sabotaged the Matchmaking Mamas by desiring Jemma for himself? He certainly hoped to find forgiveness somewhere.

CHAPTER 30

JEMMA STIRRED, WAKING BEHIND HER closed eyes. What a strange dream. Before she could sense her surroundings at all, pain shot through the back of her head, drawing a moan from her lips.

"Jemma?" Lisette's voice called to her from somewhere close.

Jemma pulled open her eyes, seeing an unrecognizable dark-wood armoire and a lavender quilt draped over her arms. "Lisette?"

"I am here." Lisette appeared at her side, taking a seat on the bed near her. "Can I get you some water?"

Jemma's mouth was a little dry. She moved to sit up, and the room swayed. "A bucket. I need a bucket."

Lisette brought a washing bowl to her just in time to catch Jemma's vomit. There was not a worse way to wake up. After she had rinsed her mouth and cleaned her face, Jemma relaxed back against the bed. "What happened? Where are we?"

By the time Lisette finished explaining how she had been hit with a ball and had been recovering in a guest room at Rivenwood the entire day, Jemma was certain she had never been more humiliated. "I thought only children were struck by balls." She groaned again. "Those poor creatures. It hurts like Hades himself jabbed me with his pitchfork."

"There is naught to be embarrassed about," Lisette assured. "You were carried off the field like a wounded queen surrounded by her undyingly loyal subjects—Brookeside's formidable cricket team."

"I do wish I could have seen that part." Jemma fingered the collar of her nightgown. "And the cricket match? Did they win?"

"Everything hinges on the welfare of their queen. They called a draw for today and will start again in the morning if you have regained consciousness."

Jemma sighed. She had caused a great deal of trouble for so many people. "On the chance of sounding ridiculous, how is my dress?"

Lisette frowned. "I am not sure the bloodstains can be removed."

Jemma nodded. "At least I paraded it around for a short while. The design was one of my favorites." She had hoped to sell the entire dress and send the proceeds to Chios survivors. She was still not certain how excited Mr. Bentley would be about his wife wanting to donate large sums of inheritance to a worthy cause, but she was determined to have an ongoing source of income for whatever charities spoke to her heart.

"The only thing you need worry about right now is recovering." Lisette stood and tugged on the bell pull for a maid. "But first thing, we are letting the others know you are awake. Your little kingdom is worried about you."

Jemma thought of Miles first. Was he concerned for her? She dismissed the thought. "Aunt and Uncle must be told first. Can we have a missive sent over straight away?"

"No need," Lisette said, perching on the bed again. "They are downstairs in the library. Everyone is here. The Sheldons, Lady Kellen, the Rebels, Mrs. Jackson, and, of course, Lord and Lady Felcroft."

Did everyone include Miles?

Oh, why did she keep thinking of him? She closed her eyes. How she hated putting people out. Her independent spirit fought against the very idea, but strangely, knowing everyone was downstairs made her feel wanted and loved as much as anything else. Soon, the maid entered, then left again to pass on the news. The women flooded her side first, fussing over her and retelling the events of the morning.

"The doctor made a few stitches on the back of your head. He thinks the ball hit one of your bonnet pins," Cassandra said from the end of the bed. "Every single brother of mine has needed stitches before, and I can tell yours were done neatly. It should mend well."

"No wonder it hurts like the devil," Jemma answered. "Pardon my language, Aunt."

"Never you mind." Mrs. Manning came over and took a chair someone had placed beside the bed, reaching for Jemma's hand. "All that matters is you getting better."

She tried to believe her aunt. She wanted to reverse time so she never took her walk. She had been so caught up in the turmoil in her heart, she had not even paid attention to the game. "I will focus on improving, but I wish this folly hadn't happened in front of so many people. Perhaps then I could recover quicker. The embarrassment alone will set me back."

Lady Kellen put her hand on the back of Mrs. Manning's chair. "You wouldn't be so flustered if you had been conscious. Your rescue was quite admirable to watch. Mr. Jackson was the first one to your side. He scooped you into his arms and, with my Ian's help, brought you safely here. They did not leave you to be stared after on the side of a field, I assure you."

Miles did that? She had a fuzzy memory of seeing him in the carriage.

"Everyone was deeply concerned," Louisa added. "Mr. Bentley fainted."

Jemma's eyes widened. "Is he all right?"

"You know he doesn't care for the sight of blood," Lisette explained as if Jemma were already aware of such a thing.

"I must have been a sight for him to faint." Jemma's hand went to her disheveled hair. "I must still be a sight."

"Nothing we cannot help with," Louisa said, her smile cheering the room. "We cannot disturb your bandage, but with a washcloth and a little soap, we could get your hair pulled into a braid."

"And perhaps put some broth inside you to bring your cheeks a little color," Mrs. Sheldon added.

"A timely suggestion." Lady Felcroft clapped her hands. "Come, ladies, let's get started. Jemma will feel better once she is properly taken care of."

The women burst into a flurry of activity, in and out of the room, and seeing to every need they could think of. A half hour later, Jemma's hair was clean and braided, she was dressed in a fresh nightgown with a shawl about her shoulders, and she was slowly sipping broth. Her stomach was settling, and the chatter of women's voices buoyed her spirits.

A knock sounded, silencing the room.

"Your heroes have arrived," Lisette said. "Are you ready for more company?"

"I was wondering what was taking them so long," Jemma joked. A wave of anticipation mixed with nerves rushed over her.

"I held them off," Louisa said, grinning, "until you were presentable."

"I owe you a great deal." Jemma produced a tired laugh, her energy already waning.

When the door opened, only Miles stood on the other side. His hair hung in limp waves as if he had run his hand through it for hours on end. His jacket was still missing, but his sleeves were cuffed at his wrist once more. Though he smiled at her, his eyes were full of sadness. Did he remember she had ignored him before the match had begun? Had she disappointed him?

Her cheeks flushed under his gaze. Where were the others so she had someone else to settle her attention on?

Before she could ask, Lady Kellen voiced the answer to her silent question. "Now that your basic needs are met, I thought we should limit the guests to one at a time so as not to overwhelm you. Come, ladies, we shall let Mr. Jackson take his few minutes first."

"Dinner will be ready shortly, and everyone is expected to stay and eat," Lady Felcroft added.

Their voices faded from the room as Miles entered. He left the door open and settled into the chair Mrs. Manning had vacated. His presence brought with him his usual air of comfort. With all the attention she had received from the women, she hadn't realized how much she needed to see him. Despite her attempt to cut him from her life, she was glad he was here. He looked at her in the quiet way he usually did, studying her before speaking.

"I heard you rescued me," she said softly, knowing several others waited in the corridor who might overhear them. Their voices carried to her, and she caught a glimpse of Louisa.

His shoulders lifted in a small shrug. "I carried you, if that's what you mean. Do you recall any of it?"

She closed her eyes, flashes of movement and pain coming back but nothing more. "Not much."

"It is how it should be. Let the rest of us remember it for you."

Miles Jackson was a perfect gentleman. No wonder her heart seemed like a lion wrestling a bear with every attempt to push him away. If only she were not too tired to keep fighting. "Thank you. For everything."

He stared at her another moment, a shadow lingering behind his eyes. "I have never been more worried in my life."

Such words shouldn't have pleased her, but they did. "Even when you thought you would have to move away from Brookeside as a boy?"

He leaned forward over his knees. "Even more than that." After a moment, he broke his heart-pounding stare—those brown eyes weakening all her resolutions and reviving her energy—and scooted his chair so his knees touched the bed. This time, when he leaned forward, he was very close to her.

She reached up, self-conscious of the straight, wilted wisps framing her face.

He caught her hand. "You are beautiful, even without your fancy dresses or pinned locks." His other hand sandwiched hers inside his own, warmth spreading up her arm and sending gooseflesh down her back and legs.

"I wasn't just worried, Jemma. I was scared. I need to tell you—"

Tom rushed into the room with Ian not far behind him. "Sorry to break up this tête–à–tête," Tom said, leaning over on his knees to catch his breath. "But our fears have been realized."

Ian stared knowingly at Miles. "I wasn't the only witness. Word is spreading."

Miles still held her hand and made no attempt to release her. In fact, his grip tightened.

"What did they witness?" She stared from Tom to Ian, finally settling on Miles. He would tell her.

Miles met her gaze, the sadness from earlier darkening his irises once again. "When you were hit, I was playing in the outfield, and as such, I was the first to reach you. You weren't even breathing. In my desperation, I kissed you."

Miles had never been one to mince words, but he might have tried a less direct answer. Her mouth fell open, and she gaped for how to respond. Miles had kissed her, and . . . and . . . and she didn't even remember it?

No wonder Mr. Bentley had fainted! She squeezed her eyes shut. An image of her beautiful, selfless cousin came to mind. The ugly truth hit the hardest.

She was the reason Lisette had never married.

It was all her fault.

She should have avoided Miles every summer. She should have fought those feelings of being drawn to him. Why had she not been a more loyal friend and cousin? But Miles . . . He should have respected her decision.

"Tell me you're lying." The words came through gritted teeth but were clear enough to get the point across.

Miles shook his head. "And I have no regrets."

She gasped and yanked her hand from his grip. "How dare you! How dare you injure my cousin." She ignored the pain her strong emotions brought to her head and the black tugging at the corners of her vision as she waited to see remorse painted across Miles's features.

But it wasn't remorse so much as a form of regret on his face. Regret that she was angry. Regret that she had pushed him aside once more. Regret that she had put Lisette before him.

She turned away from him, hating what she saw. Hating herself. Hating him for being everything she wanted.

She had made her decision, but he would not respect it. "Leave me. Now."

She knew when he left her side, not because of the sound of chair legs grating against the floor but because of the sense of loss. When she looked up, she was surprised to see Paul join Ian and Tom.

"The staff has already gotten wind," Paul said grimly, closing the door for more privacy. "Word passes quickly when there is a crowd as large as the one we had outside today. By morning, it will be blown out of proportion and nothing short of a scandal." He looked at each of them. "Did I miss something again?" He pointed to the corridor behind him. "Come to think of it, Miles looked like someone had died when I passed him just now."

"Jemma didn't take the news very well," Ian muttered, folding his arms.

Paul blanched and looked at her. "You didn't remember anything?"

Did he have to remind her? "No."

"Miles didn't mean to cause any trouble," Paul defended, his tone somber. "No one was more worried for your welfare."

Paul did not have to convince her as though she were some misinformed judge. She already knew the truth, and it hurt worse than her head. She didn't answer him. How could she? Ever since Grandmother had become sick, all her carefully plans had been trampled on. Why had Grandmother left her? Clearly, Jemma could not manage alone.

Tom tapped his leg. "Well, maybe Lisette will be glad to be rid of Miles. A man with his good demeanor and dashing looks has to be troublesome to have about the house."

Ian smirked. "You're right. What woman wants a perfect man?"

"Stop!" Jemma said much too sharply. "Lisette is bound to hear you."

"Shouldn't we be the ones to tell her?" Paul asked gently.

She sighed. "I haven't the heart." What was left of the organ was broken. She tasted her tears on her lips before she even realized she was crying. What had she done? Lisette would be crushed, and she had hurt Miles. She turned away again, shutting her eyes and wishing the men would just leave so she could sleep her pain into oblivion.

"We'll take care of it," Ian said quickly.

"He means, he will watch while we take care of it," Tom said. "We won't let Mother Hen's brisk demeanor rattle her further."

Ian's muttering was covered by Paul next words. "There's more."

"Do I have to hear it?" Jemma asked, refusing to open her eyes.

"We might as well have it out so you can sleep on your decision."

"Paul, when you speak like that, even I get nervous," Tom said.

"It is not frightening, but it might not be comfortable. There is a chance Mr. Bentley will not overlook the scandal."

"I won't marry Miles," Jemma said, turning to face them again. "I won't do that to Lisette."

Paul nodded. "No one will make you do anything, Jemma."

"We will protect you the best we can," Ian added.

Tom gave one of his winning grins. "Chin up, Vixen. I've always wanted to be in the middle of a scandal. You're making Rebel history."

"And on that note, we will take our leave." Ian directed Tom and Paul through the door. He stopped just before shutting it, his usual intimidating stare completely absent and in its place one of compassion. "Try to get some sleep. By morning, we will have a plan in place."

"Thank you, Ian."

He nodded and left her alone.

She trusted them more than she trusted herself. She put her arm over her eyes and cried. She was no stranger to Rivenwood but was as lost as she had ever been. Her head pounded fiercely, and her chest ached, and Grandmother wasn't there to comfort her. She pressed her face into her pillow, damp from her tears, and let the sweet mercy of sleep cover her like a blanket.

CHAPTER 31

MILES LEFT JEMMA'S SIDE, WANDERING through Rivenwood until he reached a dark, empty corridor. He sank against the wall. Tipping his head back, he squeezed his eyes shut. He'd let his guard down, and any progress in reaching Jemma was gone. An ache throbbed in his chest. He'd been so scared—so foolish. His heart raced remembering how still she had lain in his arms. He had almost lost her.

How he longed to hold her until his lingering nerves settled. She was out of harm's way now, and yet . . . and yet farther out of his reach than ever. Why had he deceived himself? She would never see the possibility of them together. She didn't love him. Not enough to fight for a future by his side.

Pushing himself from the wall, he sighed. He needed to speak with Lisette. His duty demanded it. All these years, he had avoided this conversation, but it was no longer possible. It was time for him to stop tiptoeing around his mistakes and take responsibility.

Somehow, he made it to the stable and blindly road his horse to the Mannings' House. The family had just retired home, relieved that Jemma was on the mend, and had not expected his arrival. He promptly requested a private word with Lisette in the drawing room. He didn't care what the family or the staff thought. Soon enough, the whole town would know what he had done. It was only right Lisette learn it from him.

"What is it?" Lisette asked. "Has Jemma worsened already?" They took seats across from each other. Lisette perched on the edge of hers, seemingly ready to leap back into a carriage and return to Jemma's side at a moment's notice.

"It is her emotional needs that concern me, actually." Miles took a deep breath, his hands sweating. "I have injured her . . . and you." When Miles finished accounting his behavior on the cricket field, Lisette paled and gripped the arm of the sofa.

Miles's own hands fidgeted for a moment. He waited for her to say something. Anything. He knew the consequences of his actions affected her as much as they did him and Jemma. They had been through a great deal together, but never something of this magnitude.

Finally, she emitted a heavy sigh. "Thank you for telling me."

He grimaced. "You alone would thank me for making such a wretched confession."

"It is grave tidings indeed." Her small smile disappeared before it reached fruition.

"I know. I am ashamed that I did not take greater pains to control myself." He would never regret kissing Jemma but vehemently regretted hurting her and his friends.

Lisette shook her head. "You mistake my words. I did not mean to imply you should feel ashamed. Only, there will be so much societal pressure to make amends."

He stared at her unblinking expression and clarified carefully. "Pressure for me to marry Jemma, you mean?"

"Yes."

Maybe if she cried, Miles would feel properly chastised. With her calmly spoken words and dry eyes, he could not gauge the level of hurt he had induced. "Lisette, for years, everyone . . . maybe even you . . . has thought that you and I, that we . . . "

"That we would marry," she finished. "Yes, I know what everyone has said about us. I wanted it, too, for a long time."

"Wanted?" Miles was stuck on the tense of her word choice.

She nodded. "It seems strange to finally speak it out loud, to you of all people." She lifted her shoulders in a dainty shrug. "I held a place in my heart for you for many years, but the constant pressure to secure your affections slowly became burdensome to me. It was only recently that I realized I am happier when we are simply friends without expectation. I can honestly say I no longer feel the same attachment toward you. Not like Tom and Cassandra love each other or Paul and Louisa."

He was relieved and ashamed all over again. It was his fault she had suffered so long. "I do not blame you if you can never forgive me."

"I already have, Miles. I am taken back by your admission but not by your partiality toward Jemma. I cannot be the only one who has noticed the way you look at her."

"You noticed?"

"I wondered off and on the last few years, but when you danced with Jemma at Kensington Park . . . Well, you have never looked at me that way before."

His face and neck grew hot, his cravat suffocating him. "I only ever wanted the best for you, Lisette, but my heart already belonged elsewhere. You deserve so much better."

She surprised him with a sympathetic smile. "*We* deserve better."

His brow hinged together in the middle.

"Forget any obligation you feel toward me, Miles, and follow your heart." Her somber expression turned resolute. "As for me, I plan to do the same."

Miles left Lisette on far better terms than he'd expected. He knew he had injured her over the years, and it still stung his conscience to think about, but having her know his feelings for Jemma was an unexpected release. Conversing with Lisette had been the right thing to do. Years' worth of harbored feelings were finally free in the world— for better or worse. So much of his future was still uncertain.

After a short sleep, he rose at dawn to ride to Tom's to meet with Mr. Bentley. With his friends gathered in the drawing room, he forced another uncomfortable confession and apology.

"I wanted to believe you were friends alone," Mr. Bentley said, shaking his head, "but now I know my suspicions had merit."

"It was one-sided," Miles said, hating the truth of it. "Miss Fielding has been hurt by my actions, and I deeply regret coming between you both." When he finished his heartfelt apology to him, Miles slipped out of the room, leaving the rest of the difficult conversation to his friends. He couldn't bear hearing Mr. Bentley waffle over his decision to marry Jemma. Miles scrubbed a hand over his face and stumbled into the library. The hour was impossibly early, but they all were eager to have some sort of plan in place before the cricket match resumed.

He suddenly hated cricket. It seemed terribly inconvenient and trite now. He draped himself over the sofa, not caring who would see him or that it wasn't his house. It was better than storming Jemma's room and pleading for her to forgive him—to see him differently—to give them a chance. But his words would fall short. There was nothing left to say that she wanted to hear.

If God wanted to humble him, it was working. Deep down, he had felt his friendship with Jemma had superseded any hold Mr. Bentley had had over her, but how wrong he had been. He'd been wrong to hope she would set aside her desires for this man or for her cousin.

Everything was wrong. Despite what he preached about not caring what man thought and only what God thought, he was undeniably guilty. Especially as the vicar of many who would gather in the crowd today. The burden of their opinions tortured him. Not to mention he had broken the trust of his closest friends.

Several minutes passed before his friends filed through the door.

"It's done," Ian said.

Miles pulled himself into sitting position. "And?"

"And he is a better man than I would be." Tom threw himself on the other end of the sofa and kicked his feet up onto a small table.

Paul shut the library door behind him. "He has agreed to marry Jemma and pretend the kiss never happened."

Miles's stomach sank like a rock. Where was the consolation in this? How could his soul know peace if the two would still marry? "Some kiss, when the girl doesn't even remember it," Miles mumbled.

"What was that?" Tom leaned nearer to him.

Miles cleared his throat. "Nothing."

"By the way, Lisette just arrived," Paul said, shoving his thumbs into his waistcoat pockets.

Miles scratched his cheek. He had told them briefly of his apology to her the night before. No one had said anything, but he knew they hoped he would fall out of love with Jemma and resolve things with Lisette. "Did she look well?"

"She wasn't crying," Tom said, as if that were the defining level of a woman's emotions.

"Because she was too worried about Jemma's reputation," Ian added. He paced to the window. "People are already gathering on the field."

Miles sighed. "Is someone going to update Jemma before the game?"

"We will let Cassandra and Louisa take care of it," Paul said. "They have volunteered to sit with her for the morning. Besides, some things come across better from the gentler sex."

"Agreed," Tom said. "Jemma will be relieved that Mr. Bentley will still have her, no doubt."

Tom hadn't meant to injure Miles with his phrasing, but the word *relieved* was like a sucker punch. Would it be so terrible if Jemma married him? Apparently, they all thought it would be.

Tom inched to the edge of his seat. "I don't know about the rest of you, but I am exhausted. Let's finish the cricket match for good today, Rebels. The worst is over."

"The worst is over for you, you mean." Miles stood. "Never mind, let's go."

"Sit down," Ian said, crossing the room to him. "We aren't quite finished here."

"Ian's right," Paul said. "Besides Miles and Jemma being at odds, and Lisette no doubt upset, the neighborhood isn't going to be excited about the scandal their vicar caused."

Miles reluctantly sat down. "Am I to be the next Rebel project, then?"

"Would you prefer we call the Matchmakers in to assist you?" Ian's top lip drew back in disgust.

"No . . . no, I don't."

Ian folded his arms, and his fingers drummed against the sleeve of his jacket. "You are supposed to be the expert on love, Miles, not me. Somehow, you've created an ugly web strung with broken hearts—the center of which is your own."

Miles shrugged. "Maybe Tom will finally cease calling me Mr. Romantic."

"Not amusing," Ian said curtly. "We need a way to deflect attention from the scandal. It might be the only way to recover a few reputations."

"Including Miles's," Paul added.

Ian rubbed his prominent, dimpled chin. "Right. Protecting your employment is essential. I don't want the hassle of acclimating this town to a new vicar."

"Always the thoughtful one." Miles smirked, but inwardly he was struggling. He had come to count on his position for security, but his job meant so much more to him than a salary. One decision had cost him so much. "Please worry about Jemma and Lisette over my place at the vicarage. I volunteer to humiliate myself again if it means protecting their names."

No one looked particularly thrilled about his pronouncement. They sat in a stupor for a moment, each lost in his own thoughts.

Tom snapped his fingers, breaking the silence. "I have it. If Miles intends to embarrass himself, there is one thing we know he hates."

Miles raised his brow. "When women ask if they can have my hair made into a wig for them to wear?"

They all stared in disbelief.

"Women do that?" Paul asked.

"It's happened a few times," Miles said reluctantly.

"Actually, I was thinking along the lines of your town role as Mr. Romantic," Tom said. "We need to think of something along that vein."

"Absolutely," Ian answered, smiling smugly. "Sacrifice hurts." He was clearly still mad at Miles for hurting Jemma and Lisette.

Miles groaned. "The very subject got me in trouble in the first place." He was already suffering from following his heart, it hardly seemed fair to wound himself further. But if it protected Jemma, he wouldn't hesitate.

"What about a charity auction?" Paul suggested. "It's a sizable distraction and something generous would go a long way in healing relations with the town and certain hurt Rebels."

A charity auction. The idea had merit. The town might grow enthused enough to overlook his ungentlemanly behavior. Most importantly, it would give them something to talk about besides Jemma.

"I like it," Ian declared, pointing at Paul. "We can offer a grand prize worthy of Mr. Romantic himself."

The pieces came together, and he groaned. "Wait, you want to auction me off?" He sank against the sofa cushion, regretting everything. "I am not sure I have the stomach for you to sell me in marriage to the highest bidder."

"Stomach . . ." Tom mumbled. "That's it. You don't have to marry them, just eat with them. A picnic with Mr. Miles Jackson— Brookeside's most *humble* and generous vicar. Chaperoned, of course."

"Won't people be displeased that I am picnicking with every available woman in town after the scandal I just created?"

Paul nodded. "I'll find a few more men willing to be auctioned for a picnic so you blend in," Paul said. "But we will set our hopes on your previous reputation. Besides, these are women who you have made yourself unavailable to in the past. You are giving them limited access. It's a diversion at its finest."

Miles gave him a flat stare. "You're doing a terrible job at convincing me."

"Only one woman would get a picnic with you, obviously," Tom said, his eyes going to the ceiling. "And it will be about the charity. It's in the presentation. Mind you, the women will have their private motivations, and we can't help that. Once they think they have a chance with you, they will forget all about your supposed interest in another."

Miles pinched the bridge of his nose. "Just tell me when it's over."

"Well done, Rebels," Ian said. "It will be an unprecedented auction. If we don't shock the town's sensibilities, it might just work."

Miles hoped for the best. He had never hurt so many people. He was sick about it. Especially when Jemma was only a floor above him and wasn't even speaking to him.

Paul clasped his hands behind his back. "It would be precautionary more than a perfect solution. But we have worked with less before."

Miles slapped his hands on his knees. "We should head out to the field and start warming up."

Tom grinned. "For cricket or for the announcement of the charity auction?"

Miles grimaced. "Both."

CHAPTER 32

WITH NO LESS THAN FIVE pillows propping her up, it was easy for Jemma to launch forward into a sitting position. "Miles did what?"

She couldn't believe what Cassandra and Louisa were telling her. They were both perched on the end of her bed, Cassandra's blonde coiffure framing her intelligent eyes and Louisa's heart-shaped face full of optimism. But neither fully understood the intricacies of the original Rebels and their lifelong friendship. They had only married their prospective husbands the year before. They couldn't know how tangled the situation was or see the pain Jemma carried.

"Miles feels terrible about kissing you." Cassandra stood and piled a few books on Jemma's nightstand with a soft thump. Cassandra had done so much to comfort her, but these words did not placate Jemma as intended. Cassandra took her seat on the end of the bed. "The auction is his way of distracting everyone from the scandal yesterday. Miles announced that the money will go to the Greek refugees."

Jemma's heart pricked, but she squashed the tender feelings as quickly as they'd come. She stared at the books to refocus her thoughts, familiar titles that normally called to her.

They did nothing for her now.

"Thank you for the books, but I cannot read while Miles is out there selling himself to the highest bidder. It may be a good cause, but this is not like him at all. He hates all the attention he receives from the women in the town."

Louisa took a pillow and plumped it before adjusting it behind Jemma. "Miles is a good man, despite his mistakes. He met with Lisette last night. I cannot imagine how hard that must have been."

"He . . . he met with Lisette?" Jemma's hand went to her throat.

Louisa nodded. "According to Paul, Lisette forgave him. They are in agreement about their future plans."

Jemma gripped her collar, her hand trembling. "What does that mean exactly?" Jemma hoped and feared for the answer.

"It means the Rebels have sorted everything." Louisa's smile was much too wide and sure for Jemma. "Normally, Mr. Jackson would be forced to marry you to protect your reputation. But Mr. Bentley is a hero in his own right, because he will not step aside. He insists on seeing right by you himself. It leaves Miles and Lisette to decide their own futures."

"I hope it means a second wedding is imminent," Cassandra said.

"I never expected any of this." Jemma wanted to cry again, but she should be relieved . . . hopeful even. The turmoil inside her was reaching a peak.

Cassandra must have noted the catch in Jemma's voice. "I know it's hard, but an unexpected event was the best thing to happen to me. I never would have guessed in a million years that my parents would arrange my marriage to the same man I decided to despise not long before. It's hard to imagine in the moment, but some good may yet come out of all this."

Louisa nodded. "A change of plans can be the beginning of an adventure. Agreeing to marry a stranger was the greatest decision I've ever made. Paul is everything to me."

"Your stories make me want to trust that things will work out, but while everything came together in the end for you both, it seems to get worse and worse around here." Jemma shook her head. "Nothing feels right anymore. Like this auction, for example. It might draw the attention away from me, but what about Miles? What if the town does not focus on his charitable nature and he humiliates himself?"

"Paul says Miles is willing to do anything to rectify his mistake," Louisa said softly. "It might settle your mind if you watch the auction for yourself."

"But how?" Jemma pointed at the lavender quilt. "I am supposed to stay in this bed."

Cassandra took on a conspiratorial look. "When Lady Felcroft heard the news, she insisted on having the auction in the front garden so Miles could stand on the house steps and make it appear official. You will be able to see and hear everything from your window."

"I suppose." Did she want to see him make a spectacle of himself? She was angry with him, but he was still her best friend. Or was he? She didn't know where they stood now.

"There is one other matter," Cassandra said carefully. "Mr. Bentley has asked to speak to you privately."

Dread filled her midsection. It had to be about their marriage. She played with her fingers, suddenly nervous. What must he think about all this? He was still a stranger to her in so many ways. She could not predict anything. She sighed. "When?"

"After the match ends today."

Louisa smiled at her. "Don't worry. Everything will work out as it should."

She could no longer fight their optimism. She let their hope buoy her own. "Thank you both for sitting with me this morning. I know my aunt and cousin will take their turn this afternoon, but I am so glad this news came from the two of you."

Louisa grinned. "And I am glad you want to watch the auction together. It will be at noon, during the players' midday break. The women and staff are in a flurry of activity trying to prepare for it."

"I hope no one is too put out."

"It's for a good cause," Cassandra said. "And the people of Brookeside who I have come to know best are always up for helping."

The women, at least, would be all too thrilled to win a picnic with Miles. Jemma wrung her hands. Certainly she could support whatever woman paid to break bread with him . . .

Dare she hope he spent the hour reading scripture to them?

Despite all her commitments against loving him, she didn't care at all for the idea of him spending time with his adoring fans. No, she did not care for it at all.

In fact, the more she thought on it, the more she hated it. Good attitude be hanged.

"We are good friends now, are we not?" she said slowly, gauging Louisa's and Cassandra's reaction.

Both women nodded.

She licked her bottom lip. "Then, I am going to need some help rigging this auction." She might have laughed at their surprised faces, but she was too serious about her intentions to feel any humor. It was time for her to spend the pin money she had so diligently promised to not spend in honor of her lesson on sacrifice. If she had to give Miles up, it would not be to his lady entourage.

CHAPTER 33

THE CRICKET MATCH HAD BEEN going in their favor all morning, Jemma was on the mend, and the weather was fine. Miles had even received a written apology from the Bradford batsman about his unintentional involvement in taking out Jemma the day before. Not to mention, no one seemed to be whispering of any scandal from the day before. It was all he could do to focus on these positives, but they fled the moment he stood on the steps of Rivenwood for their thrown-together auction.

People still dotted the sidelines of the playing field, but the majority had made the short walk to watch or participate in the charity auction. The women pushed their way to the front, coin purses in hand and reticules swinging from their wrists. He recognized several of them, but there were others he had never seen before. The plan was to start with a few lesser items to rally excitement for the prize of the hour—him.

Lady Felcroft's cook had whipped up some pies, Lisette had stockings to sell, and Louisa had donated several bolts of fabric from her brother's mills that he'd left at their home on his last visit. It could have been a spectacular event had they had more time—and had someone else volunteered to be listed as Brookeside's romantic. There were a few men who had agreed to be auctioned off for picnic lunches, but they weren't the most polished gentlemen, and Paul said they might actually have to pay people to bid on them. It didn't sound good.

Lord Felcroft stepped in as the auctioneer, and in minutes, all the pies were gone. One by one, the items sold while Mrs. Sheldon, Paul's mother, collected the money. The women were in generous moods, and the other men were bid on, despite Paul's misgivings, even if it was a pittance. All too soon, it was Miles's turn. His feet would not move. Tom looked over his shoulder and motioned with his head for him to come forward.

Ian stepped in. "Think of Jemma." With those words, he shoved Miles to the center of the steps. Cheers erupted. *Women's* cheers. This was by far the most humiliating thing he had ever done.

"Now smile and act like you like it," Ian whispered into his ear, his chuckle far too happy.

Miles tried to smile, but his grimace had to be as attractive as a donkey baring his teeth.

Tom spread out his arms. "This has been a memorable few days, has it not? And our first Brookeside charity auction is off to a good start, thanks to your generous purchases so far. For the highlight of our event, we would like to auction off a picnic with Brookeside's very own Adonis."

Clapping, whistles, and more cheers rang in Miles's ears.

"Quiet, please, while I share a short background on Mr. Miles Jackson."

Miles was too busy gagging over the sugary words to catch the whole of Tom's speech. *Elusive bachelor* stood out, as did *pious* and *diligent vicar*, and a bunch of other nonsense. There was a generous statement about how no one was allowed to ask for Miles's hair to be made into a wig for them. He appreciated it. All in all, it was a thoughtful prelude to Miles's sacrifice at the auctioneer's guillotine.

Unfortunately, there was no quick ending for him. He did not sell as quickly as the pies or the other men. Had the town not heard of his indiscretion? They were acting a little too forgiving.

Hands were raised, and women yelled ridiculous amounts. Several, he was certain, did not have the money they were spouting in the first place. He knew the Chios cause was an important one, but must they rob the women of the entirety of their precious pin money?

The numbers soared—the final bidders alarming him. It was down to Miss Hardwick, Mrs. Fortescue, and a woman he thought must be from Bradford, whose husband was arguing for her to stop. At one point, Miles glanced to the heavens to plead for the madness to end when he caught three heads peeking out of an upstairs window—Cassandra, Louisa, and none other than Jemma.

Two of them waved, and one did not. "The things a man does in the name of love," he muttered. Jemma's somber expression could not be read, but she did not seem to be especially sorrowful over their painful argument. It was unrequited love at its finest. Except, he knew a part of her did care for him. A part so hidden behind the cloak of denial that it would never see the light of day. That hurt worse than anything.

And then it was done. He had a picnic appointment with the one and only Mrs. Fortescue—a woman possibly older than his own grandmother. He had thought he had sufficiently shaken her from his trail, but by the looks of her gleeful smile, he had been terribly mistaken.

He didn't steal a second look to see Jemma's final response. She might not swoon over his sacrifice, but at least she would know his remorse over hurting her. Because even now, it was the only part he regretted.

$\vartheta\circ$

Jemma had not only financed Mrs. Fortescue's contribution to the charity but had made an older woman very happy. It almost made Jemma's lingering headache worthwhile. Unfortunately, once she had rallied her courage, she had done something else too. Something she was bound to regret. She had asked Louisa to deliver a note to Miss Hardwick's cousin. Though a veritable stranger, this cousin had been most obliging in her response, which was how Jemma had come to have Miles's book of poetry in her hands.

It was not as thick as a novel, but it was larger than the little notebooks Miles generally carried around. It was a dark green with a gold floral pattern in the background and beautiful gold script. She hugged it to her chest. She hadn't told the other Rebels about the book or even Louisa and Cassandra, but she had to know the contents. Why? Because a fierce ache tore at her insides. Because she couldn't bring herself to rest. Because despite everything, she missed Miles.

The frustrating man was still her best friend, even if he had racked turmoil inside her. It was not as if she wanted to have a discussion about his writings with him. Not when she did not plan to speak to him again until after she was married to Mr. Bentley, but she needed a piece of him near her. His book was the only part of him she could allow by her side. She had thought it over a million times. Fewer people would be hurt if she avoided Miles than if she forgave him.

A glance at the timepiece on the wall told her she had a quarter hour before she needed to meet with Mr. Bentley. Cassandra and Louisa had assured her he still intended to marry her. She had heard of far more loveless marriages than not, and it was a perfectly acceptable path in life. Fulfilling the second half of her promise to Grandmother would have to wait. It seemed falling in love was not always something a person could choose . . . just like falling out of love.

She sighed and tucked the book under her pillow to read later. For now, it was enough to have it near. She had yet to dress and had stalled far too long.

A knock sounded.

"Come in."

A maid slipped inside. "Are you ready, miss?"

Jemma had already sent her away once. Despite all her fixed resolutions, moving forward pulled the last ounce from her already depleted well of strength. She forced a nod and allowed the maid to help her change into a clean gown, one Mrs. Manning had sent over. Once Jemma was buttoned into her gown, the maid carefully fixed Jemma's hair into a low chignon. Her color was not quite right yet, but it would have to do. If she was going to have a proper conversation with Mr. Bentley, she wanted to be presentable. It was one thing for her closest friends to see her at her worst, but she would spare Mr. Bentley the sight as long as possible.

Lady Felcroft poked her head inside the room with a grin as wide as Tom's. "May I come in?"

"Yes, please. Thank you again for taking such good care of me."

"It is our pleasure." Lady Felcroft strolled to her side at the dressing table. "You have always been a special part of our Brookeside family. You know that, don't you?"

"I know you have all spoiled me, so yes." Jemma smiled.

"You look lovely tonight. Mr. Bentley has just arrived and is ready to see you when you are."

Jemma sighed, searching for her inner fortitude to take purchase. "I'm ready."

"Wonderful. Let's tackle the stairs together, shall we?"

Jemma was feeling steady enough to walk unaided, but she graciously accepted Lady Felcroft's arm. Together they weaved out of her room, which was near the stairs, and began to descend.

"Has everyone returned home, then?" she asked. The Rebels and their families had been in and out of the house and her guest room all day.

"Everyone but your aunt and Lisette," Lady Felcroft said.

"Oh? I did not know they were still here."

"They hate to leave you. They plan to stay with you for dinner and will return again tomorrow to bring you home."

She accepted the plan with a nod.

When they reached the bottom of the stairs, Lady Felcroft released her arm. "I will let you and Mr. Bentley sort things out without my hovering. I'll be back shortly to help you return up the stairs, but if you need anything, ring for a servant."

"Thank you, Lady Felcroft."

The drawing room door was open, so Jemma slipped inside, sur-prised to see Lisette sitting beside Mr. Bentley.

"Good evening," Jemma said.

They both stood, a sort of guilty look about them. Had they been discussing her? Her brow furrowed, but she said nothing. Whether she liked it or not, she was everyone's problem these days.

She took a seat on the sofa perpendicular to them, and they sat again as well. She thought Lisette would excuse herself since she was well aware that Jemma and Mr. Bentley had a great deal to discuss, but it appeared she intended to stay.

Mr. Bentley clasped his hands together. "Are you feeling any bet-ter, Miss Fielding?"

"I am much improved." She managed a smile and hoped it would deceive them. It was normally a little awkward around Mr. Bentley, but tonight, it felt unusually so. He studied her like a puzzle he could not quite understand.

He exchanged another glance at Lisette, seeming to communi-cate something beyond Jemma's own comprehension. Was this about her health? Did she appear worse than she thought? "Forgive me. Your look just now. Is there something I should know?"

Mr. Bentley cleared his throat. "There *is* something I would like to say." He shifted before beginning again. "Perhaps it will make more sense if I go back and explain my initial feelings upon arriving in England first."

"Go ahead."

"Thank you. When I began the journey home, I grew lonely for what I left behind, and I dreaded my future. I worried excessively about finding like-minded friends. Indeed, I thought finding a suit-able wife would be the hardest challenge of all. I never imagined I would move into the happiest of neighborhoods. I did not know places like Brookeside existed. It was providential for me. I found the best of people right here in this little corner of York."

His story captured Jemma's complete attention. It was the deepest conversation she had had with Mr. Bentley to date. Outwardly, he acted so confident. Had he truly worried so much? How grateful she was to her dear friends and family for surrounding Mr. Bentley and accepting him into the community with open arms.

"I owe Lady Kellen a debt," he said. "She can be a persuasive woman. Indeed, she professed to have the answer to all my problems. Before long, I was introduced to you and Miss Manning." He motioned to Lisette, stopping long enough to smile at her cousin. "I agreed to marry you, Jemma, but somewhere along the lines, I fell in love with someone else."

Jemma clutched the fabric of her skirt beneath her hands, and her response tumbled out. "You fell in love . . . with Lisette?"

Mr. Bentley's cheeks reddened. The kind, self-assured man Jemma had thought she knew was clearly still a stranger to her. She had never seen him blush before. But worse than not knowing *him* was not knowing his heart.

"I hope you will understand; I never fathomed this happening, or I never would have contracted with Lady Kellen for a wife."

Jemma nodded quickly. "You do not need to apologize. Plans change." She heard Cassandra's and Louisa's voices in her ears, assuring her that such things happened. And they happened for a reason.

Lisette had been chewing on her lip, but she ceased long enough to scoot to the edge of the sofa. "Of course we need to apologize. Whenever you left because of a headache or some other reason, I stayed behind to smooth things over with Walter."

"Walter?" Jemma repeated.

Lisette blushed. "I hope you do not mind . . ."

"It is not my place to mind," Jemma explained. "Please. Finish what you were saying about you and Wal—er . . . Mr. Bentley."

"We did not mean to spend so much time together. It only happened that way. We discovered we had a great deal in common, and conversing was so natural for us. Neither of us intended to develop any feelings for each other. But we wanted to be honest with you."

Tears formed in Lisette's eyes, and she tucked her chin and lowered her gaze to her lap.

Did Lisette truly love Mr. Bentley in return? Jemma was in complete shock. She hadn't seen any of this coming.

"Lisette and I have a connection," Mr. Bentley continued, picking up where Lisette had left off, "but . . . we will fight it, if we must."

"Mr. Bentley—"

"There is one more thing," Mr. Bentley said at the same time Jemma spoke. She motioned for him to proceed. "Because Mr. Jackson compromised your reputation yesterday, your reputation must be protected. I told him I would uphold my end of the agreement to marry you, but I said it only because I hoped to clarify a matter with you first. I have been aware for some time that you are in love with Mr. Jackson."

Jemma sputtered. Love Mr. Jackson? Her chest heaved, her heart racing to the speed of a dozen wild horses. Her eyes flashed to Lisette, who seemed to be bracing herself.

Mr. Bentley continued. "There have been several instances of proof I might offer, but the fact of the matter is, Mr. Jackson seems equally enamored with you. I cannot in good conscience give myself to you when we both have opportunities elsewhere that would satisfy our happiness far more."

Jemma squeezed the fabric of her dress all the tighter. Mr. Bentley was no fool. "Forgive me," she begged. "You are very kind to have offered for me, but as we were never engaged, please do not concern yourself with my reputation. I have money and connections enough to see to my own needs, so truly, you both must follow your hearts. There is nothing . . ." she choked on her words, "nothing I want more than Lisette's happiness."

She couldn't say anything about Miles. Not after she had cruelly sent him away.

"Oh, Jemma." Lisette's eyes welled with tears, a few spilling over, and she reached for Mr. Bentley's arm.

It was true, then. Lisette did love Mr. Bentley. How was it possible? "You deserve to be happy, Cousin. You've looked out for me for far too long. Now I will get to see you taken care of."

Lisette shook her head. "You have it wrong. You have always taken care of me. You've lent me confidence when I've had none. You've helped me secure friendships and be brave in my desires to do good in the world. It's your happiness I want."

Jemma wiped at her own tears flooding her eyes, giving a soft laugh. "Look at us. Look at you! In love!"

Lisette smiled then, too, and met Mr. Bentley's eyes. Their shared look was full of a thousand different forms of pure adoration.

"Are you certain about releasing our obligation?" Mr. Bentley turned quickly, his eyes imploring Jemma.

She nodded. "Quite sure."

He laughed and reached his hand for Lisette's. She set her long, thin fingers against his much larger ones, and he brought them to his lips, fervently kissing them.

A longing to be cherished hit Jemma with so much force that it overwhelmed her. She had to speak with Lisette. She had to tell her everything. "Lisette, would you mind speaking with me for a moment in the corridor?"

"Of course not." Lisette pulled away from Mr. Bentley and followed Jemma from the room. Jemma shut the door to the drawing room, giving them the maximum privacy an empty corridor could offer.

"What is it?" Lisette asked.

Jemma forced her hands to be still. "After your revelation, I cannot be easy until I speak of a matter of my own." She hesitated, reaching for the right words.

"You care for Miles."

Jemma's eyes widened. She forced herself to answer honestly this time. "Yes," she breathed. "I'm so sorry. I tried so hard not to care for him. I promise. I told him he should marry you." Her eyes welled up with the tears of her own betrayal.

Lisette's eyes glistened too. "Don't cry. I would never have engaged myself to Mr. Bentley if I did not think you and Miles were meant to be together."

"You say you love Mr. Bentley, but I know you love Miles too."

"Once, yes, I did, but my love for Mr. Bentley is far superior. He makes me so happy, Jemma. You might not believe me, but it's true. He is the one I want to have by my side for the rest of my life."

It would take time to fully believe. Jemma bit her lip. "Do you hate me?"

"Not even a little." Lisette wrapped her in a hug. "It's all right for you to put your own happiness first now and then. You fight so hard for what you think is right, and I admire you greatly for it. But it's time for you to put aside Grandmother's promise and the pressures from the Matchmaking Mamas and even the Rebels. It's time to choose a future you want."

Jemma gave a soft laugh. "Me? Choose? You make it sound so simple."

"You can have the wish of your youth again," Lisette said, pulling back.

Jemma swallowed. She could be a rich spinster, travel the world, and help people like she had declared for years. She squeezed her eyes shut. She knew such a life would no longer make her happy. She'd known it for a while.

"Or," Lisette continued, "you could marry Miles." She paused, and Jemma met her perceptive gaze. "Whatever you decide, you have my blessing."

Jemma wiped the moisture off her cheeks. "Thank you, Lisette. For everything."

Lisette hugged her again before returning to Mr. Bentley's side.

Jemma ignored Lady Felcroft's earlier desire to escort her to her room and hurried up the stairs. Once in the guest room, she flung the door shut and rushed to her bed. Pushing the pillows aside, she dug Miles's book out from under the pillows. After her world had been thrown upside down again, she needed—no, craved—Miles's voice.

She ran her finger over the title, *The Poems and Anecdotes of Mr. Romantic*. Her hand could not flip to the first page fast enough.

Dedicated to the Rebels of the unjust, the true lovers of hope.

She turned another page, eager to read the whole of it and let the words wash over her aching heart. She needed Miles's poetic turn of phrase to envelop her soul and give her hope that they could fix what had broken between them. The first poem told the story of a sad man resisting and fighting his heart but never being able to douse the flame of unrequited love.

An anecdote followed it, giving a short guide on selfless love. It was Miles—humble, loving Miles—to the very letter. The next poem was in the perspective of a boy saying goodbye to the girl he loved summer after summer, waiting the long seasons in between for her return.

For she took his smile with her and brought it back again every June.

She swallowed. It was about her. The whole book was about her.

"Miles . . . I didn't know." She sniffed her tears back, but they were more persistent than before, nearly blurring her vision completely. When her maid came in to see if she needed anything before dinner, Jemma pretended she was too tired to join the others and requested that a tray be sent up. There was no possible way she could cease poring over the book until she had read every last page.

CHAPTER 34

MILES SAT ACROSS FROM HIS mother in the small drawing room of his home. She made an effort to visit him once a month, and he rode to the rectory at least that often to have Sunday dinner with his family. Since he had just seen his mother at Rivenwood, he had not expected her to visit so soon. The timing allowed him to tell her his plans for the near future.

"Here I thought I was coming to congratulate you on your team's win yesterday, and now you are telling me I am to say goodbye? You cannot mean to leave so soon. I thought . . ." His mother blinked away her surprise and leaned over to pour him more tea.

"You thought what?"

"Oh, it hardly matters now." Her voice faded only to grow excited again. "But what about your friends? You have a wedding to attend."

His mother was very pretty and looked far younger than she was. She didn't have his dimples, but she had given him her dark, curly hair. He had always been close to her. Maybe it was the natural consequence after the death of a parent. The oldest child and the remaining parent had to rely on each other. Even after Mama remarried, their bond had not lessened. Still, she had no idea the suffocating hurt he was feeling. He had kept this part of himself from her all these years, and he intended to keep it that way.

He shrugged and smiled as if leaving Brookeside for a time was a natural, regular thing for him to do. "I will write a letter of congratulations," he finally said. "Mr. Bentley and Miss Fielding will not even notice my absence. They will be far too absorbed in celebrating. No one will mind if I am gone for a few months."

His mother studied him for a moment before lowering her shoulders in resignation. "I suppose my already very busy husband can step in while you are away." She gave him an exaggerated sigh.

"I had hoped it would be the case. I have a letter I wrote to him this morning. Will you take it to him?"

"You know I will." She brought her teacup to her lips and took a small sip. "Just promise me one thing."

He nodded, running his thumbs over the smooth porcelain of his cup.

"Have a good chat with your friends before you leave and tell them what is on your mind."

Her wisdom was to be respected. She could see there was more to the conversation than he was letting on. He would do his best to reassure her. "Easily done, Mama. I plan to meet a few of my friends this afternoon in fact." Not the women . . . and especially not Jemma. The men had made him agree to meet them after his picnic with Mrs. Fortescue. They had said they wanted to commiserate with him—no one had predicted she would make the highest bid—but he wondered if they really wanted to laugh at every ridiculous part of his experience.

But as soon as he finished chatting with his friends, he would be gone. He didn't plan to say goodbye to anyone else. He glanced at his undrunk tea, unable to find his appetite or even rally his thirst. He just needed time to sort himself out. He would write another book to purge his heart and return after a few months with his feelings in check. It wasn't a solid plan but a desperate one.

༄

Jemma tucked Miles's book into her reticule, not wanting to be far from it. Last night, her world had shifted again, but this morning, with the sun streaming through the window, she felt hopeful. After thanking Lord and Lady Felcroft again, as well as Tom and Cassandra, for caring for her so well, she joined Mrs. Manning and Lisette in the carriage home.

Lisette had not made a formal announcement about her engagement yet. Mr. Bentley had said they wanted a few days to talk among themselves before sharing the news with everyone. Jemma wondered if they did not speak of it out of courtesy to her—to give her time to make a plan before everyone bombarded her with their sympathies and questions. Jemma would not allow such silliness to persist, but for this morning, she let it be. Indeed, there was a great deal to think about.

Once in her room, she collapsed on her bed. The short trip hadn't tired her, but her head still throbbed. And more than this, she was lost in her thoughts.

"Pardon me, miss," a maid said from the door.

Jemma sat up. "What is it?"

"A stack of letters has collected for you in the past few days. Mr. Manning kept it until you were well enough to sort through it. Would you like me to bring it to you now?"

Mail? For her? Most of her correspondence usually came from the Rebels when they were apart. Who could be writing to her? Maybe it was an answer from the magazine! Just the distraction she needed. "I can take it now. Thank you."

Instead of handing her a few letters, the maid returned with an entire sack.

"All of those are for me?"

The maid nodded.

Jemma directed her to the small writing desk. The maid poured the contents onto her desk.

"What in the world?" Jemma picked up the first one and studied her name across the front. "That will be all, thank you."

The maid left her alone with her gigantic pile of mysterious letters. Jemma's curiosity could wait no longer. She took her file and sliced open the first seal. Bank notes fell out. She touched the money—not a small sum—before directing her attention back to the letter. She could hardly believe it. The money was for the Greek refugees!

Letter after letter, the money piled up.

And several mentioned why.

> *In response to Mr. Miles Jackson and his efforts to support the tragedy in Chios Island, we send this money to the care of Miss Jemma Fielding, as requested.*

She was not usually so emotional, but once again, she was crying. The Greek people were going to receive thousands of pounds of relief money. Even a pragmatic person could see how incredibly touching this gift was.

"Miles, you deserve someone far better." She sank back in her chair and covered her mouth with her hand. She did not know how long she stayed there, staring in awe at the unfolded papers.

A knock sounded, and the maid was back with another letter in her hand. "This just arrived for you, miss."

How many people did Miles know? And they all must love him tremendously to respond with such generosity.

She accepted the letter and returned to her desk. When she unfolded this one, however, the contents were not what she'd expected. Folded inside was a single news sheet—the gossip column. Someone had taken the time to circle the most humorous and outrageous tidbits, nothing scurrilous or vulgar or even life-changing in the gossip but just a few humorous lines to make her smile—just as she liked.

> *Lord Greene blackballed thirteen times from being admitted to Brooks Gentleman's club, only for his friends to discover he had sabotaged himself because he preferred his own company best.*

She laughed and read another.

Lord Bergren found dead in his house. Deceased for
more than six months, and yet his wife never knew it. She
was still spoon feeding him broth and porridge every morn-
ing.

"No . . . it cannot be true!" Jemma shook her head and read
another.

The honorable Bartholomew Wimple discovered to be
named after the family dog.

She giggled and set down the paper, saving the rest to read later.
She was too overwhelmed with this burning glow in her chest. Miles
had sent her the paper. No one else knew her better. The money for
the charity, the poems, the auction—he had done it all for her. Even
now he was probably assisting Mrs. Fortescue into her chair so they
could have a picnic together.

How she loved him.

Why had she forced him from her life? He not only belonged in
it, but he was also what made it worth living. She had to fix things
between them.

"Oh, Jemma!" She chewed on her thumbnail. What should she
do? Or maybe she should be asking what Mr. Romantic would do.
Surely something in his lessons could help her. Or something he had
not taught her but had demonstrated . . .

If he was willing to humiliate himself on her behalf, well, so was
she. She might regret it later, but she had an idea worthy of the next
gossip column. All in the name of love, of course.

After this, no one would mistake how she felt about Miles
Jackson—including him. Which was exactly what she wanted. It
was time for the vicar to take a wife. If all went well, Mr. Romantic
would no longer claim the title of most eligible bachelor but would
have the title of most doting husband.

If it didn't work, Jemma would likely be thrown out of Brookeside. As a Rebel, she always liked high stakes. As a woman in pursuit

of a man, she utterly feared them. She went to her closet and pulled out Grandmother's lace shawl and draped it around her shoulders. She went to the window and glanced up at the white, full clouds.

"Wish me luck, Grandmother. It isn't about my promise to you anymore." Her voice cracked. She cleared her throat to finish. "Even so, I would like you to witness my greatest effort yet."

CHAPTER 35

THE DOME, THEIR FAVORITE MEETING place, was to receive a thorough cleaning, upon Lady Kellen's insistence, so Miles and his friends went to Gibbons' instead so they could all hear about the picnic with Mrs. Fortescue. Two other gentlemen sat in one corner in deep discussion, and a single gentleman sat at a table alone with a newspaper in one hand and a cup of tea in the other. Miles collapsed into a chair at their usual table by the window and let his head fall back.

"It went that well?" Ian took a seat across from him by Tom, and Paul sank into the seat beside Miles.

"If you receive an invitation to our wedding ceremony, please have the dignity not to tell me and promptly burn it."

"What if we want to attend?" Tom's feigned look of sincerity drew a laugh from the others.

"You can go in my stead." What an afternoon. The best part being that he would never have to relive the experience. The memory alone would be torture enough.

Paul sighed. "As the vicar, you really should be at your own wedding."

"Well, this vicar is taking a holiday."

They glanced at each other and back at Miles. Ian cleared his throat. "Are you in earnest?"

A server set drinks on the table with a bowl of nuts. Miles waited for him to leave. "I need to breathe some different air for a while and clear my head."

"You mean your heart, not your head, don't you?" Paul asked matter-of-factly.

"You would be correct." Miles took a long drink, his glass clinking on the table as he set it down.

No one else seemed to be eating or drinking. Ian went as far as to push aside his glass. "Will you be back for Jemma and Mr. Bentley's wedding?"

Miles shook his head. "It is one happy occasion I am intent on missing."

"You really love her, don't you?" Paul asked.

Miles stared at his glass. "Since we were children."

Tom blew out a heavy breath. "I always knew you were the best actor among us."

Ian folded his arms and leaned back in his chair. "I never guessed it either. I'm sorry for being hard on you."

"Well," Miles said ruefully, "you all saw how thrilled she was when she found out I kissed her. There is no doubt where she stands on the matter. You can be assured, my feelings won't interfere with any wedding plans. I wish her and Mr. Bentley well."

Ian drummed his fingers on the table. "From the beginning, you were against the Matchmaking Mamas, while the rest of us were against marriage altogether. I thought it was because of your attachment to Lisette."

"We all did," Paul added.

"Lisette will always be like a sister to me," Miles clarified. "Which is one of the reasons I did not dare reveal my feelings and hurt her. But largely, I restrained myself because Jemma was against marriage. I did not think she would accept any offer from me. When she changed her mind . . ."

"You started to hope," Tom finished, shaking his head. "It doesn't seem right that our Mr. Romantic, for whom wives would leave their husbands and debutantes would throw away their reputations, ends up alone with a broken heart."

"Do try to make me sound less pathetic in the future, won't you?" Miles asked.

"It won't be easy," Tom responded. "Especially if all we can imagine is you crying in some room alone in another city for who knows how long."

"I won't be absent long. And I might be miserable, but I don't intend to stay this way," he assured them. At least his friends didn't hate him for caring for Jemma. His one consolation.

"Where will you go?" Paul asked, the light from the window making his hair more red than brown.

"To stay with my younger sister and her husband. They have begged me to visit for some time. My stepfather will oversee my duties until I return."

"And when do you leave?" Ian asked.

"When I am finished here." Miles gave a sad smile, but it was the best he could do. "I do not think I could bear to stay a minute longer."

A noise sounded in the direction of the main room of the inn, probably an argument over a guest who couldn't pay. Miles ignored the clatter by the door, too wrapped up in his own thoughts.

Tom stood. "Vixen?"

Miles looked up as Jemma marched into the room. Her eyes sparked, and her mouth pulled into a determined slant. She was a vision in a dark-pink-rose gown with her hair in a simple knot, the loose ringlets by her face swaying as she made her way to their table.

"Jemma?" Ian started to stand. "You aren't supposed to be in here."

The other guests in the room protested.

"I'll take my chances. I have important business to discuss, and it cannot wait." Jemma went straight to Miles and before he could stand, set her hand on his shoulder. Did she plan to hit him? He had never known her to be violent before, but maybe she had gotten a taste for it after his appalling behavior.

"I-is everything a-all right?" he stammered.

He saw a flicker of hesitation behind her otherwise dauntless features, but she blinked it away. "I believe it is still my move." She grabbed his jacket by the lapels and kissed him hard.

This was an offensive play he had not seen coming. For years, he had dreamed of her lips on his, but never had he imagined such fire. It was no simple kiss but a love letter to his heart. No message could be clearer. Jemma Fielding wanted him.

He leaned into her, kissing her back as if it were for the last time.

When she released him, he fell back against his seat like someone had doused him with a bucket of water. He spurted for breath while Jemma spun on her heels and left. The innkeeper yelled threats if she ever returned, and the gentlemen behind Miles growled their complaints.

But Miles drowned it all out with the sweet music ringing in his ears.

"Poor Mr. Bentley." Tom laughed. "It looks like he is officially out of the running."

"She chose me?" Miles could hardly believe it.

"You'll have to marry her now," Ian said, shaking his head with a wry grin. "Although, you will have your hands full with that one."

Marry her? Miles grinned back. Yes, it was exactly what he would do.

"If we thought a fairly concealed kiss made out of desperation was a scandal, wait until this gets out." Paul chuckled.

"It puts my ballroom kiss to shame," Tom laughed back.

Paul agreed. "But as Louisa taught me, there is always a bright side. Maybe there'll be enough gossip to draw more people out to church."

Miles vaguely heard their words, his mind was reeling over Jemma's earth-shattering kiss.

"Miles?" Ian reached over and socked him lightly on the shoulder. "You've heard our congratulations, so what are you still doing here?"

"I—I'm not sure."

"Honestly," Ian grumbled. "The man who knows the least about love has to be the one to tell you to go after her."

"Go after her. Right." Miles stood. "Wish me luck."

"Just don't rile her up again," Paul said.

"And don't let Mrs. Fortescue's undying love confuse you," Tom added.

Miles sputtered a laugh and strode from the room. Once outside, he saw a glimpse of the Mannings' carriage turn the corner. If he knew Jemma, she wasn't returning home. He collected his horse and followed after her.

It wasn't long before he steered his horse around the Mannings' carriage parked in front of the church. He tied his horse up and darted down the lane, turning at the dirt path and following it toward the trees.

His steps slowed when he saw her. She was at the bench—their bench—waiting.

When she saw him, she stood, her rosy cheeks matching the pink of her gown. She was beautiful when she was embarrassed.

"I suppose it's my move again?" he said.

She took a deep breath and nodded.

"If there were a contest for the element of surprise, you would win." He came up on the other end of the bench and hesitated. Was he interpreting her correctly? What if she was still angry and her kiss was her way of paying him back? "I, uh, thought your engagement would be announced by now, with a wedding date set for the end of the summer."

Jemma frowned. "The end of the summer is a dreadfully long time. Do you think Ian has connections to produce a special license so we might marry sooner?"

"We?" Was Jemma Fielding proposing to him now? Would wonders never cease?

Jemma sighed. "You need to keep up on the latest *on dit*. Let me summarize: Mr. Bentley is marrying Lisette. While I was busy rather inelegantly learning about love, Lisette was comforting Mr. Bentley. They grew attached in the process, and it seems they cannot live without each other."

Lisette? And Mr. Bentley? "Then, I am free?" His head fell back, and his chest rose and fell as if he had never breathed such sweet air before.

"We both are." She shrugged her dainty shoulders. "I don't suppose I will be needing any more lessons."

He climbed over the bench, his mouth pulling into a grin. "Perhaps not, but I would like to finish what we started." He stepped closer. "Lesson five . . . loyalty, devotion, fidelity, and commitment to always keep you in my heart. It's what I want to offer you in our own relationship." He put his hand out, palm up. "I cannot give you the world, but this hand is yours if you want it."

She slipped her hand into his, a smile blooming on her face. "It is everything I want. And in exchange, I give you my whole heart, though you might not believe a woman mad enough to barge into a gentleman's club, I mean every word."

Miles chuckled, wrapping her hand in both of his. "We have sufficiently rebelled against the rules of Society, have we not?"

"Our relationship is rather unorthodox. After all our secret meetings about love, it was time for us to make a public statement."

He chuckled again. "I cannot think of a more romantic gesture, Jemma." He leaned down and set his forehead against her, inhaling her scent of roses and sunshine. He brought one hand up to stroke a glossy ringlet by her face. "I can barely believe this is real."

She leaned into him. "It's no dream. I have loved you for as long as I can remember."

He pulled back. "You are lying to me."

She shook her head. "I lied to myself for too long. I have decided it is time to come clean to my vicar." She ducked her head. "I was scared to let myself love anyone. Even after I promised Grandmother, I kept fighting my heart. I wanted to keep you near me but at a safe distance. But I was only torturing myself and denying myself an even greater happiness. Those fears combined with my concern for Lisette.

"I couldn't fathom how things could work out, so even when I wanted nothing more than to be with you, I couldn't let myself. I wasn't brave enough, Miles." She lifted her chin again, her green eyes arresting his full attention. "I am so sorry." A tear trailed down her cheek. "But I promise, I'm going to be brave from now on. I love you, Miles Jackson."

She had barely uttered the words before he covered her mouth with his own. Those perfect lips had already made him so happy. He could not wait a moment longer to embrace them. He wrapped his arms around her, relishing the feel of her trim waist, slender shoulders, and elegant neck. Finally, she was his. This moment was the beginning of the story he had longed to not just write but also live. He'd fill this new book with memories of them and daily expressions of his love. It would be an epic journey where hardships only strengthened them and tragedies were weathered side by side.

His hand came up to cup her small jaw, her skin infinitely soft beneath his fingertips. Her floral scent filled every part of him as he kissed her cheeks, her throat, and her lips once more. She tasted sweeter than any peppermint or lemon drop. She was a confection in a class of her own. He deepened their kiss—a kiss he had desired for a lifetime—wanting to hold her long enough to make up for all the long winter months without her. From now on, it would be summer ever more.

CHAPTER 36

HOURS SEEPED AWAY, BUT WITH Miles, it felt like minutes. Jemma had never been happier. Miles had spread his jacket on the ground for them to sit on, both of them leaning back against the bench, with their hands tangled together. She told him about finding his poems and the dozens of letters with money for the hurting Greeks. She had kissed him again at those pronouncements. No other thank-you seemed more appropriate.

Miles Jackson was an incredible kisser. If she had not already been seated, she might have fallen over. His touch had the power to melt every part of her. If she had known, she might not have resisted him for so long. When their lips inevitably parted, she settled against him, and they traded stories about their childhood, revealing times when they had felt drawn to each other and the difficulties of hiding it.

"I always came to you for advice as an excuse to be near you," she whispered, leaning her head against his chest.

"And I always gave you advice as an excuse to impress you."

She giggled. "I thought you were trying to be a wise older brother."

He rubbed his thumb over her hand, making her skin tremble. "Trust me when I say no brother could love his sister like I love you."

She would never tire of his way with words. "What will the others think when we tell them?"

"I cannot say what our families will think, but a few of our friends were witness to some of our progression, if you recall—along with a few select gentlemen at Gammon's. I told Paul, Tom, and Ian how I felt about you after they discovered I kissed you on the cricket field. Today, I told them I would support you and Mr. Bentley just before you showed up with your sensational kiss. I was planning on leaving Brookeside until I could handle the idea of you and Mr. Bentley together. If you had arrived even ten minutes later, I would have been gone."

She drew back, meeting his warm, brown eyes. "What would I have done? I am sick just thinking about it."

He tugged her close again. "It all worked out, didn't it? And to know Lisette and Mr. Bentley are engaged makes it all the more satisfying. There's a chance Mr. Bentley and I might even be friends."

She laughed. "It would be good of you."

"Yes, well, I did have my reasons for not being thrilled with his presence here."

"Valid reasons," she said. "What about the Matchmaking Mamas? How will they react? For the first time, their plans were foiled. They put in such a good effort. I hate to disappoint them."

"Don't be too sorry. There is no changing your mind now. After kissing me in public, I am duty bound to marry you."

"Duty bound." She smirked. "You will be chasing me to the altar."

"Shall I chase you there now?"

She giggled again. "Absolutely not. We haven't even told our families."

"I agree, but first, I shall meet with your uncle. Despite your negligence of Society's rules, I intend to do this properly. In fact, there is no time like the present."

"Five more minutes?" She set her hand on his waistcoat and curled all the closer to him.

"Five minutes will turn into five hours with your claim upon my senses, but why not turn it into a lifetime?" He helped her stand and shook off his jacket. With her hand in his, they made their way to the Manning carriage. On the way, they both agreed that Lisette should be the first to hear their news once Uncle granted his permission.

An hour later, Miles came out of Mr. Manning's study, both men grinning. Jemma had been waiting in the corridor for him. She wasn't nervous about Uncle's response, just eager to be near Miles again.

Her uncle put his arms around her and hugged her tightly. "It is not often a man agrees to a marriage for his daughter and his niece in the same day."

"Mr. Bentley has come by?" Jemma asked.

"Yes, and if I am right, while we were buried in the study, my wife has gathered the neighborhood in the drawing room to tell them. I believe she sent the footmen with written invitations not long before you arrived."

"How perfectly convenient for us," Miles said.

"We'll do our best to keep the celebrations short because while I'm sure Jemma's headache is suppressed with all the excitement, she still needs her rest."

"I will make certain she gets it," Miles said, setting his hand on the small of her back.

The three of them made their way to the drawing room. The door was open wide, and sure enough, all their friends had arrived, including all the Matchmaking Mamas. Jemma's eyes naturally went to Mrs. Jackson, her future mother-in-law. To think, she would have a mother again!

She followed Miles into the back of the room, wishing he had taken her hand. Her fingers felt oddly wrong lying against her side by themselves. Her uncle joined his wife in front of the fireplace. A few of their friends raised curious brows at the sight of Jemma and Miles arriving together—particularly the men who had witnessed her brazen kiss. She did not want to think about how Society would frown on her shocking behavior.

Mr. Manning began clapping to get their attention.

"Thank you for joining us on such short notice. It has been a whirlwind few days, and you have all stood tirelessly by our sides while we've nursed our Jemma back to health. It is because of your dear friendship that we have called you to be with us again." His voice choked up, and he coughed into his hand. "I have never been prouder than I am this day," he said. "We have brought you all here to announce the wedding of my daughter, Lisette, to Mr. Bentley."

Gasps followed by cheers filled the room. Mr. Bentley pulled Lisette to her feet and kissed her soundly on the mouth.

"I think I am going to cry," Jemma whispered to Miles. "I'm so happy."

Miles reached over and caught her hand, just as she'd hoped he would, and gave it a tender squeeze.

Everyone was talking at once, demanding to know when it had happened and how. Mr. Manning got everyone's attention again. "We have all evening to discuss the news, but there is one other announcement. As proud as I am to have such an honorable man for a son-in-law, I am equally proud to marry my niece, Jemma, to Mr. Miles Jackson."

The noise level grew, and everyone was on their feet, hugging and congratulating the couples. Lisette found Jemma and hugged her tightly.

"I wanted to tell you first, before the others," Jemma said.

"I get to hug you first, does that not count for something?" Lisette pulled back, tears glistening in her eyes. "It was just as it was meant to be! The missing piece to my own happiness."

"Two weddings! I am beside myself!" Mrs. Manning interrupted, embracing both Jemma and Lisette at the same time.

When Mrs. Manning pulled back, Mrs. Jackson took Jemma's hands and squeezed them tight. "Welcome to the family! I could not be prouder of my son's choice. You two are perfect for each other." Then she pulled Miles into her arms too. "Oh, Miles, I thought you would never find the courage to marry her."

"Courage?"

When Mrs. Jackson drew back, Miles looked with surprise at his mother and then at Jemma. "You knew how I felt about her?"

Lady Kellen stepped up beside them, and Mrs. Sheldon came up beside Mrs. Manning, all grinning from ear to ear.

"What kind of mother would I be if I did not know who would suit you best?" Mrs. Jackson winked at her son.

Jemma looked from one Matchmaking Mama to the next. "You should have told the other Matchmaking Mamas and saved us a lot of runaround. By the way, I must apologize, for I truly was grateful for all your assistance. We hope you will understand."

"Understand? Why, we are exultant!" Lady Kellen put her arm around Mrs. Jackson. The two of them stood like proud peacocks.

Miles shuffled forward. "Pardon?"

Mrs. Sheldon nodded. "We were all worried you two would never come together."

"I don't believe what I am hearing." Jemma squeezed her eyes shut and opened them again. "You planned all of this?"

Lady Kellen nodded her regal head. "To the letter."

Mrs. Jackson sighed. "It was exhausting to watch. I am going to need a whole year to recover from the stress. Why, I even had to fuel a rumor about my son kissing you. I find matchmaking far more exciting when it isn't my child."

"Mother!" Miles scolded. "That was you?"

"I overhead you confessing to your friends in the library." She shrugged, clearly without bearing an ounce of guilt. "I tried to keep the story just between our families and a few trusted servants."

Jemma laughed. "This is unbelievable."

Miles set his hand on his forehead and pinched his temples. "No wonder the town was so forgiving at the auction."

"Of course, we couldn't say anything directly about our scheme," Mrs. Manning said. "We believe the matches should occur as naturally as possible."

"With encouragement," Lady Kellen added. "Which came in the form of Mr. Bentley. He did a wonderful job, for not knowing a thing. In fact, he exceeded our expectations."

"Indeed," Mrs. Jackson said. "We got two matches in one this time. I cannot wait to see what we come up with next."

"But you have yet to hear the best part," Lady Felcroft said, coming up beside Jemma and joining their circle. "Lady Kellen, tell her about Mrs. Fielding's contribution."

Jemma gripped Miles's arm. "Grandmother?"

Lady Kellen's smile grew. "Thank you for reminding me. We would be remiss not to mention it, wouldn't we? This whole arrangement started before Mrs. Fielding even passed."

Jemma shook her head. "It cannot be possible."

"Mrs. Fielding knew both of her granddaughters well," Lady Kellen continued. "She knew Lisette would not be happy with Mr. Jackson. But you would."

Tears pricked Jemma's eyes. "My grandmother said that?"

All the mothers nodded.

Jemma turned to her aunt. "And you agreed to it?"

"Wholeheartedly." Mrs. Manning's eyes filled with tears as well. "I knew if Mr. Jackson truly loved my daughter, they would have been married long ago. He is a passionate young man, but he always treated Lisette as his friend. It wasn't until your grandmother pointed out that Mr. Jackson might make a good match for you, Jemma, that I began to see how different he was in your company."

"You saw what I could not." Jemma leaned into Miles's arm, grinning up at him. The smile he returned warmed her to her very toes.

"I will be the first to admit, we are not all-knowing," Lady Kellen declared succinctly. "But no one knows their child like a good mother."

Lady Felcroft put her hand on Jemma's shoulder. "Your grandmother was one of those good mothers. She told us we could rely on your sharp intellect and determination to do right by your cousin and to see this match through. I bet she has her dancing slippers on in heaven and is celebrating how very right she was."

"The Matchmaking Mamas succeeded again." Miles's tone was one of disbelief.

Mrs. Manning batted the compliment away with the toss of her hand. "If you young people think you're romantic, remember we discovered love long before you did." She tapped the side of her nose.

They all laughed, and some of them, including Jemma, shed a tear or two.

"Our turn," Ian said, putting his hands on his mother's shoulders and gently pulling her back. "We might be the dunderheads left in the dark, but we want to properly congratulate our best friends."

The mothers filed out of the way, and the Rebels, including Mr. Bentley, who had his arm around Lisette, surrounded Jemma and Miles.

"How are we here?" Miles asked.

"We figured there would be an announcement after Jemma caused a scene at Gibbons'," Tom said. "It was Lisette's news that shocked us."

"Jemma was at Gibbons'?" Mrs. Manning's voice pitched from behind them.

"It was all in the name of romance," Tom yelled over his shoulder, as if his shocking words would placate her.

Surprisingly, they did.

"I mean," Miles clarified, "it was just yesterday that we declared war against the Matchmaking Mamas, and now look at us. Our lives are changed for the better."

"We've been through a lot together," Lisette added. "And now we're all grown up, starting families of our own."

"Except Ian," Tom said rather bluntly. "Shall we remind Lady Kellen?"

Ian groaned. "No, please, no. I have family enough in this room, do I not?"

"But what is one more?" Paul teased, elbowing Ian.

"Did you just poke me again?" Ian shook his head. She wasn't the only one who was a little shocked that the Rebel who didn't like to be touched thought it necessary to do so.

"For good reason," Paul said. "I had to get my point across somehow. There is still one Rebel against marriage who needs a change of heart."

They all laughed as Ian groaned. "I am not as easily swayed as the lot of you."

Miles cleared his throat loud enough to get their friends' attention. "Ian, please tell me, how you could resist this?" He pulled Jemma to him. She raised her brows, wondering what he was up to. She didn't have long to guess. He bent down and kissed her. She sighed inwardly with all the pleasure in the world. She didn't hear Ian's response or anyone else's, for that matter, even after Miles drew back. As she stared into Miles's brown eyes, she knew Grandmother had been right.

Love made everything more worthwhile.

EPILOGUE

A MONTH AFTER THEIR WEDDING, Jemma tumbled into Miles's office, the door banging against the wall. Miles dropped his pen and jumped to his feet. "What happened? Is everything all right?"

Jemma grinned, her bonnet strings untied and her eyes alight. "I received my first check from the ladies' magazine for my sketches!"

He laughed and came around his desk. "The poor of London are rejoicing while the rich ladies parade their fashionable wares."

"Only because we gathered such a large sum for the people of Chios."

"Speaking of them, you are not the only one with news." Miles retrieved an open letter from off a small stack of correspondence. "I received a letter confirming our aid to the Greek Revolution has been received. The government thanks us for our substantial donation and the lives we are saving because of it."

Jemma gave a happy sigh of relief. "We're doing it, Miles. We're really helping people."

"It feels good, doesn't it?"

"It certainly does." She closed the gap between them, setting her hand on his waist. "Listen. About my sketches. I have a better plan than just reaching out to London charities."

He set the letter back on the desk. "Oh? Tell me what you're scheming now?"

"I was not aware of how many were struggling in Brookeside until you showed me. I am splitting all my proceeds so the poor of Brookeside can benefit too."

He tugged her closer. "I thought you said you would be a terrible vicar's wife."

She gave a dainty shrug. "I will try to limit my scandals to yearly . . . if I can help it. Otherwise, yes, I will still be terrible. However, I will be the best supporter of you—which makes me at least a good wife in general."

He removed her bonnet, tossing it on his desk and kissed her forehead. "Not just a good wife, but the best. Now, how should we celebrate all our good news?"

She played with his cravat. "Couldn't you recite a bit of poetry for the occasion? Perhaps a ballad to my name?"

He studied her, never growing weary of every detail about her. "Let me guess—you would like each stanza to include my undying love for you?"

"If you would be so gracious."

He laughed. "I no longer have the need to vent my feelings through poetry when I can kiss you instead."

She lightly punched his arm, but her feigned anger disappeared with sudden wide eyes. "I almost forgot. Lord Kellen is insisting Ian go to London for the Season. There is a strong rumor he has found Ian a wife."

Miles frowned. "You never put so much stock into gossip before."

"This rumor did not come from any newspaper. There has been a musical meeting called."

"The Matchmaking Mamas?" Miles pursed his lips. Ian would not like this at all.

Jemma nodded. "It appears there is to be an unofficial contest between Lord and Lady Kellen."

Miles did not know whether to smile or cringe. "You know what this means? Ian does not stand a chance."

Thank you for reading the third book in my Matchmaking Mamas series! I hope you enjoyed Miles and Jemma's story and have the chance to experience all the Rebels' romances in this collection.

Read about Paul and Louisa in *Bargaining for the Barrister*. Louisa is eager to meet her match, but Paul has a secret past and is bent on thwarting marriage at all costs. Will the cunning Matchmaking Mamas win against Paul and his Rebel friends? Or will true love be the victor?

Read about Tom and Cassandra in *An Unwitting Alliance*. Cassandra's parents engage her to a complete stranger, but when the couple meets, they realize they aren't strangers at all. Cassandra cannot possibly marry the man she despises.

Coming in 2025: Ian meets his match!

∄UTHOR'S ∖OTE

MY RESEARCH FOR THIS BOOK included learning the game of cricket, fun facts about fashion, and historical and modern recipes for making English biscuits (more like shortbread or cookies than American biscuits). The tone of this series is meant to be romantic, witty, and uplifting, but my research tends to include all sides of history, even the dark and heavy. One of the more poignant themes of this particular story is the Rebels' desire to be charitable to their fellow man—even those thousands of miles away. I would like to share with you what I learned about a tragic event that inspired my characters.

The Chios Massacre of 1822 (pronounced key-Os) could be considered the first modern-day Holocaust. It started with a Greek revolt against the Turks in March 1822. Greeks came from the Island of Samos, gathered some of the Chios Greeks, and attacked the Turks there, but the majority did not participate. As backlash, the Turks destroyed the inhabitants of Chios to make an example of them in an antirebellion movement.

The Turks' fleet arrived on Holy Thursday, April 11, 1822. Nearly 100,000 Orthodox Christians were killed, enslaved, or forced to take refuge elsewhere by Muslim troops from the Turkish Ottoman Empire. The Turks were ordered to kill all infants under three, all males over twelve, and women over forty, but the carnage reached far beyond this. The enslaved survivors were forced to deny Christ or be beheaded.

May we always remember the tragedies of the past so we might learn from them. May we also recall the stories of love and kindness, even the fictional ones, that inspire humanity to rise above greed, selfishness, and desire for power, to fight for a better future.

ACKNOWLEDGMENTS

BEHIND EACH BOOK IS AN army of people who battled to get this book into shape. I won't salute them only because I am more of the hugging type. So here is a virtual hug to all those who helped Miles and Jemma get their HEA in print! Special thanks to the amazing team at Shadow Mountain! My editors, designer, and marketing team are all fantastic. I have loved working on this series with them.

Hugs to my readers, who were many on this project! My critique partners: Laura Beers, Laura Rollins, Sally Britton, and Mindy Strunk. My beta-readers: Mandy Biesinger (two hugs for reading it twice!), Katie Stone, Tiffany Odekirk, Aurora Walker, Addalyn Walker, Heather Okeson, Taylor Riddoch, Lauren Winzenried, and Heidi Riddoch. Your ideas and feedback made this story shine!

Hugs to my ARC team—you know who you are! And to my sweet readers! Thank you for reading, reviewing, and sharing this with your friends. You make all the difference.

My family always deserves the biggest hugs. I keep waiting for them to tell me to find a new hobby, but their support seems never-ending. How can I not love them forever?! Last of all, I am thankful for a loving God, who gifted me another story to share with you. He is the ultimate master storyteller, and His work promises a happy ending for all.

Photo by Megan Waldal

ABOUT THE AUTHOR

ANNEKA R. WALKER is a best-selling author of historical and contemporary romance. With humor and an abundance of heart, she crafts uplifting stories you won't soon forget. She is the winner of the Swoony Award and various chapter contests. Her books have received praise from *Publishers Weekly*, Historical Novel Society, *Midwest Book Review*, and Readers' Favorite. She graduated with a bachelor's degree in English and history and hopes to never stop learning. She is a blessed wife, proud mother of five, lover of Jesus, connoisseur of chocolate, and believer in happy endings. Subscribe to Anneka's newsletter at mailchi.mp/a278fdec4416 /authorannekawalker, and follow her on social media.

Facebook: @AnnekaRWalker

Instagram: @authorannekawalker

To see a complete list of Anneka's books, view her website at www.annekawalker.com.

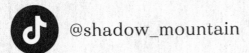
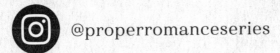
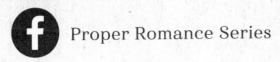